eyo

ABIDEMI SANUSI

First edition copyright © 2009 by
WordAlive, Nairobi, Kenya
This edition copyright © 2014 by Piquant
PO Box 83 Carlisle UK CA3 9GR
www.piquanteditions.com

Mobi format: 978-1-909281-32-5
Epub format: 978-1-909281-33-2
Print ISBN: 978-1-909281-31-8

For Parakletos
for the journey

Don't you see that children are GOD's
best gift? The fruit of the womb, his generous legacy?
Like a warrior's fistful of arrows are the children of a
vigorous youth. Oh, how blessed are you parents,
with your quivers full of children!

Psalm 127:3-5 (*The Message*)

A word from the author

Eyo is my attempt to draw attention to the twin issues of child trafficking and sex slavery in the United Kingdom. While it is true that this is a work of fiction, any African child trafficked to the UK will encounter, at one point or another, some or all of Eyo's experiences.

There are thousands of Eyos in Europe. In your country, there may be children's charities working to safeguard the lives of children like Eyo by campaigning against child trafficking and sex slavery. For the most part, they work on limited funds and need all the help they can get. You might not be able to support them, but please, keep an eye out. For every Eyo that is rescued from human traffickers, scores more are trafficked out of Africa and into Europe.

Do something. Keep an eye out.

African
Flower

One

"Ice water! Ice water! Don't let the heat of the day take you down! Buy ice water!"

The girl calling out her wares walked carefully and purposely, with the confidence of someone used to negotiating her way around plastic bags of human waste on the road. She held on to a boy walking next to her. The boy looked about eight and carried a tray filled with melting ice, too.

The girl couldn't have been more than ten years old, although it was hard to tell. Her eyes were brown—"Clear," the girl's mother said—fringed with long lashes. Her nose wasn't anything special—rather snub, if truth be told—hovering above full lips. If she was indeed ten, then she was rather small in size for someone her age, thin as opposed to underweight, with even thinner arms that looked like reeds. There was strength in her arms; you could tell by the way one hand held on to the tray on her head, while the other held on to the boy's hand, with the tenacity of a warrior queen from days past.

"Ice water!" the girl called out again in a nasal singsong. Her voice rang out clear at first, before it was drowned out by other hawkers.

"Slippers! Buy fine slippers!"

"Fresh bread! Buy tasty, fresh bread!"

Not to be outdone, the girl and the boy cried out again in perfect nasal symphony.

"Ice water! Fresh! Let our ice water cool you in the sun!"

By the roadside, stalls were lined up cheek by jowl against each other, their brightly coloured cornucopia weighing down the rickety tables. They offered many wares from meat and biscuits to car parts, watches and other unidentifiable items. The road itself belched with cars, lorries, vans, motorcycles and herds of animals stuck in tedious traffic. The incessant din of car horns, bus conductors, and haggling traders and buyers all rose up to the ears of the sun, which responded by beating down its merciless rays on the seething mass of humanity below, as if to remind them that they were its captive. Like they needed reminding.

The girl and the boy were in Ajegunle, a seething, sprawling slum on the swampy marshes of Lagos Lagoon, west of Lagos Island. It was separated from the opulence of Apapa and Tin Can Ports by a canal and had a reputation for being the most violent, notorious and criminal ghetto in Nigeria. Called AJ City by its residents and aptly named Jungle City–which the residents preferred to Ajegunle–by others, with its narrow, untarred streets, winding alleys and shanty settlements, Ajegunle stood defiant on reclaimed marshes, surrounded by decomposing garbage, burning wood and rotting animal carcasses–the latter being remains from the abattoir on the fittingly named Malu (Cow) Road, the entryway into Jungle City.

The boy whom the girl was holding attempted to break free from her hold. The girl looked around for what prompted his action. She didn't have to look far, before she spotted it: a punctured ball, black with dirt, a few feet away from them.

"No, Lanre," the girl said firmly.

"Eyo, let me," the boy pleaded, twisting his arms and wriggling to break free.

"Lanre, I said no. We're almost done. We're going home soon," Eyo said.

Lanre didn't answer. He jerked his arm with determined force and freed it from Eyo's hand.

"Lanre, no!" Eyo called out.

Lanre ran towards the ball, one hand balancing the tray on his head. He stopped short, when he came against a dark brown shirt stained with grease. He looked up and encountered a cruel face.

"Give me your money," the face said, pushing him. Lanre staggered back, with his hand still on his tray. He looked back at his sister in fear. She held out her free hand towards him. Lanre hastened back and grabbed it.

"You have to kill me first," Eyo said to the man, and she meant it. The thought of going home empty-handed and facing her father gave her the strength of Samson. She tightened her grip on her brother and on her tray.

"*Olé*! Thief! *Gbomogbomo*! Child stealer!" she screamed, pointing at the man.

Heads turned. Frayed tempers, the splitting din of traffic and even the heat seemed suspended temporarily. The smell of blood stirred the crowd. The man tried to walk away without drawing attention to himself. But it was too late.

"*Olé*! Where? Get him!"

Eyo pointed to the man who had started running. The crowd gave chase.

"Somebody get a tyre!" someone shouted.

"Let's get him first!" another hollered.

"Are you all right?" a woman asked Eyo and Lanre. They both nodded.

"Don't worry. They'll catch him and he'll get a tyre," the woman continued.

Eyo and her brother nodded again. The 'tyre' was a peculiar trademark of Lagos street justice. It was handed out to people who were caught breaking the law and were unfortunate enough to be seized by the horde and not by the police. Victims of this mob justice had car tyres thrown around their necks, which, in turn, were doused in petrol and set on fire. Afterwards, their charred bodies were left on the ground for wild dogs to feast on and, at other times, to rot in the scorching heat, the smell a reminder to passers-by of the rules of the street and what happened to those who broke them.

"Ice water! Drink! Fresh from the tap! Ice water!" Eyo called out.

Nobody paid her any attention, as all eyes and running feet turned toward the direction of the man who was now surrounded by a jeering crowd. Eyo and Lanre could hear him begging.

"Please, have mercy. They're lying. I'm no child stealer. Have mercy."

They heard a dull thud and then a searing gasp of pain. Eyo and Lanre joined the crowd. They could just make out the man, a lone figure in the middle. He was on his knees, crying and pleading, his clothes now mere shreds. The mob surged towards him. Eyo and Lanre could see some people holding batons poised above their heads. Someone with a tyre was making his way through the rabble.

Eyo turned her brother's face away and started in the opposite direction.

"Can we go home now?" Lanre asked, his voice subdued.

"No. We haven't sold all the ice. Papa will be mad," Eyo replied. "Don't worry. The man is gone now. He won't trouble us again," she said, shaking his hand reassuringly.

"Ice water!" she called out.

"Ice water!" Lanre echoed.

They both disappeared into the heaving humanity of Jungle City. Behind them, someone lit a match. It was followed by a blood-curdling scream and the jeers of onlookers.

*   *   *

Eyo rounded the corner of her street, her hand still holding Lanre's. Her tray was empty and so was his. Papa would be pleased. It was dark, the darkness alleviated by the timid candlelight of roadside stalls. She navigated the crater-sized potholes easily, each crater and its location committed to memory. Her feet danced over plastic bags and the open drains overflowing with effluent. Her brother's steps matched hers, his mind filled with thoughts of what he would do once he got home.

Sounds of highlife music boomed from a neighbourhood beer parlour, an edifice of four concrete pillars supporting a corrugated steel roof that sheltered plastic chairs and rusty tables underneath. Eyo stole a glance at the place. Sure enough, her father was there. She walked on quickly.

Suddenly, from the dark recesses of the street corner, a shadow stepped out and stood in front of them. It was an 'area boy', a local gangster. His teenage eyes were bloodshot.

"Eyo, Eyo," he said, his voice high-pitched. Eyo could tell he had been sniffing glue.

"Leave me alone," she said. She held her brother and tried to sidestep the area boy, but he blocked her.

"Would you like me to show you something?" he asked, his hands grabbing the bulge of his trousers.

"No. Just leave me alone," she answered. She pushed past him, dragging her brother along. Behind her, she heard his piercing cackle.

"Eyo! I'll catch you one day and show you a good time!" he called after her.

Eyo ignored him. Inwardly, she hoped that he wouldn't chase after her as he sometimes did. He was like all the other addicts in Jungle City, unpredictable. She waited, then breathed easier when she didn't hear his running footfalls behind them.

Eyo and Lanre soon approached their house, a type of building locally known as face-me-I-face-you. Face-me-I-face-yous were rectangular in shape, sometimes uncompleted, with rows of single rooms facing each other, divided by a corridor with an open doorway at either end. There were ten rooms in Eyo's building, with at least ten people living in each. All but Eyo's family's and the landlord's rooms measured ten feet by eight feet.

Eyo's family had the smallest room, so they paid a slightly lower rent. Like most of the houses in Jungle City, their building lacked electricity, running water and a bathroom, so the tenants bathed very early in the morning or late at night, in the 'backyard', the outback. The *shalanga*, the pit latrine, was also in the backyard, in a windowless hut, hence people didn't hang out too long in there. The latrine smell only eased during the harmattan season, when the cold winds of the Sahara Desert rolled across West Africa, leaving a fine cloud of red dust in its wake.

Eyo let go of Lanre's hand and they both walked over the open drain outside the building. She ignored the man who was lying down languidly on a rickety bench in front of the house and was watching her and her brother with hooded eyes.

Lanre ran to their front door. He opened it and came out a minute later with a battered ball in his hand. A lady came out of the room, wearing a *wrapa*, a long piece of cloth tied across her chest. She was a large woman, with luminous skin and with eyes that told anyone who dared look that they saw everything and missed nothing.

"Lanre, at least eat before you play ball!" the woman called out.

"Mama, you know what he's like. By the way, the landlord is outside. I'll just drop this off and go and watch over Lanre," Eyo said, going into the room.

"That man should be ashamed of himself. No child is safe from him. No child!" Her mother spoke in a loud voice that carried outside to the ears of the man lounging on the bench, just as she intended.

"Yes, Mama," Eyo said. She stacked the tray against the wall and did likewise to Lanre's, which was on the floor. She looked around.

"Where's Sade?" she asked.

"Mama Fola took her out. That's the only person you care about in this house. Your five-year-old sister," her mother replied, although she smiled when she said it.

Mama Fola occupied the room opposite theirs. She was also Mama's best friend.

"Somebody tried to take our money today," Eyo said.

"I hope you showed them," Mama said.

"I did the *gbomogbomo* thing," Eyo replied.

"Good," her mother said. "They won't get a chance to steal from hard-working people again. Now go and watch your brother."

Eyo took an *apoti*, a wooden squat stool, from behind the door and went back outside. She set it in front of the house, a few feet away from the landlord, and focused her eyes on her brother playing street football with his friends. Not once did she acknowledge the landlord. A while later, the front windows of their room opened out to where she was sitting.

"Lanre! Eyo! Food is ready!" her mother shouted.

Eyo called out to Lanre and they both went inside, with Lanre dripping sweat, to his mother's irritation. "You think water grows on trees?" she grumbled.

*   *   *

Everyone was asleep. Eyo could hear their rhythmic breathing. Mama was on the bare mattress. Eyo, Lanre and Sade were on the sleeping mat on the floor. Outside, the moon peeped through the slit in the thin curtains–two pieces of local *adire* cloth folded over the curtain rails and held together by wooden pegs–and cut the room in half with its sliver of grey light. It was humid, and the closed windows did not keep out the dank smell of rotting garbage, which permeated the house. Eyo wiped her forehead and turned on her left side. Sade's hot breath drove her to turn to her right, where she encountered Lanre's flailing arm. She turned on her back and looked up at the ceiling. Cobwebs dangled from the corners, and flies buzzed above her. She swatted a few and turned on her left side again, deciding that Sade's sweet, hot breath was better than Lanre's pummelling limbs. Eyo heard the room key turn in the lock and immediately shut her eyes.

A dark figure entered the room. It waited at the foot of the mat. Eyo kept her eyes shut, though she could sense the figure's eyes boring into hers, willing them to open. After what seemed like an eternity, the figure made its way to the mattress and descended on Mama, fumbling clumsily with her *wrapa*.

"Wale, please. The children..." Mama's voice was sleepy.

"Olufunmi, it's nothing they won't discover themselves."

Papa's voice was slurred.

He mounted her and positioned himself. Soon enough, a grunt of satisfaction escaped his lips. Eyo kept her eyes steadfastly shut. She turned her face slightly towards Lanre because Sade's breath on her face was getting too hot, and her eyes opened for the barest moment. In that instant, she caught Papa's eyes and he angled himself and Mama—just as she knew he would—in such a way that she could see what they were doing. The moon's silvery light illuminated their sweat-slicked bodies, as they both moved in rhythm with each other. Eyo shut her eyes. She heard Mama's unconscious, plaintive moans and then Papa's shuddering gasp as he collapsed on her.

Eyo turned over and Lanre's leg came thundering down on her arm. She moved it away gently.

Two

Eyo's eyelids fluttered open. She could hear people moving around in the corridor. Silently, she got off the mat and made her way to the door. It was dark and she groped her way out from memory, guided by the flickering light and a smoky smell from the corridor. When she got to the door, she paused, as she always did, to take another look at her two siblings before opening the door quietly and stepping into the passageway. Mama was bent over a small stove, turning the *ogi*, fermented corn porridge, in the blackened pot. The air was thick with the smell of kerosene. Olufunmi adjusted the fire. It flared for a few moments before settling down again. Eyo moved closer to her mother.

"Careful," Mama said. There were half a dozen other women in the corridor, in various stages of cooking and cleaning. The air was filled with black smoke from the kerosene stoves.

"Have you greeted everybody?" Mama asked. It was a rhetorical question.

"Good morning," Eyo said.

"Good morning, Eyo," the women chorused.

"Go shower quick, quick. And be careful with the water," Olufunmi said.

She turned away from the *ogi* she was stirring and nudged a small bucket of water next to the stove towards Eyo. A few of the women were already making their way to the backyard, each carrying individual water containers. A small bowl bobbed in each pail.

Eyo followed them, half carrying and half lugging her own bucket. Behind her, her mother warned, "Watch the water! Watch the water! Eyo, I said, 'Watch the water!'"

The women walked down the corridor, past the landlord's room. His was the biggest room in the house, with double windows that opened into the backyard.

"Eyo," one of the women called out.

"Mama Fola, I'm here," Eyo responded.

Mama Fola reached out and took Eyo's hand in hers and they stepped into the morning darkness together. Somebody lit a candle and placed it on the low concrete wall a few feet away from them. Without speaking, all the women stepped forward, until they were approximately one foot away from the wall. They turned their backs towards the landlord's windows and undressed grimly and quickly, hanging their towels on the same wall as the candle. In perfect unison, they bent over to pour water on themselves, using the small bowls. As if on cue, the landlord's windows opened. There was the flare of a match and then a cigarette glow.

"*Olosi*! Foolish man," Mama Fola hissed.

"You wait till I tell my husband," another woman said.

"He won't complain; he owes me money," the landlord retorted as he dragged on his cigarette.

"As God is my witness, you will dic from that poison," Mama Fola prophesied to him.

The landlord laughed and exhaled smoke.

Eyo didn't have to look behind her to know that the landlord was watching her. She ignored him and concentrated on her bathing ritual: a few handfuls of water to lather the sponge, one bowl of water to rinse off the lather and the last bowl to rinse off its remnants. That left enough water in the bucket for Lanre and Sade to bathe as well. Water was expensive; she knew that and was grateful that she could bathe every day. Not everyone could. Eyo tried to imagine what that would feel like and decided it was too horrible to think about. She and Lanre rarely came home from the day's hawking without being caked in dust and grime. Some children in the building didn't bathe daily, and it showed because they stank.

It was the cusp of dawn, although it was still dark. From where she stood, Eyo could see flickering candlelight and lanterns dotting the settlement, reminding her of fluttering butterflies. In the distance, the occasional growl of a passing car had turned into the steady roar of the infamous Lagos traffic.

On the other side of the fence, Eyo could see the women of the next-door face-me-I-face-you bathing as well. The neighbours' building was on a plot set way back from the street. It was dominated by a three-storey building in front, which doubled up as a mosque and a church. The ground floor was a mosque and the top two each hosted individual churches.

The face-me-I-face-you was not visible to everybody, dwarfed as it was by the three-level structure. Only Jungle City residents knew that it was accessible from the street by walking down the narrow corridor on the left of the 'building of worship', as residents mockingly called the mosque-cum-church.

"Eyo!"

Mama's voice jolted Eyo from her reverie.

"Ma, I'm coming!"

She nodded to Mama Fola and went back to the house, carrying the bucket and its depleted contents easily.

"Quick, quick. Eat the *ogi*, before it gets cold. I'll get your brother and sister ready. Here," Olufunmi held out the bowl of *ogi* to Eyo.

Eyo took the bowl from her mother and went into their room. The fetid smell hit her afresh as it did every morning after bathing in the open air. Her building, like most in Jungle City, was built on solidified garbage. She dared not open the two windows in the room for fear of mosquitoes and the outside stench. It was worse during the rainy season, when the building seeped its putrefying foundations into the rooms, sometimes flooding them. She and her family would then have to find shelter elsewhere, usually under a flyover, until the rain stopped. But not today. Today, the room was just humid and fetid.

The door handle turned and Eyo's mother came in. Eyo sat cross-legged on the mat, as far as she could from her brother and her sister, while balancing the bowl of *ogi* carefully in her hands. Lanre's waking movements were as legendary as his sleeping ones. She ignored her siblings' forms on the mattress.

"Eyo, don't take too long. I want you to be the first person at the ice company today. That way, you can start early and come home early. Sade will be coming with the two of you today. Lanre, *oya*, come on!" Olufunmi shook Lanre as she dragged him out of the room.

Eyo nodded and turned her eyes to the side window on the left, which faced the building of worship. She craned her neck a little and made out the face-me-I-face-you behind it. She turned her head back to the building of worship.

"Today is your day of victory." The six a.m. prayer meeting had begun. The loudspeaker screeched as its frequency was adjusted.

"Amen!"

"I said, 'Today is your day of victory!'"

The frequency was fine. Eyo felt the loudspeaker thundering in her head. She looked at Sade, still sleeping blissfully on the mat, and shook her head. *How did she do it?*

"Amen!"

"I said, 'Everywhere your feet shall touch today, you shall conquer.'"

The sleeping form on the mattress stirred and yawned. Quickly, Eyo got up, carrying her bowl of *ogi*.

"Yes, Jesus!"

"Every plan of the enemy for your life shall come to nought, in the name of Jesus."

"Am…"

The door creaked as someone opened it slowly from the outside. Only one person opened a door like that, with cat-like stealth. Eyo put her bowl of *ogi* on the floor, stood up and wrenched the door wide open. The person on the other side almost tumbled into the room.

"Eyo," the landlord said, smiling.

Without a backward glance at her father lying on the mattress, Eyo shouted, "Mama! The landlord is in our room!"

Several doors opened, including Mama Fola's. When Mama Fola saw Eyo in the doorway and the landlord standing awkwardly in the corridor, she cried out, "Olufunmi! The landlord is in your room!"

Standing in their own doorways, the other women echoed her cry.

"Olufunmi! Come and guard your child!"

The landlord looked at Eyo for a few moments. He could also make out her father getting up from the mattress. "You think you're clever, don't you?" he said before scampering to his own room at the end of the corridor, shooting Mama Fola and the other women dark looks en route.

Eyo ignored him, muttering, "*Olosi*! What a foolish person," under her breath. She bent down to pick up her bowl of *ogi*.

"If I see you in my room without my permission or anywhere near my children again, I will kill you," her mother shouted from afar. "Useless man! You think you own us? *Olosi*!"

The voice of Eyo's mother drew nearer and nearer, until she charged into the room, with Lanre. He was dripping with soapsuds. Olufunmi pushed him towards Eyo.

"Wale! Wale! What were you doing when the landlord came into our room? Have you forgotten that we have children?" Olufunmi exclaimed. "Lanre, dry yourself and let your sister dress you. Since your father refuses to deal with this man, I'll have to do it myself."

Olufunmi stormed out the room. Eyo put aside her now cold *ogi* and started drying her brother.

"The landlord likes Eyo," Lanre said, giving Eyo a toothy grin.

"Everybody likes Eyo," Papa said, his leering eyes boring deep into Eyo's back.

* * *

Wale swung himself off the mattress. He yawned and then scratched his belly. He took a peep at the left window. All was quiet at the building of worship. It wouldn't last long, though. The street and even his room would soon resound with the muezzin's call to afternoon prayer, no doubt to be followed by the church loudspeakers, determined not to be outshone by the mosque in the business of worship.

He surveyed his home, a square box of inhabitable space. He yawned again and made his way out into the corridor. He saw the landlord lounging on a bench. He drew up a wooden chair alongside him and yawned some more.

"Are they all gone?" the landlord asked.

Wale nodded and swatted a fly. They didn't speak for a few moments. A car screeched to a halt, narrowly missing an *okada*, a motorcycle cab. In a flash, both drivers jumped out of their vehicles. Their passengers sighed wearily.

"*Na* your father build this road?" the *okada* driver taunted the car driver, sweat streaming down his face.

"Please come back to the motorcycle and let's just go. I have an important appointment," his passenger called out to him.

The *okada* driver went up to the car bumper and banged on it. "*Na* me and you today!"

The car driver shook his head and got back inside his car. As he drove away, he shouted at the *okada* driver, "You're ignorant!"

The *okada* driver kicked the rear end of the car as it went past him. He went back to the motorcycle and drove away.

From their ringside seats in front of their face-me-I-face-you, the landlord and Wale chortled.

"You tell me where else in Lagos you can get such drama for free," the landlord said.

"Nowhere else. It's only in Jungle City, the city of dreams," Wale agreed.

He wasn't wrong. Every day, thousands of people poured into the urban jungle from all over Nigeria and the rest of West Africa, lured by glitzy Nollywood images and other people's embellished tales of success. They came, convinced their tenure would be a short one. Eventually, though, like millions before them, they melted into the sweltering Lagos metropolis.

Wale yawned again.

"I'm still waiting for the rent," the landlord said.

"You'll get it," Wale replied.

"Eyo is growing up to be a young lady."

The landlord spoke with his eyes on the street.

Wale stood up.

"You'll get your money," he said, walking back inside the room.

Wale quickly got dressed and made his way to the beer parlour. He didn't have to wait long before Femi, his oldest friend, appeared. He was about five-foot-nine, with a trim body that was peculiar to the well-fed and the rich. He walked with the assured gait of a man who knew his way well around Jungle City.

"*Alaye*! The man!"

"*Oga*, master, rich man! You've come back to your friends in Jungle City!"

The inhabitants of the beer parlour hailed Femi and he acknowledged them all with a smooth wave of his hand.

"Drink well. They're all on me," he said.

His voice was drowned by the hearty thanks they gave him. He spotted Wale at the back of the beer parlour and headed towards him. They shook hands, patted each other's backs and sat down. The barmaid put two bottles of ice-cold Guinness on the table, dropped two glasses and slinked away.

"How body?" Femi asked his friend.

"We *dey* manage," Wale replied, looking at his friend's expensive-looking shirt, trousers and leather shoes. Everything about him spoke of breeding, wealth and elegance. There was no trace of the thirteen-year-old boy abandoned by his mother almost twenty years ago at Ajegunle bus stop, crying because some men with guns had stolen his money. Wale had run into Femi, now a Jungle City orphan, and they'd remained friends ever since. But Femi had made it out of the jungle, while Wale hadn't.

"Look at you, big man," Wale said, taking a sip of his beer.

"Are you sure about this?" Femi asked, referring to the real reason for their meeting.

"She has to go. We cannot continue living like this. The rent is due."

"I can pay the rent," Femi interrupted.

"It's not just the rent. It's everything. At least, in London, she'll be able to go to school. She will have a better life than the one she has here," Wale said.

"It's not as easy as you think it is."

"I don't care what you say. She'll be getting paid for something she does for free here: taking care of her siblings.

If she can take care of someone else's children and get paid for it in pound sterling *and* get free education to boot, then why not?"

"Wale, all you're seeing are the money signs. I still think you should think about it," Femi cautioned.

"There's nothing to think about. You send people over there and I'm asking you to do the same for my daughter. Look around you. What future does she have here?"

Femi leaned back on his chair and fingered his chin thoughtfully. The diamonds on his watch caught the sun's rays and glinted at Wale, who watched him intently. Femi sighed.

"I've never taken a child before," he said.

"There is always a first time," Wale responded.

They both reached out for their beer glasses and drank. The barmaid inserted a popular highlife CD into the player and the sounds of an Ajegunle musician filled the beer parlour.

*   *   *

The sun was setting when Wale made his way back to his home. He found the landlord in exactly the same position as he had left him earlier that day: on the bench, outside the face-me-I-face-you. He nodded to him and went inside. He nodded at the women cooking in the corridor and then opened the door to his one-room home. As expected, his wife had gotten home before him. She was putting aside ingredients for their supper.

"The children not back yet?" he asked.

Olufunmi shook her head. "Did you go to that man for that *alabaru*, goods carrier, job?"

Wale had forgotten all about it. He waved his hand and sat

on the mattress. "Forget all that. I have something to tell you," he said, taking off his rubber slippers. The soles were crusty with hardened dirt.

"And I have a lot to tell you, too. That landlord…"

"Forget about the landlord. This is important."

Something in Wale's voice made Olufunmi take notice. She put aside the onions, garlic and chilli she was sorting and joined him on the mattress.

"I told Femi to take Eyo to London," he told her.

Olufunmi's hand went to her chest.

"We don't have a choice. With the rent and everything… She'll have a better life."

"What is she supposed to do in London?"

Olufunmi could barely get the words out.

London. The word reverberated around their room like the forbidden fruit, as if it were meant to be spoken in more salubrious surroundings.

"She will take care of small children, like she does her siblings here, except that she will be paid in pound sterling, which they'll send to us. Just like Mama Fola's sister. Her daughter is taking care of children there, too."

"Wande has not heard from her daughter in over a year," Olufunmi reminded him.

Wale carried on as if he didn't hear her. "Imagine! She will have a better life."

"Wale, I don't know…"

"In London, she will go to school. It's free there. She'll finally be able to read."

Olufunmi was silent.

"She will have a better life. Think of all those people that go and come back every year with money. Our daughter will be one of them."

"But how…"

"Femi will be here soon. He'll explain everything. He said that, if all goes well, she can even be in London at this time tomorrow. Imagine that. Our very own Eyo, in London."

Olufunmi looked around their home. It was the dry season. Even then, she still slept with one eye open because of the threat of fire. They didn't have electricity, so they used candles. The close proximity of buildings and shacks in Ajegunle made fire a constant threat. It was not uncommon for settlements in Ajegunle to be wiped out by fires from unattended candles. When this happened, entire families would camp by the roadside and under bridges, until they sourced enough money to build new shacks.

In the rainy season, Olufunmi lived in fear of their one-room home being flooded–which it did frequently. The wooden planks they laid on the floor did nothing to disguise the fact that their building was built on solidified garbage. The lack of drainage facilities in Jungle City didn't help either. Two years ago, their home, a wooden shack in another AJ City settlement, was washed away during the rainy season. After that, they joined other families sleeping at the Isale Eko end of the Third Mainland Bridge. It had been their home for a year, until Femi helped them out–again–by finding them this room and paying the requisite two-year upfront rent. Cholera, malaria and other diseases were rife. She didn't know which she feared most: fire, floods or disease. And now, the rent was due. In fact, it was three months overdue and Wale wasn't working. She sold food by the roadside, but it wasn't enough. It never was.

London. The land of white people. Everybody who went there made money. She knew some women from Jungle City that Femi had taken there. Every Christmas, they came back to visit their relatives in Ajegunle, with money, clothes and jewellery. Some of them had even built houses on the Victoria Island extension, otherwise known as Millionaires Quarters.

London. If Eyo went, she would have a better life, one where she wouldn't be watched by a perverted landlord while bathing. She would sleep on a bed, not a sleeping mat. She would never have to flee her own home in the middle of a rainy night, when it flooded with sewage. She would get an education and support her family when she grew older. She would escape the curse of Jungle City.

Wale followed his wife's eyes. He was looking at what she saw: a hovel, not painted, its concrete walls darkened by years of filth and grease. He saw the mattress on the floor, the only furniture in the room. To the left of the door were two cardboard boxes: one filled with clothes and the other, with pots and plates. Next to the cardboard boxes was their cooking stove. Propped alongside the wall were more pots and pans, Olufunmi's work tools. To the right of the door were two sleeping mats. A few flies buzzed around the oppressively hot room. On alternate days, their eardrums resonated with trumpet calls from the neighbouring mosque and churches.

It wasn't much of a life. But then, Wale's life hadn't amounted to much either, unlike Femi's. Femi had seen a way of getting out of Jungle City by exporting people to Europe. He was now a millionaire, on the verge of launching his own property development company. He had cited the unsavoury characters flooding the people export business as his reason for diversifying.

"I need time to think about it."

Olufunmi's voice intruded on his thoughts.

"Femi will be here tomorrow. He'll explain everything," Wale responded.

"Will Eyo be all right?"

There was a tinge of fear in Olufunmi's voice. Wale didn't speak for a few moments.

"Of course, she will be all right. Anything is better than this."

*   *   *

Eyo wiped her face. Her body was slick with sweat. In the dark, she could hear frogs croaking in the drain outside. She turned to Sade and almost immediately turned back towards Lanre. She was rewarded for her trouble when he flung his arm onto her chest. She put his arm back on his side. Their bedroom door opened quietly. Immediately, Eyo shut her eyes. She sensed someone crouch at her feet and then felt the person shake her ankle. She refused to open her eyes or even acknowledge the figure. Then she heard a whisper.

"Sade."

Quietly, Eyo got off the mat and followed the person out of the room. She trembled slightly when the person held her hand and led her down the dark, unlit corridor to the outback. She could just make out the garishly coloured mat he'd set on the ground. Her father gave her a gentle shove towards the mat and she lay down on it, determined not to let her tears fall. Woodenly, she took off her nightdress and waited for him. He came towards her and thrust his hips at her. A whimper escaped Eyo when he took her hand and shoved it inside his trousers. He moaned softly when Eyo released his manhood and bent over it. She had barely finished before he pushed her back on the mat and roughly parted her legs. When he was spent, Eyo got dressed and got off the mat.

"You're a good girl. Imagine what would happen if anyone ever found out. And your poor sister," her father said.

Eyo didn't answer. Wale sighed heavily before getting up. He rolled the mat and went to the *shalanga* hut, propping the mat against the wall. He came back and took Eyo's hand in his. She resisted the urge to break free and run. She couldn't run away, though. She had to think about Sade.

They entered the room as quietly as they had left it. On the mattress, Olufunmi heard them come back in. She bit her lip when she heard Eyo's involuntary squeal of pain as she sank back on the sleeping mat. When her husband joined her on the mattress, she turned her back to him and faced her daughters' direction. In the dark, as her eyes settled on Eyo, she fought back the memories of herself at Eyo's age and her father leading her to a secluded spot at the edge of the village. She could hear her mother's voice, "Olufunmi, you must endure because you are a woman. That is what women do. We endure."

Olufunmi turned away from Eyo and faced the ceiling. On the mat, Eyo turned to face her younger sister. Tears streamed down her cheeks. She wiped them away without taking her eyes off Sade.

Three

The next day, Eyo got off the mat gingerly, her intimates stinging. She could hear the women in the corridor as they called out morning greetings to each other and prepared breakfast for their families. As she got off the mat, she took a customary look at her siblings and, as was equally customary, ignored the sleeping form on the mattress.

She reached out for the door handle and turned it. Mama was stirring the *ogi* and sweating heavily in the corridor. Eyo looked towards the open doorway to the right. It was dawn.

"Go back to bed. You're not working today," Mama said.

"Let me help you stir the *ogi* then," Eyo said.

"I said you should go back to bed. I know you're illiterate, but don't you understand Yoruba as well?" Mama's voice was sharp.

"Maybe if you'd sent me to school, I wouldn't be illiterate," Eyo answered.

Her mother gave her a dark stare and Eyo retreated to the room. She felt feverish, her insides stinging badly. He had been rougher than usual with her last night. As she entered their one-room home, she had a strong urge to descend on the prone figure and kick him into oblivion, screaming and laughing manically while doing it.

Sade stirred on the mattress and Eyo went to her. She ran her hands through her braids. Mama came inside the room and sat on the mattress. She didn't look at the person on it. Eyo could tell she was mad at *him*.

"Eyo, we need to talk urgently. Your father…" Olufunmi cleared her throat. "We've both agreed that Femi should take you to London."

"The London you see on the mechanic's television?"

"Yes."

Eyo didn't see how that was possible. She was in Jungle City and London was far away, a land inhabited by white people.

"You'll be helping somebody with their children. You'll also go to school yourself…"

Mama's voice was getting hoarse. She cleared her throat.

"It will be good for you. You will have a better life," she continued.

The body on the bed spoke, "Imagine that, Eyo. You, in London."

"What about Sade and Lanre?"

"They'll remain here," Mama answered. "When you're older and settled in London, you'll send for them and they will be educated, just like you."

Eyo didn't understand. *Why were they sending her away?*

"I'm not going anywhere," she said.

Eyo could tell that Mama didn't like what she said by the way her ample bosom heaved.

"Eyo, you will do as you're told," Mama's voice roise with each word. "How many people from Ajegunle think about going to London, much less are offered the opportunity to do so? Your Uncle Femi wants to do something good for you and you want to throw it back at his face."

Sade and Lanre stirred. Eyo shook the two of them awake violently. "They want me to go to London," she told them. "You'll never see me again."

Sade rubbed her eyes. "I want to go to London," she said sleepily.

"You'll never see me again," Eyo warned Lanre.

"Send me a football when you get there," he yawned.

Eyo faced her parents. "I'm not going. I'm not leaving Sade. I don't want…"

"Eyo, look at me," Mama's voice was soft. "Your sister will be *okay*."

There was a look in her eyes that Eyo couldn't read. From the mattress, her father spoke again, "Femi will be here shortly. He'll explain everything. He said he might be able to get false documents for you within two weeks, but it could be less than that. You're going to London, whether you like it or not. This is an opportunity of a lifetime for you, for Sade, for Lanre, for all of us. Don't ruin it."

Wale turned his back on all of them, seeming to sleep again.

"Imagine that, Eyo. You, in London!" Mama mimicked Papa's earlier words.

"I want to go to London," Sade cried out.

Eyo tried to carry her, but she resisted, preferring instead to walk to Mama, her arms outstretched. Mama got off the mattress and picked her up. She stopped in front of Eyo who was still sitting on the sleeping mat, her eyes down, a tear glistening from the edge of her nose.

"You will understand when you're older," she heard her mother say.

*　　　*　　　*

Everything was packed. The only thing that remained was for Uncle Femi to come and pick her up to take her to London. Mama Fola, Mama, Sade and Lanre were all in the room. Her father was outside, waiting for Uncle Femi.

"Your life will be better," Mama assured Eyo. "You will go to school. You will be with white people and learn new things. All you have to do is help Femi's friends with their children. That's it. That's all you have to do. And then, when you're older, you'll help your siblings. Maybe even bring them over to London with you. That's a good thing, isn't it?"

Eyo nodded. It was a good thing. She had been selfish before, thinking only of herself. She would endure. She would go to London, work hard, go to school and send for Sade, Lanre and Mama, when she was older and had money. They would all live in London together, away from her father.

"Your Uncle Femi, has done something very good for you. Don't give him any trouble, you hear? On your way to London, be quiet and don't say or do anything that will bring attention to yourself. You know what your father and I always tell you about your sharp mouth. Always having an answer for everything. But not in London, with the people you'll be helping, you hear? Your uncle has paid a lot of money to do this for you, money that we will never have or hope to repay. You understand? You must *endure*," Mama emphasised the last word.

Eyo nodded again.

Mama Fola stepped forward. She embraced her.

"You've heard everything that your mother has said. Remember: Endurance is everything. You're going somewhere new, somewhere nobody in this family has ever been to before. It will be strange, but you must endure. For your sake and for the sake of your family. Remember: Your uncle has done a great thing for you. Don't forget it."

Eyo turned to her brother who was fiddling with his football.

"Don't forget to send me a better football when you get there," Lanre said.

They heard a car horn. Mama Fola and Olufunmi looked at each other anxiously.

"Sade, aren't you going to say bye to your sister?" Mama Fola chided the little girl.

Sade continued to play with the Barbie in her hands. "I want to go to London," she said.

"To think that Eyo gave you that doll as a leaving present," Mama said.

The room door opened and Wale's head popped out from behind it. "Femi is here," he said.

Eyo followed him out of the door, on legs of lead. Mama, Mama Fola and Lanre followed her, their steps muted. As she came out into the early morning sun, she paused and looked at the narrow street with its cavernous holes. She looked back at their face-me-I-face-you, her gaze committing every unpainted crack and greasy wall to memory. She then looked up again to the street where her uncle was standing by the car. Suddenly, she ran back to their room. Inside, Sade was on the mattress, playing disconsolately with the Barbie. Eyo embraced her and kissed her forehead.

"I want to go to London," Sade whined.

"Bye, Sade," Eyo whispered.

Then she was gone, out of the room, out of the building and into the open car, crying. As the car pulled away, she waved to her mother, Mama Fola and Lanre. They waved back, tense smiles on their faces.

"She hates me," Wale said as the car disappeared down the street.

"She hates all of us," Olufunmi said.

"Nonsense," Mama Fola said. "She has resigned herself to her fate in the last two weeks. Besides, when she's older, she'll understand."

*   *   *

In the car, Femi drew Eyo close to him, murmuring comforting platitudes. Eyo didn't respond. She didn't want to go to London. She wanted to stay in Jungle City with Mama, Lanre and Sade. She wanted to make sure that Sade would be safe from Papa.

She cried even louder.

Four

"There," Femi pointed ahead of him. "That is what is called an airport. Remember what I told you about them. They're processing centres for people who travel. It is also where planes–those things that fly in the air, which Lanre likes chasing after–are parked."

Eyo looked up and saw the building Uncle Femi was pointing at. It was big and had what looked like stadium lights outside it. There were a few policemen milling about. Cars were pulling up alongside the structure. People would get out quickly, grab their bags out of the boot and give the car's occupants a swift wave, before scurrying inside.

Eyo heard a crash and she and her uncle turned in the direction it came from.

"I said, 'No parking in front of the airport!'" a policeman shouted. "There's a car park downstairs!"

The officer's baton was on the now dented hood of the car in front of them. A young man got out and a heated argument ensued.

"You just drop us here and go back. Drive safely," Uncle Femi told their driver.

"Yes, sir." The driver parked and immediately ran to the boot. By the time Eyo and Femi disembarked from the car, he had their luggage on the pavement. He ran back inside the car and drove off, just as another policeman with a swinging stick reached the car.

"You shouldn't be too free with that baton," Uncle Femi advised him.

"I don't have time for this," the officer replied, walking off.

A minute later, Eyo and Femi heard him barking again.

"No parking in front of the airport. You think you're special? I said, 'Move the car!'"

Eyo held onto her uncle's hand. She was rewarded with a reassuring tap on the shoulder. They saw someone wheeling an empty trolley and Femi called out to him.

"In London," Uncle Femi said as he hoisted their bags onto the trolley, "these things are free at the airport. But here, you have to pay to use them." He counted some money from his wallet and handed it to the trolley man. "By the way, this is called a trolley. Repeat after me: 'trolley'."

"Trolley," Eyo echoed.

Femi nodded approvingly. They made their way inside.

Eyo looked around her and blinked at the bright lights. When she opened her eyes again, it was in awe. She didn't think she had ever seen such a grand place. She was in a big room with many people carrying bags, walking around. There were some people behind desks, talking to people in front of them. Every so often, they would hand them a piece of paper which they looked at before leaving the counter.

Femi bent down to Eyo's height.

"I need you to be quiet for now, while I confirm everything is okay with our flight—that's what you call going to London by plane. You see that area?" he pointed to where the people behind the counters were. "We'll be talking to them soon, after we've queued. You've been brave so far and we've not long to

34

go now. I need you to be strong and quiet. Can you do that for your uncle?"

She would not bring shame on her uncle and family after everything he'd done for her.

Eyo nodded.

"Good," Uncle Femi said, smiling. Eyo smiled back, trying to mask the wave of sadness that came over her. She wouldn't think of Sade, Mama Fola, Mama and Lanre. They wouldn't be in the house now. Mama and Mama Fola would be at the roadside, selling food. Sade would be with them, on her special mat, hopefully playing with her new doll. She wondered who would accompany Lanre when he went hawking. Tears pricked her eyes and she wiped them off furtively. Uncle Femi was taking her to London, helping her, and she was crying like an ungrateful person. She wasn't enduring. Mama would not be happy.

They joined the queue. A man in a uniform came up to them.

"Passport?"

Uncle Femi gave him two small booklets, which the uniformed man looked at for a very long time. He left them standing and went to a computer on a table at the head of the queue. She knew it was a computer because that was what they were called on the films shown on the battery-powered television of the neighbourhood roadside mechanic. She knew that computers helped people do many things. Exactly what, though, she didn't know. The man came back and handed the booklets back to Uncle Femi, his face unsmiling. He looked at Eyo and back again at Uncle Femi.

"Is there a problem?" Uncle Femi asked.

"I'm sure there is. I just have to find out," the uniformed man said. He left them in the queue.

"Passport?" Eyo heard him say to the couple behind them.

"Ignoramus," Uncle Femi muttered under his breath. Eyo clutched his hand and he smiled at her reassuringly.

When it was their turn at the counter, the uniformed man hurried over and stood beside them.

"Could you move please?" Uncle Femi said irritably.

"I work for this airline, so I have every right to be here," the man said.

"Passports and tickets please," the lady behind the counter said, her hand outstretched to them.

Eyo thought the lady was beautiful. She spoke English like white people did. Eyo thought she would soon speak like that. Mama would be so proud of her and her education. The counter lady caught Eyo staring at her and smiled.

"Yours?" she asked Uncle Femi as he handed over the booklets and some pieces of paper stuck in between their pages.

"Not strictly speaking, no. She's my niece," Uncle Femi replied.

"If I was you, I would keep my eyes on their passports instead of making idle chit-chat," the uniformed man said.

The counter lady's smile disappeared. Her movements became brisk. She studied their passports and tickets officiously.

"Have you got any sharp instruments or anything of that sort in any of your luggage?"

"No," Uncle Femi answered.

"Did you pack the two suitcases yourself?"

"Yes."

"Can you put the first suitcase on the scale for me please?"

Uncle Femi put his suitcase on the scales. Red numbers flickered on a screen on the front side of the counter. The lady pressed something and the rubber surface under Uncle Femi's bag started moving, taking it away from them. Eyo gasped.

"It's okay. It's taking it straight to the plane," Uncle Femi said. He then turned to the counter lady.

"It's her first time on a plane," he explained.

The uniformed man snorted.

"You can put the second suitcase on there as well," the counter lady said.

Uncle Femi obeyed and, in no time at all, the second piece joined its sibling on the magic roller. The counter lady handed Uncle Femi the booklets and pieces of paper.

"Enjoy your flight," she said.

"Thank you," Uncle Femi said. He led Eyo away and patted her back.

"Well done. Your parents would be proud of you. There's just one more thing we need to do before getting on the plane to go to London."

He led Eyo to another counter. This time, there was a policeman standing behind it. He yawned as he looked at their documents and waved them through to a hall with another queue. They took their place in the queue. Eyo could see what looked like four counters at the front end of the line, manned by uniformed men. Every so often, she would see people from the queue go up, hand over their passports–she hoped she got the name right–to the uniformed man who would bang something on them and then hand them back to the individuals in front of him.

"After this is London," Uncle Femi whispered to her as they waited to be called forward.

Eyo tried to stop the sudden terror that rose inside her as she thought about the journey. *What if the plane came down from the sky, while she and Uncle Femi were in it? After all, there was nothing to hold it up in the air.*

The uniformed counter man motioned for them to come forward. Uncle Femi stepped to the counter.

"For a minute, I thought we would be sent to another counter," he said to the uniformed counter man.

The man's face was unreadable.

"Passports?" He held out his hand.

Uncle Femi gave him the passports. "The money *dey* inside," he whispered.

The uniformed man took something–which looked stained with ink–from his table and stamped the passports with it. With a practised hand, he slipped out the money from between the pages of one passport, while his nearby colleague discreetly looked away.

The uniformed man handed the passports back to Uncle Femi.

"Enjoy your flight," he said.

Femi nodded. Holding Eyo's hand firmly in his, he led her to the hand luggage check. They made it through without any trouble and continued walking to the departure lounge. Eyo looked behind her, until she couldn't see the uniformed counter man anymore. She wanted to tell him that he should take her passport back and allow her to leave the airport and go back to Jungle City.

"And now, to London!" Uncle Femi said. "But first, some food. How about we get you a taster of the kind of food you'll be eating in London?" he asked her.

Eyo shook her head. "I'm not hungry," she said.

Her uncle crouched on the airport floor to her level. "You're thinking of everybody in Ajegunle, aren't you?"

Eyo nodded, her lips quivering.

"Don't worry. You'll see them again," Uncle Femi said. "How about I get you some Coke and biscuits?"

Eyo started shaking her head but stopped; she remembered her promise to Mama that she wouldn't make trouble for Uncle Femi.

"Maybe later," she said.

"Yes, on the plane," her uncle said.

A voice announced a ten a.m. flight to Manchester, over the Tannoy. Femi got up and reclaimed Eyo's hand in his, and they both walked to the boarding gate. Eyo took one last look behind her and whispered softly to herself, *Bye, bye, Ajegunle. Bye, bye, Nigeria.*

*   *   *

"Remember, I'm your uncle and this is your first time in the UK. Yes, *uukaay*. Say it like that: u-u-k-a-ay."

"*Uukaay*," Eyo pronounced after him.

Femi nodded satisfactorily. She was doing well. A bit too quiet but that was the inevitable result of her parent's priming.

There was one point, just before boarding the plane, when she had balked in terror.

"Everybody in this thing? What will hold it up in the air?" she asked.

"White man magic," he'd replied.

Eyo's grip on his hand was hard. Femi consoled himself with the fact that he knew the family she was going to stay with very well. The couple were good people, with two children aged ten and six years. The mother owned a Nigerian restaurant in east London, while the father was a jack of all trades, including part-time work as a people exporter. Eyo would be all right.

At his side, Eyo thought of her brother. She wondered what Lanre was doing now, which was probably playing football while waiting for Mama and Sade to come back from selling food on the roadside. She hoped he wasn't anywhere near the landlord. Mama would kill him. Suddenly, she felt low. Then she reminded herself how fortunate she was. Many people dreamed of going to London, but few actually made it. And here she was ready to cry. Because she was in the uukaay and she didn't think she liked it. Mama wouldn't be happy at all if she knew.

She would be quiet. And she would not draw any attention to herself, even when it was so cold and everybody seemed to speak through their noses. She wanted to cry because she missed Mama, Lanre and Sade. But she would be quiet because she wouldn't want to cause trouble to anyone. She held on even tighter to Femi's hand as they stood in the queue, awaiting their turn at the counter.

"Passports please."

Femi handed over their passports. There was a brief pause when the officer looked from Femi to Eyo and back again. Then she looked at their passports.

Femi waited.

"And is this your first time in the UK?" the officer directed her gaze to the young girl dressed in dated jeans and sweater. The girl looked back at her with clear eyes.

"Uukaay," Eyo said.

The officer arched her eyebrows.

"It's her first time in the UK," Femi explained.

The officer looked at Eyo with trained eyes. Eyo was holding on to Femi's hand. There was implicit trust in her grip and eyes. No sign of enforced closeness as was common with trafficked children. Eyo and Femi waited. The officer stamped the passports and handed them back to Femi.

"Welcome to the UK," she said, waving them through.

*   *   *

In the back of the car, Eyo stole fleeting glances at the man that came to pick them up from the airport. He was tall, extremely dark, with a big belly and a booming laugh. They were on a motorway that kind of resembled Third Mainland Bridge in Lagos, except this one was wider, with no traffic and no hawkers selling anything to anybody. Above her, the motorway lights threw shafts of brightness across the back seat and her lap. Uncle Femi said that in London, people had electricity all the time. Eyo thought of Sade and their father in their dark room in Ajegunle. A feeling of utter wretchedness came upon her and she huddled deeper into the car seat, trying to flee from the awful despair her imagination was inflicting upon her. From his mirror, Sam glanced at her before turning his attention back to the road.

"Femi, she's a bit thin. Are you sure she can work?"

"Sam, she's taking care of your children, not selling things in the market," Femi replied.

"This journey…" Sam began.

"Gatwick and Heathrow are no-go areas now. Immigration and child protection people have set up shop there. They watch Nigerian flights like people on a mission. You know that, so don't complain."

"I was just saying, that's all," Sam explained.

Femi didn't answer. Sam said it all the time. That was the problem. He knew as well as Femi did that there was no way they could've gotten Eyo past immigration at Heathrow or Gatwick. Too many questions. Still, Sam had to complain. Just because.

"Try driving from London to Manchester and back in one day," Sam continued.

"*You* try bringing in people, especially a child from Nigeria, into any country in Europe nowadays and see how far you get," Femi retorted.

"Eyo, you like London?" Sam asked her in Yoruba, looking at her from his rear-view mirror.

Eyo nodded.

"We're now going to the real London. You landed in Manchester earlier, you see," Sam said.

Eyo nodded again. She didn't really understand what the man was saying about the different Londons but thought it would be good if she pretended to do so. If she appeared stupid, the man might decide he didn't want her anymore and tell Uncle Femi to take her back to Nigeria. It would make her happy, of course, but make Mama sad and mad at her at the same time. Eyo didn't want that. Besides, she didn't want to look ungrateful for what Uncle Femi had done for her, paying all that money for her to come to the uukaay. Eyo wiped the tears that gathered in her eyes. She was cold. And she wanted to go back to Ajegunle. To see her mother and siblings. She leaned on the car window and looked outdoors.

It was dark outside. It must be really late. Papa would be at the beer parlour by now. Lanre and Sade would be sleeping and Mama would be getting her pots and pans ready for the next day. When she finished, she would usually lie down and pretend to sleep, so Papa wouldn't disturb her when he came back. As if he cared. He did what he always did anyway: climb on top of her and start grunting away like the animal he was. It was because of him she was here in this cold, clean country, where people spoke through their noses and she was away from her mother and siblings. A sniff escaped from her.

*   *   *

Femi heard the sniff and turned round from the front seat to look at Eyo. *It was all Wale's fault*, he told himself. He was her father, the one who wanted his daughter in London, "the land of white people, where she will have a better life".

He turned back and faced the motorway ahead of him.

Sam heard the sniff. He hoped she wouldn't cry all the time. Somehow, he didn't think his wife would have the patience to placate a thin, snivelling, illiterate girl from Nigeria.

*　　　*　　　*

Someone was shaking her.

"Eyo, wake up! You're in London."

Eyo opened her eyes and yawned. Sam was leaning over her, while his hand rested on her thigh. She had an image of another hand there and moved away slightly. His hand fell limply on the car seat. Her eyes went to the front seat of the car and outside it. *Uncle Femi wasn't there.* She fought the fear that came upon her and looked around again.

"He's gone. Now get out of the car. We haven't got all night."

Sam raised his hand as if to shake her thigh again, so Eyo scrambled out of the car and shivered in the cold. She stole a quick look around her as if expecting her uncle to emerge from somewhere.

They were in a large compound with lots of dark-brown concrete tower blocks. The overhead street lights beamed on the clumps of grass trying to live within their allotted few square feet. Their futile existence added a desolate, pathetic air to the place. Eyo looked up, expecting to see stars in the sky. There were none, so she quickly looked back down again, anxious not to anger the man who had brought her to the *real* London. Looking at stars had been one of her favourite pastimes with Lanre who was back in Ajegunle and had probably forgotten all about her. Loneliness pounded her afresh in waves.

Sam had parked the car in one of the parking bays in front of a block. She watched him as he started taking some bags from the car boot. She shivered, unsure of what to do. When he finished, he came up to her.

"Come on; let's go. Unless you want to die out here in the cold. Look at you; you're shivering."

The last sentence was a statement. He gave her a small push and walked past her, clutching his bags. Eyo wrapped her arms around her chest and followed him. *What about Uncle Femi? Where is my uncle?* She wanted to ask.

The man's mobile phone rang.

"We'll see you in a few moments. We're just downstairs," he said in Yoruba to the person on the phone before hanging up.

"Will I see my uncle again?"

"Didn't I tell you to hurry up and walk?"

Eyo bit her lip. Mama always said she asked too many questions. She decided to be quiet. She didn't want to cause trouble and be sent back to Nigeria. By now, they were right outside a tower block. Eyo waited, while he punched what looked like numbers on the left side of the building's entrance, a steel door. The door opened and they both walked in. Eyo found herself facing a lift. She knew what it was because she'd seen it on a Jungle City mechanic's car battery-powered television. She stopped.

Sam pressed something on the wall. The lift made a noise and its doors opened with a ping. Sam pushed her towards it. Eyo took a few steps and stopped again. Suddenly, Sam understood.

"It's a lift. Just enter it," he nudged her inside and they went in together. "Tell it where you want it to go by doing this: Press a number. This one." Sam pressed a number on the far right of the top row of buttons. The number meant nothing to Eyo. "And then you press this button here." He pressed what looked like two arrows facing each other. "Understand?"

Eyo nodded like she understood. She knew that after today she wouldn't enter this moving box by herself. She would find another way to get to where they were going. She nodded, though, because she didn't want the man to think she was stupid and send her back to Jungle City. Her father would kill her.

"Good," Sam said. "You'll be doing this yourself from tomorrow."

Eyo nodded again. She tried to quell the sick feeling that arose in her stomach, when the lift started moving.

After what seemed like forever, a mechanical voice spoke and the doors opened. They stepped out and Eyo gulped the fresh air in relief. Lanre would've enjoyed the lift journey. Unlike her, he had no fear.

She found herself in a long balcony punctuated with doors she guessed led into people's homes. She turned to her right and only then did she realise how high up the building they were. Immediately, she focused her attention on Sam's back. She reminded herself not to look down again the next time she came outside and was on the balcony. It made her feel ill. They walked past a few doors and eventually stopped in front of one. Before Sam could do anything, the door flew open and a boy about Lanre's age ran out and threw himself on him.

"Daddy!"

"Joshua! Come back inside! It's cold and you're not wearing shoes!"

A woman wearing a *wrapa* and a cardigan walked out hurriedly after the boy.

"It's okay," Sam said. "You've missed your daddy, haven't you?"

Sam dropped his bags and lifted up the little boy in his arms. He squealed in delight. Eyo drew back, not sure what to do.

"This boy…" the woman stopped and stared at Eyo. "What are you waiting for? Carry the bags inside!" she ordered in Yoruba.

Eyo bent down immediately and started picking up Sam's bags.

"Joshua, this is Eyo. She will be helping mummy take care of you. Say 'hello'," Sam said. "Lola, those bags are too heavy for her. I'll take them inside myself, once I've taken care of Joshua."

"Hello, Eyo," Joshua said in English. Sam shook his son playfully. "Come. Let's go inside. It's cold. Eyo, leave those bags. Joshua, you have to get down. Daddy needs to pick up the bags. Come on, everybody, inside." Sam alternated between speaking in English to his family and Yoruba to Eyo.

Eyo followed her master and his family inside her new home.

At least it was warm inside was her first thought when she entered the flat. The front door opened into a small hallway. To her immediate right was a half-open door through which she could see a kitchen. Directly in front of her was another half-open door through which she could just make out a booming television. To her left was a clothes rack on the wall, with several coats and jackets hanging from it. Directly underneath was a family-size shoe rack.

Eyo noted the number of children's shoes on it. Femi had told her the couple had two children. *Surely, the two of them didn't own all the children's shoes on that rack?* Back in Nigeria, she and her siblings owned just one pair of rubber slippers each.

A few feet away was another door, which she guessed led into the bathroom. She sensed Sam's wife watching her and turned back quickly, keeping her eyes down. Mama often told her off for "looking at people disrespectfully".

Sam dropped his bags in the hallway and Joshua ran inside the living room.

"Children, no television. Bed. Immediately," Lola called out after him. She turned to Eyo. "Follow me, but first, shoes off," she said in Yoruba.

Eyo removed her shoes. Suddenly, she felt like she could sleep all day. She also wanted to know where her uncle was and why he disappeared without saying goodbye. Had he gone back to Nigeria already?

"Eyo, am I going to repeat myself every time I ask you to do something?" Lola folded her arms as she spoke.

"No, madam."

"Then why are we still here when I asked you to follow me? Sam?" Lola turned to her husband who was veering to the bathroom on their left. He opened the door and Eyo caught a glimpse of a bath and toilet. Just like the ones she'd seen on television. A shower hose had been attached to the wall above the bath. She wondered how they used the shower to bathe and hoped they had a bucket and small bowl that she could use. Femi had showed her how to use the toilet on the plane. "In London, every family has their own private bathroom, so you will never have to bathe outdoors again. And look," he said, flushing the toilet, "you won't need to use a *shalanga* ever again in your life either."

"Uncle, it's loud," Eyo had told him. The toilet's whistling sound scared her.

"Only airplane toilets are this loud. Now show me once again how you flush toilets."

Eyo showed him and Femi had nodded in approval, which made her happy. She couldn't believe it; she would be bathing indoors using bathroom taps, just like on television. Sade would love it! At the thought of her little sister, the beginnings of Eyo's smile faded and her tiredness returned.

"Leave me out of it. You wanted a girl to help you; I got one for you. Now leave me alone."

Eyo was brought back to the present by Sam's voice. Lola walked inside the sitting room and Eyo followed her. Joshua was sitting on the floor, his eyes glued to the cartoon on the television screen. There was another girl in the room, about Eyo's age, curled up on a sofa alongside a wall to the left. She was reading a book.

"Tolu, don't you think you should go and greet your father?"

"In a minute. I've almost finished my book."

Tolu turned another page and made herself more comfortable on the sofa. Lola walked up, took the book from her and threw it on the floor.

"Now," Lola commanded.

"Mum!"

Tolu got up grudgingly and left the room.

Lola turned to Joshua. "Bedtime," she said.

"Mum!"

"No arguments. Eyo, start tidying up this place. When you finish, wait here." She motioned to the living room doorway.

"I'll be with you as soon as I finish with him."

Eyo's stomach rumbled. Lola shot her a glance and motioned to Joshua to follow her. He obeyed, giving Eyo a wondering look.

The living room was roughly double the size of her home in Ajegunle. It was dominated by the large television and computer and chair at the end of the sofa. She bent down and started picking up the toys. There was a doll with long blonde hair. It looked like the one—the Barbie—in Jungle City, which she had found by the rubbish heap, cleaned up and given to Sade. She stroked the doll's hair and her fingers traced its face. A few moments later, the doll was snatched from her. She looked up. It was Tolu. The girl went back to the sofa, still holding the doll, and picked up the book her mother had thrown to the floor.

"Tolu!" It was Lola calling her.

Tolu pretended not to hear.

"If I call you again, you'll see!"

Tolu groaned and made exaggerated dragging movements towards the door just as her father came inside the room. "You've said 'hello' to Eyo? She will be helping your Mummy take care of you. Remember: She doesn't understand English," Sam said in English.

"I can take care of myself, Daddy," Tolu replied.

"I'm sure you can, but your brother can't. Come on upstairs, before your mother loses her temper."

"Goodnight."

"Goodnight."

Sam sat on the sofa and watched Eyo picking up the toys, for a few moments. Her movements were ungainly.

"Leave all that and come and sit down," he said, patting the space next to him on the sofa. "You must be tired."

"Madame says that I should tidy up the room and stand there," Eyo pointed to the door.

The sofa did look inviting, but then she also remembered his hand on her thigh, in the car. She shut her eyes for a moment to block out the unbidden images of her father and then opened them; Sam was looking at her strangely.

"Well, I'm telling you that you should come and sit down." He patted the sofa again.

Eyo hesitated, then remembered what her mother had said about not being the cause of any trouble. She joined Sam on the sofa. A few moments later, her body relaxed and her head dropped to her shoulder. When Lola entered the living room and found her sleeping on the sofa, she gave her husband a questioning look.

"Leave her. She's tired," her husband said.

"The girl is thin," Lola commented.

"You can learn from her," her husband replied. Lola threw a cushion at him and they both roared with laughter.

Five

Bola joined Michael, her husband, on the living room sofa.

"The kids?"

"Out like a light," she answered him.

They sat in silence.

"What are we going to do?" Bola asked. "We can't go on living like this. People are starting to avoid me because they think I will ask them for money."

"There is, of course, another way," her husband said, not meeting her eyes. Bola shook her head vehemently. She knew what he meant.

"Well, we can't just sit here staring into space. All you have to do is go there for a year or eighteen months and come back with money, just like the other women. It's either that or we die of hunger. You won't be the first graduate to do this. Everyone is talking about Stella. You've seen the house she's building."

"You're my husband. How can you ask me to do this?"

"Would you rather we starved to death? I'm not working and, in any case, is it bad for you to do something noble for your family?"

"There is nothing noble about prostitution," Bola replied.

"Money does not discriminate," her husband answered.

They debated the issue far into the night. In the end, Bola gave in. At dawn the next day, her husband hurried to the house of the local *italio*, people smuggler. They negotiated the terms: false papers, flights, accommodation in Italy and the fees of the *italios* and an Italy-based madame. It came to just over fifty thousand US dollars, payable over two years. A month later, Bola was on the plane to Madrid via Ghana. In Madrid, she was met by one of the *italio's* agent. He met her at the airport. Straight after, they caught the train to Italy. That night, she joined the legions of Nigerian women on the Turin roads.

Bola had only ever slept with one man: her husband. She justified her reason for being on the streets by thinking of her children's future. It didn't stop her from vomiting all over a grassy bank off the main road the minute her first client left. But afterwards, she got up and rinsed out her mouth with water from a small bottle in her handbag. She then went back out on the main road. By the end of the night, she'd had sex with six men. A teetotaller, she went to bed amply aided by the Chianti that a street veteran had given her.

"It gets easier after the first night," the girl said as she handed Bola the bottle. Bola wasn't sure about that.

The second night *was* easier. After her third client, she had told herself that the men were having sex with her body and nothing else. By detaching her feelings from the body on top of her and the action taking place below her waist, she could take her mind back to Nigeria, to the real Bola: a married woman with two daughters. *Very soon*, she thought, *I would have enough money to pay off the* italio *and provide my family with the kind of life they deserve, a life free from lack and from the curse of poverty.*

All she had to do was grit her teeth and hold on. She almost believed she could do it.

Six

Tolu's mother–Mama Tolu, as she insisted Eyo call her–came to the kitchen. The children weren't at home. Joshua was playing football on the estate grounds with his friend, and Tolu was at Toni's, her best friend, a mixed-race Nigerian girl who lived in another housing block on the estate. They were both due back home within the hour.

Eyo set the wet dishes on a rack before wiping her hands on a kitchen towel.

"Look at her, wiping her hands on my kitchen towel as if she's been in London all her life!" Mama Tolu said, as if she spoke to an audience instead of just Eyo.

Eyo put the kitchen towel on the counter.

"If you don't want me to use it, I won't," she said.

Something in her voice irked Lola.

"I think you should mind your manners," Lola spoke sharply to her.

Eyo muttered something under her breath. Lola came closer to where she stood by the sink.

"What did you say?"

"Nothing, madam. I just want to know when I can go to school," Eyo said.

"Did you go to school in Ajegunle? Did you?"

"Isn't that the reason I'm here?"

Eyo realised she'd spoken out loud when she saw Mama Tolu's face change to rage. She grabbed hold of one of Eyo's ears and dragged her to the sitting room. Eyo twisted and howled to no avail. Mama Tolu's grip on her ear was tenacious.

Sam was on his computer, muttering to himself about people packages and rescheduled planes.

"You hear that, Sam? The girl wants to know when she can go to school," Lola said.

Sam kept his eyes on the computer screen. He spoke without looking up, "Lola, deal with her. Don't bother me."

Lola gave Eyo a blow that threw her against the back of Sam's chair before falling on the floor, on all fours. Eyo heard a buzzing sound in her ears. A moment later, shafts of pain exploded in her head, while the room spun around her. She lay still on the floor. Sam scrambled up from the chair in alarm.

"Lola, you and your temper, stop it!"

Lola wasn't listening. She lunged at Eyo's still body on the floor and *dealt* with her. When Sam eventually managed to haul her off, Eyo's face was swollen, a mass of multicoloured bruises. Her lower lip was bleeding where Lola's wedding ring had found a particularly soft target.

"Lola, what were you trying to do? Kill her?"

Lola wiped her brow, breathing heavily. "You didn't hear the way she spoke to me in the kitchen. An illiterate girl from Ajegunle, somebody of my daughter's age, talking to me like that. How dare she? She won't make that mistake again."

Lola left the room and came back a minute later with

something in her hand. She threw them at Eyo's still body. "I want her to start wearing this wig and scarf every time she leaves the flat. Too many nosy people around," she said, still breathing heavily.

*   *   *

Eyo raced out of the kitchen. Joshua and Tolu were waiting for her by the front door.

"You forgot our lunch," Tolu reminded her. Eyo ran back to the kitchen and grabbed the two lunch boxes by the sink.

"Eyo, we're going to be late!" Joshua flew out of the flat. Tolu ran after him shouting, "Joshua, wait for Eyo!"

Eyo adjusted the wig and headscarf on her head. She made sure her coat was buttoned all the way up to her neck before going after Joshua and Tolu. She kept her eyes down, as she half walked and half ran. She had just gone past the flat to their right, when she heard its front door open and close and someone shuffle out. She veered to the left, leaning slightly on the balcony railings, and waited for a few moments for the person to walk past. From the corner of her eye, she could see the two children ahead of her, waiting by the lift.

"Go on, dear," the voice said.

It was their elderly neighbour, a white woman with silver hair. From the rare occasions she saw the lady, Eyo figured that she lived alone.

Eyo didn't answer the woman. Not that she understood what she said as she spoke in English. The neighbour rested her hand on Eyo's arm and nudged her forward. "Go on," she said.

Eyo understood. She nodded and caught up with Joshua and Tolu by the lift.

"Mummy said you aren't allowed to talk to the neighbours," Tolu said in broken Yoruba.

Sometimes, Eyo felt that Tolu understood more Yoruba than she let on. She could never tell with Tolu because the girl changed moods as abruptly as uukaay weather.

"I didn't talk to her," Eyo replied in equally broken Yoruba, so Tolu could understand what she said. The lift pinged open and they all got inside. The doors were about to close, when the elderly neighbour approached.

"It's all right, dears. I'll wait for it to come back again," she said, looking at Eyo who looked away. The woman's bespectacled eyes were too penetrating. The neighbour turned to Tolu. "And who did you say she was?"

The lift doors closed, cutting her off.

Tolu said to no one in particular, in English, "We're going to have to tell Mummy that Mrs Richards saw Eyo."

"Okay," Joshua said, playing with an imaginary sword.

Their meaningless English words washed over Eyo. She leaned weakly against the lift wall. She hadn't had breakfast and she hadn't had dinner either the night before. Sam and Lola's visitors hadn't left the flat until well past midnight. Between waiting on and cleaning up after them, she didn't get to sleep until the early hours of the morning. It seemed like she had just closed her eyes for five minutes, before Lola woke her up to get the kids ready for school. The children. She was the same age as Tolu was and she looked after her. She might be illiterate, but something about that didn't seem right to Eyo.

Ping! The lift doors opened. They were on the ground floor. Eyo made sure she held on firmly to Joshua's hand, before they left the lift. He had the tendency to tear off, if he wasn't restrained. *Just like Lanre.* At the thought of her brother, she breathed in deeply, swallowing her tears. She adjusted the wig and scarf once more and stepped out of their tower block, with Tolu leading the way. The school was a mere ten-minute walk from their flat, which Eyo liked. The school walk was the only time she ever left the flat. That, or whenever Mama Tolu needed her help at the restaurant.

They weren't the only school walkers on the road. Most of the children on their estate went to the same school as Tolu and Joshua. In fact, there was a steady exodus of buggies, children and mothers from their estate, walking towards school. Eyo held on to Joshua's hand and walked, her eyes to the ground. Tolu was in front of her, chattering away to Toni. Joshua alternated between walking with his sister and Toni and hopping back to Eyo. At the school gates, Tolu took her brother's hand and waved goodbye to Eyo.

"Bye," she said in English.

Eyo waved back.

"No, say 'bye'. You have to learn English," Tolu said. "You've been here a year and still can't say a word in English. Say it: 'Bye'."

It was one of Tolu's favourite games to teach Eyo to speak English. If Eyo didn't know better, she would say Tolu's favourite pastime was teaching anybody anything: how to use the microwave oven, satellite television controls, the music player… It didn't matter what it was; everything was a teaching game or, as Eyo privately thought, a bossing-around opportunity.

"Bye," Eyo said in a low voice. She still didn't trust herself to say it right.

Tolu nodded satisfactorily and ran inside the school, her

brother in tow. As she ran, a thought came to her. By the time she dropped her brother off to his classroom, the thought had become a plan. Years later, when asked why she decided to do what she did, she wouldn't have any answers for her interrogators. The only one she could give was, "Why not?"

Right now, though, the plan seemed like a good way of filling in the interminable days, when she didn't have any books to read. She loved to read. She had already decided to be either a writer or a teacher when she grew up. She had told her mother as much. Lola had laughed and said that teaching would suit her because she was so bossy.

Eyo turned around and started walking briskly back home. She raised her head from the pavement for a few moments, when she got to the traffic lights by the roundabout. When she saw the elderly neighbour on the other side of the road, she turned her eyes back to the pavement and walked quickly back to the flat, abandoning all thoughts of extending her tenure outdoors by a few seconds.

Back inside the flat, she went straight into the kitchen. The children's bowls still had some milk and cereal flakes floating in them. To her now loudly rumbling stomach, they looked like a feast fit for a king. She grabbed one bowl and poured its contents down her throat. She then reached for the next. When she heard Sam coming down the stairs, she wiped her mouth and started washing the dishes.

"They're gone?" Sam appeared in the kitchen doorway.

"Yessah."

"I keep on telling you to call me 'uncle', not 'sir'," Sam told her.

Never, Eyo thought. "Yessah," she said.

"Make me some coffee and bring it to the living room."

"Yessah."

While the kettle was boiling, Eyo quickly downed the contents of the other cereal bowl. A wave of nausea came over her. She held onto the kitchen sink for a few moments while waiting for the nausea to subside. The kettle clicked and she prepared Sam's coffee. The inclination to spit into the coffee was so strong; she felt nauseous again. She fought it off by holding on to the kitchen sink. She then took the coffee into the living room. Sam was on the computer, his back towards her. He turned around when he heard her footsteps.

"Thank you," he said, taking the coffee from her. "You can go now."

"Sah."

"Yes?"

"My mama…"

"I've told you. You can't speak to her because she doesn't know how to use the mobile phone that Femi bought her. It's very difficult to call them. I've explained all this to you before."

He was lying. She knew that he hadn't spoken to Uncle Femi in a long time. The last time her uncle came to the flat, there had been a heated argument between him and Sam. She wasn't sure, but she thought it had something to do with her. Uncle Femi had stormed out of the flat, saying that Sam had better give him the money for Eyo or else. When Eyo ran after him, Mama Tolu screamed at her to go back inside the flat. She had obeyed, wondering when he would return.

It wasn't the first time he'd stormed out of the flat after an argument with Sam. When she first arrived in the uukaay, she could tell when he was coming to visit because Mama Tolu and Sam would start saying things like, "See everything we've done for you, taking care of you in London. Don't start mouthing off to your uncle, when he comes to visit you. Okay?"

After a while, they stopped saying that and started saying something else. Like the things they would do to her if she told Uncle Femi lies about them. When the arguments between Sam and Femi started becoming more frequent, Mama Tolu said she could tell her uncle anything she wanted because they would call the police and say that he was bringing people into the country illegally. The police would then take him to prison. As for Eyo, she would never see her Mama again because they would throw her out of the flat and leave her to fend for herself in this cold uukaay.

Mama Tolu would go on and on like that. And so, whenever her uncle came to visit, Eyo would smile harder and wear the clothes that Mama Tolu gave her to wear especially for him. She would hop into the kitchen to help Mama Tolu, and when Mama Tolu insisted that she sat on the sofa next to her uncle, she would shake her head shyly and insist that she wanted to take special care of her uncle's food in the kitchen.

Mama Tolu only ever gave her long sleeved blouses and dresses to wear whenever Uncle Femi came to visit. It was the only way of covering the bruises on her arms and the welts on her back. When Uncle Femi asked her about school, Mama Tolu said they'd just missed the year's intake, but the headmistress of the local school had said that Eyo would definitely be taken in the following academic year.

Uncle Femi's visits gave her news of her family in Jungle City, which she soaked up and replayed in her mind as she lay on the mat in the living room where she slept. Lanre was still playing football and Sade was getting bigger.

"A spitting image of you, by the way," he said.

At the mention of her sister, Eyo would always want to ask, *Uncle Femi, is she okay? Has Papa...?* but she would stop and catch herself just in time. As for Mama, Uncle Femi made her laugh with stories of her fights with the landlord.

"Your mother's tongue can cut steel. She's still levelling the landlord, with her words. That's who you take after: your mother. You have the same busy mouth," Uncle Femi would say, pulling Eyo to him affectionately.

In all the time she'd been in the uukaay, she'd spoken to her mother only once. Uncle Femi dialled a number on his mobile and placed it against her ear. The minute she heard her mother's voice, Eyo had burst into tears. She cried all the way through Femi's visit and, even after he'd gone, she didn't stop crying, not even after Mama Tolu threatened to beat her senseless. Not that Eyo cared. Her mother's voice had brought memories of her one-room home, the familiar smell of rotting garbage in Jungle City which, at that moment, was what she wanted to smell and where she wanted to be more than anything else in the world.

And now, here was Sam telling her that her mother didn't know how to use the mobile phone that Uncle Femi had bought her. Had he forgotten that she was there that night, the week after his last argument with her uncle? Uncle Femi had come late at night, shouting her name through the letterbox—Sam wouldn't let him inside the flat—telling her to pack her bags. The children had woken up and started crying. Mama Tolu told Eyo that if she dared move a muscle, she would personally make sure she never saw Mama again. The next thing Eyo knew, the police came and took Uncle Femi away because he was causing a *deesterbance* and the neighbours had complained.

When they first heard the police siren coming into the estate, Mama Tolu told Eyo to stay in the bathroom until she told her to come out. Eyo had waited and waited, not daring to sleep, worried about her uncle. Tolu said the police in the uukaay were good people, not like the ones in Nigeria, but Eyo was not so sure. Even in the bathroom where Mama Tolu had locked her in, she had heard the way they spoke to Uncle Femi and how they physically took him off the estate. If she closed her eyes now, she could still hear him shouting as the police physically dragged him off.

"Eyo, I'll come back for you. I promise."

That was quite some time ago. She hadn't heard from him since. Now Eyo remembered all this as she stood in front of Sam.

"When did you speak to Uncle Femi?"

"Are you questioning me?"

Eyo's initial boldness quelled.

"No, sah."

She turned to go back to the kitchen.

In there, she wiped the surfaces and put the dishes back in the cupboards, ensuring that she banged the doors shut as loudly as she could. Next, she cleaned the cooker. She was reaching out for the mop, when she heard the master bedroom open. A few moments later, Lola came into the kitchen, yawning. She dragged her finger across the kitchen surface and examined it.

"Hmm," she said.

Eyo ignored her and proceeded to mop the floor.

"My children got to school all right?" Lola asked.

"Yes."

"Yes, Ma."

"Yes, Ma," Eyo repeated.

"Make me some tea and bring it to the living room. And take off that ridiculous wig and scarf. You're supposed to wear it only when you leave the house."

"Yes."

Eyo carried on mopping, knowing she was courting danger and not caring. She wanted her mother, to speak to her and tell her that she would find a way of paying back Uncle Femi's money. *I would do anything, just please let me come back to Nigeria*, she pleaded with her mother, in her thoughts.

Lola looked at Eyo's thin arms as she manoeuvred the long-handled mop. A splash of water from the mop landed on her ankle as Eyo spread the mop into a fan and started moving it up and down the kitchen floor. The water felt cold and dirty. Lola had a suspicion but decided against acting on it. Eyo was strong-willed, but even she wouldn't dare spray her mistress with dirty water.

"Didn't you hear me?"

"Yes, Ma."

Eyo wrung out the mop in the bucket, then dragged the bucket to a corner of the kitchen. When she finished, she looked at Lola as if daring her to do something. Exactly what, Lola wasn't sure, but she chose not to give Eyo *another* lesson. It was too early in the morning.

Seven

Lola stretched out her legs and yawned. She still had a few hours to kill before the children came back home. But first, her idea. It was so simple and obvious that she wondered why she'd never thought of it before.

"Sam, do you remember what Rachel said when she was leaving last night?"

Sam shook his head, his eyes on the computer screen.

"She said that we should let her know if we wanted to open a babysitting service, what with Eyo being here and all. I know she said it jokingly, but what do you think?"

"What do I think of what?"

"Have you been listening to me?"

Sam smiled to himself before turning away from the computer and facing his wife. He had been listening but had pretended not to, to get a reaction from Lola.

"Are you serious?" he asked her.

"Why not? Eyo is here. She can take care of the children. She's been here for a year. Do you know how much money we'll make? People are desperate for babysitters, you know."

"This is a two-bedroom council flat. Are you mad?"

Lola sighed impatiently. "Think about it. When Tolu and Joshua are in school, Eyo can take care of those not old enough for school. By the time Tolu and Joshua are done for the day, it will be time for the mothers to pick up their little ones. We'll start with four little children and see how things develop from there."

It sounded like she had already made up her mind.

"Four little children? Eyo's ten. How will she manage?"

"She *was* ten when she came here. She *could* be eleven now. Anyhow, she's from Ajegunle. Those people start haemorrhaging children when they're eight. In any case, we don't know how old she is. After all, she is illiterate."

"What about Femi?"

"What about him?"

"He sent me another threatening email."

Lola brushed her hand in the air impatiently, as if shooing a pesky fly. "Forget him. Block his email address from your inbox, change your mobile number–yes, again–and tell the police that he's still harassing you. You've already served him with an injunction. If he continues being a nuisance, call the Home Office. Let's see how far he goes with his threats, with them on his tail. By the time we finish with him, he will never come to this country again."

"I just hope that Eyo girl doesn't get ideas about running away or doing something."

"Run to where? She can't read. Nobody knows who she is and there is no record of her in the country because of her false passport. She's not registered with social services, a doctor, or anything like that. As far as everybody is concerned, she doesn't exist. And she doesn't leave the flat without wearing a wig and a scarf. I've told everybody that she's my Muslim niece from Nigeria, on an extended holiday. That's why she covers her hair and doesn't like looking at people's faces when she's walking. If the questions get too much, we'll just lock her in the flat."

"You've really thought about this, haven't you?"

Lola paused for a few moments. "I have. Rachel's comment just got me thinking, that's all. All our years of grafting in this country and what do we have to show for it? Nothing. We might as well make use of the opportunities presented before us."

Sam went to sit next to her on the sofa. He put his hand underneath her pyjama top and caressed her. "Opportunities like now," he said.

Lola laid back and sighed contentedly. Eyo wouldn't dare come inside. She knew better.

*   *   *

In the kitchen, Eyo heard them. She put her hands over her ears, but that didn't drown the noises coming from the living room. She prowled the kitchen for a few minutes, picking up things and putting them back again.

Whoosh! Whoosh! She heard the sofa inflate and deflate with each thump. She stood by the closed kitchen window, her hands still on her ears, intending to engage in her favourite pastime: looking at the world outside.

A minute later, she stepped away from the window and stood by the wall next to it. She had heard a shuffle. She leaned forward and peered through the window at the same time her elderly neighbour looked up. The woman smiled and Eyo stepped back again, her heart in her chest.

If Mama Tolu found out about this! No, she mustn't think about it. She peered through the window again. The neighbour was knocking on their immediate neighbour's door, the one to the left.

Was she telling the woman about me? Eyo wondered. She prayed not. She didn't want to get into trouble. A loud moan came from the living room.

This was it, Eyo thought. This was her chance to escape to Tolu's and Joshua's room, unheard and unseen.

She took slow, light steps towards the kitchen door. At the doorway, she stood still for a few moments. She could see the half-open sitting room door from where she stood. Heart thumping, she crossed the hallway quickly, keeping her eyes away from the living room when she went past.

The children's room was two doors down from the living room, right next to their parents'. Eyo ran inside and closed the door in relief. Once inside, she picked up Tolu's Barbie and played with the doll's hair. Sometimes, she wished she had yellow hair like Barbie's, which she could play with and brush all day long. She sat on the bedroom floor for a while, playing with the doll's hair, trying to erase the image of Sam suspended above his writhing wife on the sofa. At some point, Sam became her father, fumbling with Mama's nightdress in the dark. She could hear Mama saying to him in a low, urgent voice, "Wale, the children…"

She shouldn't stay too long in the room. There was a lot to be done. Mama Tolu's restaurant was open from late afternoon until midnight. The plantain had to be sliced thinly, ready for frying as soon they were transported to the restaurant. The meat had to be cut and seasoned. Onions, peppers and other ingredients needed to be prepared as well. The restaurant itself had to be cleaned before they opened for business that day. She hoped she wasn't needed at the restaurant today; otherwise, she would have to go and pick up the children from school, prepare their dinner and leave them with their father before joining Mama Tolu to go to the restaurant.

When she finished helping her set up the restaurant for the day, she would walk back home, a journey that sometimes took over an hour. Mama Tolu refused to show her how to use public transport. Eyo knew it was because she was scared Eyo would run away. Eyo wondered how far she could run and where she could go without having any money and knowing no one.

When she got home from the restaurant, she would help the children settle in for the night. She didn't know what Sam did, but she knew that he operated sometimes as a night-time minicab driver. Night-time was her favourite time, when the children were in bed (or when Tolu *allowed* herself to go to bed) and Mama Tolu and her husband were away. Eyo would then switch on the television, put it on mute—as Tolu had taught her—and watch the flickering screen. At the sound of the key turning in the front door, she would jump up, turn off the television and start tidying the room frantically.

Mama Tolu's moaning had stopped. Eyo parted Barbie's yellow hair tenderly and put her back gently in her pink house.

Barbie was lucky.

*　　　*　　　*

It was early evening. Tolu and Joshua were both in their beds. Tolu was reading a book and Joshua was playing a computer game. The bathroom was clean; the kitchen, spotless; and the hallway, free of family debris. She'd been to the restaurant to help Mama Tolu set up for the day and now she was back in the house, tired. The morning's leftover cereal was a memory as distant as her mother's voice. She thought of going to her favourite hiding place: the bathroom, where she sometimes sat on the floor for a few minutes of the day, but decided against it. Joshua was bound to come looking for her once he got bored with his game. Besides, if she went to the bathroom, she knew she would fall asleep in there. She'd done it once. Mama Tolu had found her like that, sleeping on the bathroom floor. Sam had to physically restrain her from beating Eyo senseless.

Eyo decided not go to the bathroom; she would go to the sitting room instead. As usual, Sam was glued in front of the computer. She asked him if there was anything he would like her to do. He swivelled the chair and looked at her for a full minute. Eyo cast her eyes down.

"You saw Mama Tolu and me on the sofa, didn't you?"

Eyo was silent. It had taken her a while, but she eventually figured out that Sam didn't necessarily require a response when he spoke to her. That was why he spoke in statements.

"I saw you when you walked past. You tried to cover your eyes, but I saw you."

Eyo remained silent.

"I'm sure you've seen people, even your parents, do it, living in that one-room shack in Jungle City."

Eyo kept her eyes on the floor. She heard him swivel his chair back to face the computer screen.

"That'll be all," he said, without looking at her.

Eyo fled back to the children's bedroom. Tolu put her book down on the bed when Eyo entered. She watched as Eyo headed straight for Barbie's house and straightened the toy furniture. Her hands lingered a bit too long on Barbie's hair when she put the doll in the miniature dining area.

Tolu got off the bed and motioned for Eyo to sit on it. Eyo shook her head. Joshua was still engrossed in his PlayStation. Tolu motioned to the floor. Eyo's heart sank. Another teaching game. Her stomach rumbled loudly and hungrily. She sat down on the floor and watched Tolu motion to the book on the bed and back to her. She then made scribbling movements with her hands and pointed at Eyo. When Eyo looked at her blankly, Tolu stamped her foot in childish frustration. *This was going to be much harder than I thought*, Tolu thought to herself.

Tolu sat on the floor next to Eyo, took her hand and traced her finger alongside a line of text inside the book. She looked at Eyo, pointed to her eyes and back again to the line of text, smiling. Eyo's stomach rumbled again. Tolu left the room. When she came back, she had three thick slices of bread heavily layered with butter on a side plate. She gave the plate to Eyo and gave her a conspiratorial smile. Eyo took the plate gratefully. She even gave Tolu a ghostly smile when she pointed to her eyes and the book again.

A few feet away, on his bed, Joshua let out a huge shout. "Scored! Just like Beckham!" And he went back to his game. On the floor, Tolu and Eyo smiled at each other. This time, Eyo's smile was more pronounced.

"Repeat after me. Ay."

Eyo wiped the breadcrumbs from her lips and carefully put the side plate on the floor.

"Ay," she repeated slowly and quietly, testing the letter on her lips. Embarrassed, she looked downwards.

71

"Very good, Eyo," Tolu said, smiling like the cat that got the cream. "'A' is part of the alphabet. Repeat after me: al-fa-bet."

"Al-fa-bet," Eyo pronounced.

Tolu smiled again.

"Eyo!"

Eyo raised panicked eyes to Tolu and got up quickly, stepping on the side plate. The last slice of bread overturned and breadcrumbs littered the bedroom floor.

"Dad, she's coming!"

Tolu looked at Eyo. *Don't worry*, her eyes said. *It's okay.*

Joshua put his game aside and stretched himself on the bed. "I want to sleep," he said, closing his eyes.

"Go!" Tolu motioned for Eyo to leave.

Eyo hesitated, picked up the bread from the floor and stuffed it in her mouth. She then started picking up the breadcrumbs.

"Eyo!" There was a tinge of impatience in Sam's voice.

"Yessah!" Eyo called out before hurrying out of the room, breadcrumbs and side plate in hand.

*   *   *

When she closed her eyes, Eyo could see her home in Jungle City as clearly as she felt the mat she slept on in the cold living room. She could feel the scorching Lagos sun on her back and the hardened dirt encrusted on the soles of her feet, flattened by her rubber slippers. If she tried hard enough, she could hear herself call out, as she pounded the Lagos metropolis with her brother.

"Ice water! Don't let the sun take you! Drink our ice water!"

Up and down the streets they would walk, dodging pickpockets and area boys, until their ice water was all sold. They would then head back home to Jungle City. Back to the settlements on reclaimed marshland, back to the sounds of highlife music thundering from stereos on street corners, and candlelit stalls in the evening. She could see her untarred street with its crater-size potholes and plastic bags filled with human excrement floating in the open drains. That was her home. Yes, the unpainted face-me-I-face-you right next to the building of worship.

In her mind's eye, Eyo could see the rickety, long wooden bench in front of the house and the landlord lounging on it, watching her and Lanre with hooded eyes, as they walked past him and turned to the right, to their one-room home. She saw her hand hurriedly turning the key in the lock, while her brother hopped impatiently to enter, get his football and escape next door to play football with his friend.

Eyo could see all these things as she lay on the mat, on the floor of the living room, that late October night, a year after she had arrived in the uukaay. She covered herself with a thin blanket, trying hard not to sleep, in case Sam came back and wanted her to do something or decided to use the computer.

And now, she could hear the key turning in the front door. She held her breath, hoping it was Sam. In his own way, he was kinder to her than his wife. If he got home late at night before Lola, he usually told her to sleep in a corner of the living room, while he worked on his computer or watched television. When his wife returned, he would tell her to let Eyo rest. If Mama Tolu got home before him, Eyo knew she was in for a long night.

It was Sam. She could tell from the way he turned the key in the lock. He turned it the same way he came inside the house: quietly and methodically. His wife did not do things that way, preferring instead to make her presence known *before* she stepped indoors.

"Eyo!" she would cry out the minute the key turned and she flung the front door open, standing in the doorway, with bags of leftover food from the restaurant.

Eyo! Pick up the bags!

Eyo! Why is there water on the bathroom floor?

Eyo, is this how you prepare food for human beings? This is not Ajegunle, you bush girl!

Eyo!

Eyo!

Eyo!

Eyo put her fingers in her ears to drown out Mama Tolu's shrill voice in her head. She could hear Sam's quiet footfalls in the corridor. She was just getting off the mat when he appeared in the living room doorway, his silhouette illuminated by the hallway light.

"It's okay. Don't get up. Sleep. The children didn't give you too much trouble?"

"No, sah." Eyo stood in the corner, her eyes down, her manner subservient.

"Don't worry. I won't turn on the living room light. Sleep." Sam gestured to the floor.

Eyo nodded and lay on the mat, her back to Sam, expecting him to leave. He didn't. He continued standing in the doorway, watching her. Eyo could feel his eyes boring into her body. She wrapped the blanket even more tightly around herself and tensed, her heart beating so loudly, she thought he could surely hear it.

She didn't know how long he stood, watching her, but it felt like a lifetime. Finally, he left.

Eyo didn't sleep that night.

Eight

"Lola, we'll see you on Monday. Patrick, say 'bye' to Aunty Lola."

Patrick waddled to Lola and put his arms around her right calf.

"*Aah*," his mother and Lola said at the same time. Lola picked him up, kissed him and handed him to his mother.

Eyo waited by the front door. She didn't care if it showed; she was happy that Patrick was going home. He was one of five children—each averaging three years between them—she'd babysat today. Their mothers usually brought them round about nine a.m. and came to pick them up in the evening, around the time Sam was preparing to go to work. Sam also picked up Tolu and Lanre from school.

"I don't know why you're waiting by the door, when you can help Rachel with her stuff," Lola said waspishly.

"It's okay. I haven't got much anyway," Rachel replied.

"Rachel, let her help you. That's what she's there for," Lola said firmly.

Eyo remained standing by the door. Lola shot her a baleful glare, which she ignored.

Rachel noted Lola's look and Eyo's affected ignorance. She bent down to pick up her bag, held Patrick on her hip more securely and headed for the door where Eyo was.

"Goodbye, madam," Eyo said, opening the door.

Rachel looked away. She couldn't bring herself to look into Eyo's eyes. After all, it was her fault she was babysitting all these children, including hers. And she knew more children were coming Eyo's way because Lola had said as much. She'd seen the bruises on Eyo's gaunt arms. She'd heard the way Lola spoke about "the illiterate girl from Ajegunle" and, knowing how short-tempered her friend was, she could only guess at the verbal and physical assaults Eyo was subjected to. Which was why Eyo's wilfulness had such a sense of tragedy about it.

Rachel caught herself. Whatever went on in this flat was none of her business. But sometimes, she would find herself replaying in her mind those few moments when she made the throwaway comment about Eyo being a babysitter. *Had she meant it? No. Yes. No, it had been made in jest. Yes, she had meant it because childcare was so expensive…*

"Eyo, take the bag from her and take it to her car."

Lola's voice shook Rachel out of her reverie. Eyo hesitated for a brief moment, as if deliberating whether or not to obey, before taking the bag from Rachel. Lola pursed her lips, marched up to the door and twisted Eyo's ear before pushing her out of the flat with a rough shove.

"Lola, easy on the girl. And as for the wig she's wearing…"

"I've told her to start wearing it around the house now. Our neighbour, Mrs Richards, once asked about my niece who likes looking out the kitchen window. I've told her that particular niece has gone back to Nigeria. This one is her younger sister. She's a nosy old cow, Mrs Richards is."

"But that wig is awful."

"It does the job."

Patrick let out an impatient cry. Rachel gave him a kiss and wiped his brow.

"I'd better get him home quickly. Well, I'll see you on Monday."

They hugged.

"Let me know if Eyo gives you any trouble," Lola said.

Rachel had no intention of doing such a thing. Nevertheless, she nodded and stepped out of the flat. In the extended balcony, she peered down to the car park below. Eyo was walking towards the car, a strangely solitary figure in oversized clothes, a coat fully buttoned up to her neck and a badly made wig of plaited extensions covered by a black scarf. If this was Lola's way of not drawing attention to Eyo, she was doing a terrible job. Rachel drew in a deep breath and headed for her car, eager to dispense of any interaction with Eyo. She didn't want to admit to herself why the girl made her feel so guilty and uncomfortable.

*   *   *

Ping! The lift doors opened and Eyo stepped out, as if she'd been walking out of lifts her whole life instead of a year. To think she was so scared of using it her first night in the uukaay! She smiled to herself when she thought of that night. The smile faded when she spotted Mrs Richards waiting for the lift. The elderly lady started smiling and saying something, but Eyo didn't wait. She brushed past her and ran back to the flat, straight into Lola who was fiddling with the clothes rack behind the front door.

"I was watching you with Rachel downstairs. You wait till Sam gets home. We'll see how you manage in London with your Ajegunle body out on the streets. All the *wahala*, trouble, you've been giving me recently? I've been marking them up in my head. I've had enough of you. Your day of retribution is coming. You mark my words."

Lola was still fiddling with the clothes rack as she spoke. When she finished, she brushed past Eyo and headed for the sitting room. A moment later, the television came on.

Eyo went into the kitchen. Once there, she went behind the door, leaned against the wall and started crying.

"Eyo! What are my children going to eat when they come back? Air?" Lola's shrill voice resounded in Eyo's head.

Eyo sniffed, and she wiped her eyes. "No, Ma," she called out.

She got off the floor, opened the fridge and took out an onion. She started chopping it.

"Madam, I'm making their dinner," she said.

"Good."

A minute later, the television volume was turned up. Eyo put the knife and onion aside. Silently, she walked towards the kitchen door and pushed it so that it was almost shut. She then went behind it and, with her back against the wall, sat on the kitchen floor. With shaking hands, she wiped the tears streaming down her cheeks.

"Eyo, bring me tea!" Lola's voice cut through her tears.

"Yes, Ma!"

Eyo wiped her eyes and got off the kitchen floor. She went to the sink and splashed water on her face. Next, she filled the kettle with water. When it finished boiling, she made Lola's tea. She didn't even have the energy to spit in it.

Nine

"Olufunmi, anything yet from Eyo?"

"I'll let you know when I find out, Mama Fola. What about your niece, the daughter of Wande?"

"My sister hasn't heard anything either. The people my niece was staying with told Wande that her daughter had run away."

"It's been over a year. And now, we can't even get hold of Femi. He's become a big man with all his money. Do you think my daughter is okay?"

"Of course, she is. She's in London. What could possibly happen to her?"

Ten

On Sundays, the whole family would go to church, leaving her alone and locked up in the flat. Eyo wondered what the church minister would make of Lola and her family life outside of the church walls. Once, she overheard Lola on the telephone, trying to dissuade the minister from making a pastoral visit to the flat. She knew it was the minister because her voice was fawning and she kept on repeating herself, each time more firmly than before.

"Pastor, there's no need for a visit. We're all fine. God is really kind to us. No, don't trouble yourself."

Sometimes on Sundays, a paralysing fear would overcome Eyo when she thought of the fires in Jungle City and wondered what would become of her should the flat ever catch fire with her locked inside, unable to escape. That was the only reason she was relieved on the occasions Sam stayed behind in the flat with her, rather than going to church with his family. This relief waged war with her increasing discomfort around him. If she found herself alone in the flat with him, she spent her time in the children's room, playing with Tolu's Barbie, going through the alphabet books that Tolu showed her… Anything to take her mind off the fact that Sam was a few feet away, somewhere in the flat. Lately, he'd started watching her the way her father used to–like a lion watching its prey before pouncing.

"Eyo!"

"Yessah!"

Today was Sunday and they were alone in the flat. Eyo put Barbie back in her house and went to the living room reluctantly. When she saw the television screen, she turned her eyes away, quickly. Sam laughed indulgently and motioned for her to stand in front of him. Eyo remained rooted where she was, her eyes fixed to a faraway point on the wall behind Sam.

"Eyo, I won't tell you again."

She walked on legs of lead and stood in front of him, her back to the naked, coupling image on the television screen. Sam grabbed her by the arms and turned her around so she faced the television. Eyo put her face down. Sam forced her head up, towards the screen. Even then, Eyo tried to look away, but Sam's grip was like concrete, unyielding. On the television, the lady was now on her knees, her face between the man's legs. The camera bobbed up and down with each stroke, forcing back buried memories for Eyo. Bile rose in her throat as she tried not to gag. Sam released her face and started unbuttoning his trousers. He then took Eyo's hand and put it inside his boxer shorts. An ecstatic moan escaped his throat as his manhood sprang to life in Eyo's hand. He spread his legs wider and drew Eyo closer to him.

"You've seen the film," he said.

Eyo knelt down and brought her face closer. She opened her mouth wide and came down, her teeth clamping down hard like someone hanging on for dear life.

*   *   *

Lola flung the front door open.

"Eyo!" she called out.

Tolu and Joshua ran inside the flat and headed for their bedroom. A moment later, Joshua came running out, a visibly shaken Tolu behind him.

"Mummy, Eyo is on the floor of our room. She's not moving or answering anybody," Joshua looked up at his mother, frightened.

In the sitting room, Sam waited for a few moments before pushing his chair away from the computer screen and joining them in the hallway.

"Children, don't worry. She's fine. She was naughty and daddy had to teach her a lesson, that's all," Sam said, herding the children towards the sitting room. He looked over his shoulder and gave his wife a loaded look.

Lola dropped her handbag in the hall and marched to the children's bedroom. Sure enough, Eyo was on the floor. She heard her husband come up behind her.

"Sam, what happened?" she asked.

"I taught her a lesson. That's what happened. I've had enough of her rudeness. After today, she won't cross me again."

No kidding, Lola thought, looking down at Eyo. She was curled up on the floor, in the foetal position. Her body was still, her back to the door. Lola could see the welts across her back and the bruises on her cheek. She felt that there was more than Sam was letting on but decided to let it go. He would tell her what happened in his own time.

She sighed. "Fine. How long has she been like this?"

Sam shrugged and left the room. Lola sighed again. A fleeting image of herself at Eyo's age, in another house, went through her mind. She drew her breath sharply. She was irritated and just a little angry with herself for allowing the memories to arise and weaken her. She looked at Eyo again and left the bedroom. On her way to the bathroom, she heard the children.

"Daddy, will she be okay?" There was a hint of worry in Tolu's voice.

"Of course, she will," Sam answered soothingly.

Lola could hear Joshua playing games on the computer. The children weren't allowed to play their computer games on Sundays, one of Sam's rules. The fact that she could hear Joshua on the computer meant he'd resorted to bribes to get his son's mind off Eyo.

"Daddy, I think she should go to hospital."

"Tolu, I think you should read your book," Sam's voice was curt.

Eyo didn't turn around, even when she heard the bedroom door shut. She felt someone turn her round and start dabbing disinfectant-soaked cotton wool on her back and arms. It stung. She lay limply on the floor, her tears splashing the bedroom carpet. When Lola finished, she rolled Eyo almost tenderly on her side and covered her with a cotton sheet. She then got off her knees and left the bedroom.

Eleven

Tolu placed her finger underneath the word and spoke slowly, "B-o-o-k."

"Book," Eyo repeated.

Tolu nodded. She turned the page and placed her finger under a word, moving it slowly along the surface.

"Cat, dog," Eyo read each word confidently, in unison with Tolu's finger movements.

There was a sound of quick footfalls marching towards the bedroom. The door opened and Lola stood in the doorway, arms folded. She took in the scene: Eyo and Tolu on the floor, Joshua's old alphabet books spread in front of them. Eyo stood up quickly.

"What do you think you're doing?" Lola addressed her daughter.

"Nothing. Playing teacher with Eyo," Tolu answered quickly.

Lola turned to Eyo. "Get out!"

Eyo fled. Lola turned back to Tolu. "Joshua said you've been teaching Eyo to read."

"No, Mummy, I've been playing teacher."

This time, Tolu's voice was defiant. Lola waited and, sure enough, she relented.

"Mummy, it's not fair. Why shouldn't she be able to read?"

"We've talked about it. She needs to go to a special school for eleven-year-olds who can't read and we can't afford to send her there just yet," she said.

"Mrs Simmons said that she doesn't need to go a special school or anything."

"You've been talking to your teacher about Eyo? How many times have I warned you not to talk to strangers about our family business? If social services knew Eyo was here…"

Lola drew in another deep breath and forced herself to calm down.

"I haven't. I just told her I knew someone who couldn't read and would like to go to school."

"What did she say?"

"She asked if it was the girl who wears the scarf and brings Joshua and me to school every day."

Lola sat down on Tolu's bed. "Oh dear God," she said weakly.

Tolu went to sit next to her on the bed and attempted to stroke her shoulder.

"Mummy, it's okay."

"No, Tolu, it's not. If anyone finds her here without immigration papers, we'll be in trouble. Why do you think we go through so much trouble to disguise her and stuff?" Lola paused and thought for a while. "When did you speak to your teacher?" she asked.

"Yesterday."

"Then Eyo will not take you and your brother to school anymore. She will stay in the flat and she will not go anywhere, unless she's accompanied by either me or your father."

"Mummy, I was just trying to help her."

Help her with what? Lola wanted to ask.

Tolu crawled under the duvet. She turned her eyes away from her mother towards the wall.

"Mummy?"

"Yes?"

"You don't have to beat her all the time."

"I don't beat her all the time and you know what Eyo is like: stubborn."

"I don't like it when she goes all quiet and lies on the floor when you and daddy…"

Tolu stopped talking and turned back to Lola. "I don't think you and daddy would like it if somebody did that to me."

Lola felt as if she'd just been splashed with cold water. *Eyo.* She was at the bottom of all this, learning to read and turning her daughter against her. Whatever next?

Tolu watched the array of emotions flit across her mother's face. She sighed and turned back to the wall. Great. Eyo was in trouble. She would probably get beaten. Again. And all because of her.

"Mummy, please don't do anything. I won't talk to anybody about her or teach her to read again. Just don't beat her."

Lola gave Tolu a hug. She spoke lightly, "Look at you, getting all upset. Of course, I'm not going to do anything. Come on now. Stop all this. It's okay." She patted Tolu's back.

In the kitchen, Eyo busied herself with rewashing the clean plates on the dish rack. She heard the children's bedroom door open and Lola's footsteps coming towards the kitchen. Her heart started beating rapidly. She picked up a damp cloth and began wiping down the sink. Lola darkened the kitchen doorway.

"You think you're clever, don't you?" she sneered.

Eyo didn't answer. She carried on wiping the surface. Lola watched her for a few moments before leaving. When she left, Eyo stopped wiping the surface. She raised her head to the window above the kitchen sink and looked outside. The sun was out. Its rays reached out towards the tower blocks. Eyo wrapped her arms around herself. She felt cold.

"Eyo!"

It was Lola, summoning Eyo from the sofa in the sitting room. Eyo looked back down at the kitchen sink and placed the damp cloth on its surface.

"Coming, madam!"

She hurried to the sitting room.

*　　　*　　　*

Eyo turned, half asleep. She froze when she saw a shadow coming towards her. Next thing she knew, a hand covered her mouth and her lungs constricted as someone sat on her chest, pinning her down. Her chest started burning and she tried breathing with difficulty. She flailed her arms to push off the person.

"If you make a sound, I'll kill you," Lola spoke quietly and fiercely. *Smack*! Her hand went across Eyo's face.

"You think you can do your Ajegunle magic and turn my daughter against me?" Lola's voice was angry.

Eyo tried moving to her side to dislodge Lola from her chest, but the older woman held Eyo's two hands in her left hand and gave her another slap. Eyo shook her head, her tears splashing on Lola's right hand that firmly clamped down on her mouth. Lola moved her hands away and wiped Eyo's tears on her *wrapa*. She then got off Eyo's chest, breathing heavily.

"Get up." It was a command.

Eyo got off the mat.

"Now take off your clothes," Lola commanded her.

Eyo started crying. "Madam, please. I beg you."

Lola looked towards the closed sitting room door. "If you wake up my children, I swear, you'll regret ever coming to London. I said, 'Take off your clothes!'"

Eyo flung herself at Lola's ankles, crying. "Madam, please."

Lola kicked her away. "Eyo, I won't tell you again."

Still weeping, Eyo took off the nightdress she was wearing and handed it to Lola. She stood in the middle of the sitting room, naked and cowering.

"Pass me the blanket as well," Lola ordered.

Eyo didn't move. She stood where she was, crying softly. Lola pushed her aside roughly and grabbed Eyo's blanket from off the mat.

"Let this be a lesson to you," she said. "The next time I see you with my daughter learning to read or anything, I won't be responsible for what will happen." She went to the sitting room door and reached out for the door handle. "You will get your clothes back in the morning," she said on her way out.

Eyo sank to the floor.

∗   ∗   ∗

Sam turned the key in the lock and walked in, careful not to make any sounds that might wake up his family. He'd been unusually busy for a Monday night. His last passenger had been a drunk woman who lived on the other side of London.

The return journey had taken him over an hour. He looked at his watch; it was one a.m. A noise in the sitting room made him walk towards it. When he got to the doorway, he stood and looked. Eyo was in the foetal position, naked and crying in the middle of the room. Her thin body shook with each cry. He spied her rumpled sleeping mat in the corner of the room. Its haphazard position showed evidence of an earlier tussle with somebody, probably his wife. Sam came inside and shut the door behind him quietly. Eyo's head shot up. Even through her tears, Sam could see a quiet resignation on her face. He sat on the sofa and undid his trousers. He then spread his legs wide.

"Come," he motioned to her.

Eyo got off the floor and walked towards him, wiping her nose. She stood in front of him, shivering. Sam looked at the ripening buds of her breasts and her sprinkling of pubic hair, and desire rose within him. He took her right hand and put it inside his boxer shorts. He took her left hand and pulled her down so that she knelt, her body between his legs.

"You know what to do," he said.

Eyo opened her mouth wide and bent over, her tears wetting his penis. When he came, his semen sprayed the inside of her mouth, threatening to poison her.

"You've done this before," he said.

She remained kneeling, his seed swimming in her mouth, trying hard not to gag. Sam fell back on the sofa and waved his hand.

"You can go and spit it out," he said.

She left and came back, standing by the door, awaiting orders, her mind and body on automatic mode, just like they were whenever she did *it* with Papa. Sam motioned for her to sit on the sofa with him. Eyo wondered if he knew how ludicrous he looked, sitting on the sofa, with his trousers around his ankles, his boxers halfway around his thighs and his limp manhood flopped to one side like a spineless dragon. She sat next to him obediently, still shivering, expecting him to place a hand on her back just like her father used to do, but Sam didn't touch her. He took her right hand and laid it on his penis. The dragon jumped back to life.

"Just play with it, eh?" he said.

She obeyed.

*   *   *

The next day, Lola sprang out of bed and half ran to the sitting room. She wasn't quite sure what she expected to find, but she knew what she didn't want to find: Joshua watching television as he sometimes did before being dragged to his bath by Eyo. Lola didn't want to explain to him why Eyo was naked and without any blanket on her sleeping mat.

She opened the sitting room door. Eyo was on the mat, her naked back to the door. She knew Eyo was awake because she saw her tense her shoulders when she heard the door open. Lola flung the nightdress and blanket at her.

"The children will be up in half an hour. You get Joshua ready for school and make sure their breakfast is ready. From today, I will be taking them to school, while you stay here and wait for the other little children to come. There will be two extra children today."

Eyo didn't answer. Her tense back said it all. Lola contemplated giving her a kick but decided against it. She wouldn't give Eyo the satisfaction. She left the sitting room and shut the door behind her.

When she heard the door shut, Eyo reached out for the nightdress and flung it across the room. She then reached out for the blanket and huddled underneath it, her knees to her chest. She felt the coldness of the sitting room extend to her heart.

Twelve

Eyo heard the key turn in the lock and someone walk into the flat with ungainly steps. It was Sam, and he lurched toward the sitting room. On the mat, in the far corner of the room, she curled up in the foetal position, paralysed with fear. She knew drunkenness and what it made men do. Drunkenness led Papa to fumble with Mama's clothes most nights and launch himself inside her, with Mama protesting half asleep that he "shouldn't wake the children". Drunkenness made her former landlord bold with little children. She dreaded to think what it would make Sam do.

The sitting room door opened silently, just like it did most nights. Sam staggered in and launched himself on the sofa.

"Eyo," he slurred. She didn't answer.

"If I call you again…" he threatened.

Eyo got off the mat and walked to him as one walking to her grave. Sam motioned to his trousers and Eyo started unbuckling his belt. When she reached out to unbutton his trousers, he suddenly lifted her by her waist, laid her on the sofa and held her there by his weight on her. He held her two hands in a one-handed grip above her head. Eyo kicked and struggled to no avail. Sam was like a mountain, unmoveable. Instead, he lifted himself up slightly and, with his free hand, unbuttoned his trousers and pulled down his boxers. He then lifted Eyo's nightdress and pulled down her underwear.

"I will tell madam."

Sam stopped and gave her a blow. Immediately, everything went black for Eyo. When she came to, Sam was on top of her, grunting the way Papa used to do with her and Mama. She became aware of a burning sensation and something between her legs. Understanding dawned on her. She opened her mouth to scream, but Sam put his free hand on her mouth and started grinding her even harder and faster. Her face felt like it had exploded and shattered into tiny pieces. Her arms were still imprisoned in his hand, held above her head, on the sofa armrest. Her wrists throbbed painfully.

Sam started shaking, he gave a restrained groan and went inside her one final time with a deep thrust. He ejaculated and collapsed on her. He then released her hands. Through her fog of pain, Eyo chose her next words carefully.

"I will tell madam and your daughter."

Sam laughed quietly, indulgently, like the drunk he was. "By the time I finish with you tonight, you will not be able to walk, much less talk," he promised.

He honoured his words.

*   *   *

Sam stilled for a moment. He thought he heard something. He turned his head back to the person underneath him and put his finger to his mouth. Eyo nodded in understanding. Sam waited for a few more moments and resumed his coupling. He shuddered and collapsed on Eyo, spent. She pushed him away silently and went to the bathroom. Inside, she took a flannel and ran it under the cold water. Next, she wrung the the flannel and placed it between her legs, allowing its coolness to penetrate her stinging insides. She held the facecloth under the cold water and pressed it against her insides again. At times like this, it was like she was back in Ajegunle. The only difference was that it was her father who would hold the flannel against her insides, when he finished with her. He usually did it when he put his fingers up there for too long. One day, he played a game. He said he wanted to know if his hand could fit in there. He stopped after putting the hand halfway through and she started screaming.

She couldn't stay too long in the bathroom. Sam would surely get annoyed and come looking for her. There was a set pattern to their routine and she still had one more thing to do before Sam went back to his matrimonial bed. Eyo returned to the sitting room. Sam patted the space on the sofa next to him and she sat down. Her right hand went inside his boxers and Sam sighed, his head falling back on the sofa in contentment. Eyo's stroking became harder and faster, while Sam's breathing became more laboured. A minute later, he came, his semen spurting all over Eyo's hand. She withdrew it from his boxers.

"Honestly, Eyo, you're getting way too good at this," Sam said.

Eyo went to get a roll of paper towels and came back to the sitting room. She tore off a few sheets and handed them to him. Sam wiped himself and stood up, yawning. He looked at the clock on the wall. It was half past two a.m., time to go.

When he left, Eyo went to the kitchen and took out the ice-cube tray from the freezer. She took it to the bathroom and wrapped the flannel around it. She then sat on the covered toilet and held it between her legs. Ten minutes later, she went back to the sitting room and lay on the mat. She had to be up soon.

On waking, she would roll up the mat and sweep the sitting room. Afterwards, she would bathe Joshua and get him ready for school. But before that, she would set the dining table and prepare breakfast. Usually, it was cereal or toast. After breakfast, Lola would take the children to school. She had twenty minutes to bathe and get ready to babysit the toddlers. There was a stable group of five children who came to the flat every weekday. Eyo knew Lola wanted more but Sam had refused. "You really want Mrs Richards on our tail, don't you?"

Eyo shut her eyes and tried to picture her mother's face. It had been blurry for a while now, which sent her into a wild state of panic. It was her mother's face she clung to when she would hear the sitting room door open silently as it did most nights, when Sam would fumble with her underwear.

When he went inside her, she took her mind to happier times in Ajegunle. When sometimes, the pain became so unbearable she felt she would surely be split in two, she would lie still, her mind focused on remembering the letters of the alphabet that Tolu had taught her. Or she would think of happier times in Jungle City.

Now, in the bathroom, on the toilet seat, Eyo started crying silently, as she did most nights after Sam's visits. She got through her days by pretending she wasn't a human being but a robot, like a character in one of the Japanese cartoons that Joshua liked to watch so much. *Robots couldn't think or feel*, Tolu had explained to her. They just did the things they had been built to do and that was it. They couldn't feel, cry or laugh like human beings because they weren't human. In fact, Tolu had concluded, with all the knowledge and wisdom of a future teacher, that robots were really quite stupid.

Eyo didn't agree. She thought robots were rather clever because they couldn't feel anything. That was when Eyo decided that she would be a robot. She would do what was required of her and try very hard not to feel anything. Perhaps if she tried long and hard enough, she would be like a robot at night with Sam and during the day with his wife and the children she had to take care of. It worked but not all the time. Like tonight. She had so many thoughts going through her head she felt she would surely go mad. When she tried desperately to picture Mama's face, her head ached with the effort.

In that moment, it came to her that she would spend the rest of her life in the uukaay, in this flat with Sam, Lola and their children. She would never go to school and certainly never see her mother and siblings again. She turned her head to one side and wept even harder. When the tears stopped coming, she wiped her nose resolutely, a little of her Jungle City spirit restored as a plan formed in her head.

The next day, she woke up and performed her usual duties as normal. Finally, the house was silent. The kids were in school and Lola wasn't home. Three mothers had called to say that they wouldn't be bringing their children round for babysitting. Sam hadn't emerged from the bedroom since he waved off the children to school with Lola.

Eyo wiped down the fridge with a damp cloth and wiped her hands on her jumper. She usually avoided Sam whenever he was in the house but not today. If everything went according to plan, she would walk out of the flat and never come back again. As for where she would go, she didn't know. Once she got outside, she would ask someone to take her to the police who would take care of her. Tolu had said they could be trusted in this country. Not like the ones in Nigeria. She went to knock on the master bedroom.

"Sah?"

"What?"

"I need to take the bin downstairs to the garbage shed."

She heard him yawn and shuffle to the door. The door opened and he stood in the doorway in his boxers.

"If you see Mrs Richards, just smile and come straight here. No need to run away, okay?" He gave her the keys to the flat.

"Eyo?"

"Sah?"

Sam was watching her thoughtfully. "I'm watching you. If you're not back here in five minutes, I'll come downstairs myself."

"Yessah."

She turned round and headed for the kitchen, a triumphant smile on her face. In the kitchen, she took the half-empty bin liner in one hand and held the flat keys in another. She thought about going to the children's bedroom to get Tolu's Barbie but decided against it; it wasn't hers to take. When she got to the front door, she gave the flat one last look and inserted the key in the lock. She stepped out, elated. Her heart was beating so fast she was convinced it would burst out of her chest. Behind her was the flat door. She looked up at the sky. It looked better in the open outdoors than from the confines of the kitchen window. She took a few steps forward and peered over the balcony railings. That was the kind of thing Lanre would do: lean over the balcony railings on the tenth floor of a building.

Eyo, look! he would've exclaimed, pointing to the cars parked below them in the square. *I bet I can kick a ball straight into an open car window,* he would've added, pointing excitedly.

"Eyo, is it?"

The voice brought Eyo back to reality. It was Mrs Richards, watching her intently from her own open kitchen window.

Eyo smiled and made signs to let her know that she didn't understand English. The flat keys jangled in her hand. She took a few steps towards the lift and stopped when Mrs Richards started talking again.

"I know you don't. You look so much better without that awful wig," she said kindly, still in English, smiling at her.

There was a sudden burst of wind and the bin liner flapped in Eyo's hand. In the distance, Eyo heard the lift ping as its doors opened and Lola's unmistakeable march headed their way. She suddenly became aware of the wind in her hair. She touched her head. She wasn't wearing the wig. A cold fear came upon her. *She'd been caught. Lola would kill her. She would die in the uukaay, in this flat. She would never see her mother or her siblings again.*

∗　　　∗　　　∗

Lola hurried to the flat. She had been halfway to her food supplier when she realised she'd forgotten her ATM cards at home. She stopped short when she saw the scene in front of her flat: Eyo standing outside minus wig and scarf, holding a half-empty bin liner, and Mrs Richards smiling at the girl through her open window. It looked like she'd interrupted something, exactly what though, Lola wasn't sure.

"Sade?"

Eyo stepped back from the balcony nervously and clutched the bin liner. "Madam, I was just taking the bin to the rubbish shed," she said.

Mrs Richards saw the look of fear that came over Eyo. She turned to Lola. "I was just telling Eyo–that's her name, isn't it?–what a beautiful day it was," she said.

"I've told you; this isn't Eyo. This is her twin sister, Sade. And just like Eyo, she doesn't understand English either," Lola said.

Mrs Richards smiled. "Of course," she said. She withdrew back in her kitchen and shut the window.

"Get back in the flat," Lola ordered Eyo. Clutching the bin liner, Eyo went back to the flat, her footsteps heavy. In her flat, Mrs Richards dialled a number.

"Safeguarding Children please," she said to the person on the other end of the line.

*   *   *

The house was silent again. Lola had gone back out. Sam was still in the bedroom; she could hear him on his mobile. The last two mothers had called to say that their children wouldn't be coming in that day either. Eyo prowled the kitchen, trying hard to ignore the growling pains in her belly. After a particularly loud growl, she went to knock on the master bedroom.

"Sah?"

"Yes?" Sam opened the door, still in his boxers, mobile in hand.

"I was going to make you eggs and bread for breakfast," Eyo said.

"Fine," he said and closed the door.

Eyo raced to the kitchen and cracked open four eggs. After ten minutes, she took a tray laden with an omelette, half a loaf of bread and a steaming cup of coffee and carried it to Sam. His eyes widened appreciatively when he saw the tray.

"You're trying to please your *oga*, your master, eh?" he said, moving aside so she could bring the tray into the bedroom.

"Yessah," Eyo replied, steering clear of him when he reached out to grab her.

Sam smiled to himself. Eyo set the tray on the bed and made as if to leave the room.

"Eyo, I'm expecting a friend in an hour or so. He'll be staying for a few hours."

"Yessah."

Eyo raced to the kitchen and headed for the bin. Inside was a rolled-up newspaper, with grease leaking through it. Quickly, she unrolled it. Inside was a steaming egg sandwich. She rammed the sandwich down her throat, praying Lola wouldn't come back while she ate. Lola monitored the food content in the kitchen. It wasn't that she didn't feed Eyo. She did but just enough food to enable her to function. No more, no less. "I didn't bring you to England so you would eat me out of house and home and get fat," she would say, as she checked the fridge with beady eyes.

Eyo felt the sandwich warm up her insides. Slowly, her energy returned. She filled a glass with water and drank, looking out the window. When she finished, she went to the children's bedroom. She made sure her ears were tuned to the room next door where Sam was. In the bedroom, she headed for the bookshelf. It was easy to tell which books were Joshua's; they were the bright-coloured ones. Tolu considered herself a mature reader. She refused outrightly to read books she thought were too brightly coloured for her intellectual palate.

Eyo ran her hands across the bookshelf, her fingers brushing the book spines. She took one book off the shelf, sat on the floor and opened it. Her finger traced the first word slowly on the page.

A-p-p-l-e. On the page opposite was a big drawing of an apple.

D-o-g. She tasted the word on her lips. There was a drawing of an impossibly big dog on the page opposite. She didn't like dogs. In Nigeria, dogs bit people and gave them diseases. They also ate the remains of the human recipients of Lagos mob justice. But not here. She didn't believe Tolu when she said that in the uukaay, people shared their beds with their dogs, until she herself had seen a dog licking its owner's face, to the evident delight of the owner. Eyo shuddered and turned the page. The next letter was E, which accompanied by an egg drawing.

E-g-g. She pronounced the word to herself the way she thought Tolu would pronounce it, the way white people spoke.

The doorbell rang. Eyo put the book back on the shelf and got up reluctantly. She heard Sam's bedroom door open and close. He had to open the front door because she didn't have the key. She left the children's bedroom and went to the kitchen. Soon enough, Sam would come inside and tell her what he would like her to cook for his visitor.

"Come in."

Eyo heard Sam say to the visitor. The person—a man—said something she couldn't hear and he came in.

"This way," Sam said, his back to the kitchen, his hand outstretched towards the sitting room. The man followed Sam's direction and Sam walked after him. Eyo could see the man's outline from the kitchen. She didn't know who he was. He certainly hadn't visited the flat before.

"Eyo!"

"Sah!"

She hurried to the sitting room. The visitor was sitting on the sofa. He turned to Eyo when she came inside. He looked at her speculatively. Sam was standing by the sofa.

"Eyo, this is my friend. I've told him a lot of good things about you. I saved you from Lola's beating this morning with the garbage situation. If you cause me any trouble with this man… Anyway, we both know what happened the last time you gave me trouble, don't we?"

There was a distant ringing in Eyo's ears. She took a step back. Sam went to her and nudged her towards the man on the sofa. Eyo shrank back, but Sam gave her a shove.

"Remember what I said. No trouble."

He left the sitting room, locking the door behind him. The visitor started unbuttoning his trousers.

Thirteen

Tolu was counting down to her twelfth birthday.

"T-w-e-l-v-e," she said that morning as she got dressed. "Repeat after me: t-w-e-l-v-e."

Eyo repeated after her. She could always tell when Tolu was trying to teach her something. She spoke slowly, dragging her words with exaggerated lip movements. That evening, their parents were out, leaving all three of them alone in the flat. Tolu came into the sitting room where Eyo and Joshua were watching cartoons. Tolu had chosen the time well. It was Joshua's favourite programme. She knew there was no way he would move away from the television. She motioned to Eyo to be quiet and to follow her. Eyo followed her into the kitchen.

Tolu went to the fridge and took out the milk. She pointed to the writing on the plastic bottle. "M is for m-i-l-k. Milk," she said.

Eyo was unable to stop the smile that spread across her face. "M-i-l-i-k."

Tolu shook her head. "No, it's pronounced milk in England, not *milik* like in Nigeria. Now, say it again, m-i-l-k." This time, Tolu dragged the word even slower on her lips.

Eyo pronounced it and got it right. Just. Tolu went to the bread bin and took the bread. "B is also for b-r-e-a-d. Bread."

"Bread," Eyo said. Just then, Joshua wandered into the kitchen.

"What are you two doing?" he asked.

"None of your business," Tolu said imperiously. "Mummy's boy, always running to mummy for everything." She started mimicking Joshua's voice. "Mummy, Tolu is teaching Eyo to read. Mummy, I'll tell you everything because I'm a baby."

"I'm not a baby!"

"Yes, you are!"

They started bickering. Eyo left them and went into the bathroom. She sat on the floor.

M is for milk. M-i-l-k. B is for bread. B-r-e-a-d.

Eyo tasted the words on her lips and smiled to herself again. Tolu had just started teaching her to write when Lola found out about her lessons. Eyo traced an M on the bathroom floor.

Em. She knew it was an em because of the way Tolu pronounced it. Sometimes, it sounded like *erm.* She could still hear Tolu and Joshua squabbling in the kitchen. She left the bathroom and went back to the kitchen.

"Just think, Eyo, you've been here almost two years already," Tolu said. "And I'm going to be twelve." Tolu held up her two hands in front of Eyo and wiggled her fingers. "Twelve. Repeat after me: twelve."

Eyo repeated after her, not sure what Tolu was doing. The front door handle turned and Lola and Sam entered the flat.

"Mum! Tolu is teaching Eyo how to count!" Joshua said, running to them.

"No, I'm trying to show her how old I'm going to be!" Tolu glared at her brother. She shot Eyo a pitying look. Eyo went to the hallway.

"Welcome," she said, taking Lola's handbag from her. Lola grunted. Eyo gave Sam a cursory greeting and took Lola's handbag to the sitting room. The whole family followed her. Lola and the children settled on the sofa and Sam switched on the computer.

"Madam, would you like some tea or dinner? I've made rice and stew," Eyo said.

Lola waved her away. As Eyo was leaving the sitting room, Joshua whispered to Lola, "Mummy, Tolu is teaching Eyo again."

"Mummy, I'm teaching her how to speak English. There's a difference," Tolu said.

Sam barely glanced at his two children before turning his attention back to the computer screen. Lola wiped her forehead wearily. She and Sam had gone to visit Sam's sister who lived in Peterborough. The woman depressed Lola at the best of times. As for the husband, he wasn't any better. He gave her the creeps, but she endured the monthly visits to their home because she didn't want them anywhere near hers in London. They also had a three-year-old daughter. Lola hoped the poor girl hadn't inherited any of her parents' attributes. She would be doomed for life.

Lola yawned and stroked Joshua's back absent-mindedly. "Joshua, I haven't got the energy to deal with this today. Come on. It's bedtime."

"Mum, it's Saturday," Tolu said.

"And it's nine p.m. on a Saturday. That means bedtime." Lola got off the sofa and yawned. "Bed!"

Her voice brooked no arguments. Tolu and Joshua got off the sofa reluctantly and followed their mother out of the room.

"Night, Dad," Joshua called out.

"Night, son," Sam replied.

In the kitchen, Eyo waited. Ten minutes later, Lola joined her. She went to the cooker and opened the pots on it. She nodded in approval and Eyo breathed a bit easier. Next, she ran her finger on the kitchen surface and checked it; it met her approval too. She opened the fridge and closed it. Then, she stood in front of it and yawned.

"Very tiring day today," she said.

"Yes, madam," Eyo said.

"Sam might want something to eat later, so don't pack away the food yet," Lola said.

"Yes, madam."

Lola yawned again. "I'm off to bed. You've done well today, Eyo. Have some food to eat and, if Sam doesn't need you, you go to bed as well."

"Yes, madam."

Lola stifled another yawn and left the kitchen. Eyo helped herself to some rice and stew from the cooker and sat on the kitchen floor to eat. She was about to put the first spoon in her mouth, when she heard Sam call out her name. Her first inclination was to pretend she hadn't heard anything but she decided not to. The consequences would be too grave. She put the loaded plastic fork back on the plate and went to the sitting room, making sure she stood by the doorway.

"Sah?"

Sam looked away from his screen. "Come in. Why are you standing by the door?"

Eyo moved a few feet inwards.

"The man that came the other day is very happy with you," Sam said. Eyo waited, but there was nothing more.

"That'll be all," Sam dismissed her. Eyo went back to the kitchen.

*   *   *

It was Tolu's birthday. The flat was so filled with children and parents that there was barely any room to move.

Eyo! Come here and change this baby!

Eyo! Have you served Rachel?

Eyo!

Eyo!

Eyo!

Eyo ran between the kitchen and sitting room, serving food, wiping spilt drinks off the floor and trying not to lose her balance among the excited, active children. The doorbell rang and Lola went to get it. A woman came in with a toddler and a young girl about Eyo's age. Eyo could see them from the open, packed kitchen. The woman pushed the young girl towards the kitchen.

"Seyi, is this the girl you were telling me about?" Lola asked. She had to shout above the din.

"Yes," the woman said, giving her coat to Lola who hung it on the clothes rack behind the door. "She just arrived last week."

"How is your husband?"

"Glad to have the house to himself," Seyi responded. They both laughed.

"Eyo!"

"Madam!" Eyo hurried to Lola.

"Take…" Lola looked inquiringly at Seyi.

"Lara," Seyi completed.

"Take Lara to the kitchen. She'll be helping you there."

Lola pushed the girl towards Eyo. There was a slight commotion and the sound of something crashing in the sitting room. A woman came hurrying into the hallway.

"Lola, I need kitchen towels," she said.

Eyo went into the kitchen with the young girl and came out a few moments later by herself, holding a damp cloth. "I'll clean it," she said.

The woman nodded briefly and they both went into the sitting room. Seyi carried her toddler on her hips and, from the hallway, watched Eyo clean up the spilt drink.

"So," she said. "How are you managing with her?"

"Well, I think we understand each other better now," Lola said.

"I'm thinking of sending Lara to school."

"Are you mad? If she goes to school, who will take care of your children?"

Seyi stroked her daughter's head. She was asleep. She moved her to her shoulder and stroked her back. "I don't know. I'm just trying to figure how this whole thing works."

They were both silent for a while. Several screaming children ran around them.

"Busy today, eh?" Seyi said.

"Very. A few words of advice: You send that girl to school and you can end up with more problems. Social services, Home Office–you name it. They will all come knocking on your door for one reason or the other and make you regret your decision. You see Eyo? She's been here about two years now. Do you see me sending her to school? It's bad enough coping with nosy neighbours. How do you think I would cope, knowing that government offices were going through my business?"

Seyi nodded thoughtfully. "You're right. But you know my husband, he's a do-gooder. He promised her parents that she'll be educated."

"We all make promises we wish we could keep."

"Mum!"

"The birthday girl is calling. We'll chat later," Lola said.

Seyi nodded and followed her to the sitting room. As they were going in, Eyo was coming out, holding a soggy flannel in her hand. Seyi took note of her face. It was closed, the face of someone who'd decided to wall in all expressions, emotions or anything that could endanger its wearer. It looked macabre, even eerie on a child, which was what Eyo was, despite her circumstances.

Eyo was wearing Tolu's cast-offs. That much was evident. They hung on her thin frame like leaves hanging from a tree in autumn. The girl kept her eyes down. Her movements were calculated not to draw attention to herself, but somebody else was watching Eyo. Seyi could sense it and she perceived that Eyo could as well, not that the girl gave any hint that she knew.

Eyo carried the flannel and kept her eyes to the ground, but her shoulders gave her away. They were upright. And the sudden, slight tilt of her head upwards was designed to let her watcher know that she knew she was being watched and why, but she didn't care.

Seyi shifted her daughter on her hips as she looked around the packed sitting room. Sam was by the hi-fi, his hand poised to change the tracks. He also had his eyes on Eyo. It was the way he was looking at her that made Seyi slightly uneasy. He looked at Eyo the way one would look at a possession. There was also something else about his look that Seyi couldn't put her finger on.

"Seyi!"

The voice shook Seyi out of her reverie. It was Rachel, with her son, Patrick, on her hips.

"Rachel!"

They hugged, their toddlers hanging off their sides.

"I hear you've got a girl, too," Rachel said. She had to shout to make her voice heard above the din.

"Yes, her name is Lara. She arrived last week from Nigeria," Seyi answered.

"She's settling in okay?"

"Very well. She's helping Eyo out in the kitchen. I'll bring her to you in a while," Seyi said.

Eyo wrung out the flannel in the kitchen sink. There were several women in the kitchen, either helping themselves or serving others with food. People wandered in and out.

"What would you like me to do?" Lara asked her. She had a soft voice. She couldn't be more than a year or two older than Eyo, with more meat on her body.

"I'll give you a bin liner. Take one to the sitting room and put any rubbish you see there inside," Eyo said. "When you come back, I'll give you a tray with food and drinks on it to take there and start offering to people."

Eyo handed Lara a bin liner, and she took it. In the sitting room, Rachel and Seyi found two empty chairs in a corner and watched everyone around them. They placed their sleeping children on their laps and sighed in contentment.

"Thank God. I thought I would have to carry him forever," Rachel said.

A young girl about Eyo's age came into the room, holding a black bin liner. She started picking up empty cans and half-eaten plates of food and putting them inside. She worked quietly, navigating her way around the packed sitting room with expertise.

"Is that the girl you just brought from Nigeria?" Rachel nodded towards Lara. Seyi nodded.

Rachel fell silent. She had finally succumbed to her conscience and stopped bringing her son to Lola's for babysitting. There was no getting away from the fact that Lola maltreated Eyo. She'd seen it herself and she wanted no part of it. While she acknowledged that what Lola did in the privacy of her home was her business, Rachel slept better knowing that she wasn't contributing to it in any shape or form.

By the stereo, Lola was trying to persuade Sam to dance with her. Rachel and Stella watched her pulling Sam's arm. He kept on shaking her off good-naturedly. On the 'dance floor', the middle of the room, Tolu was wagging her finger in someone's face.

"That is not how to dance," she was saying. "I will teach you."

"That girl is something else. Her parents make me laugh, too," Seyi said.

"Yes, Lola has come a long way, hasn't she?" Rachel said.

Lara left the sitting room with a half-filled bin liner. She came back a few minutes later with a tray filled with snacks and fizzy drinks. She was followed by Eyo. The two of them picked their way gingerly through the crowd, offering their wares to the party-goers.

"She has, hasn't she?" Seyi agreed. She turned to Rachel, her manner serious all of a sudden. "I am not sure about Eyo," she said. There was an unspoken question in Seyi's statement, one Rachel was not sure she should or even wanted to answer, without implicating herself. She chose her words carefully.

"You know what Lola's like."

"Yes."

Seyi's response was an unspoken agreement that they had both taken the conversation as far it could go.

"Lara will go to school. We'll also tell social services about her, tell them we're fostering her privately," Seyi added after a while. "It's the right thing to do."

Rachel drew her sleeping son closer to herself and gave him a kiss. He was her son. She would kill anyone who dared lay a finger on him.

Fourteen

At the doorway, the gentleman brought out his wallet and gave Sam some notes. Sam pocketed the money and waved the man out. In the bathroom, Eyo sat on the covered toilet seat and held the flannel firmly between her legs. Outside, across the hall, through the closed sitting room door, she could hear the children joining in a cartoon DVD singalong.

A tear escaped Eyo's right eye. She sniffed and brushed it away. The man had been quite rough with her, pinching her nipples. Plus, she had hit her head on the toilet handle. She had been on her knees, bent over on the covered toilet seat. The man had mounted her from behind and she had given a small gasp of pain, her arms wrapped rigidly around the toilet sides. Her cry seemed to stimulate the man even further because he became rougher. At one point, she had found herself with one half of her body dangling off the toilet seat.

There was a quiet knock on the bathroom door. "Eyo, it's almost three. I will be leaving to pick up the children from school soon," Sam said.

Eyo pressed the ice-wrapped flannel even more firmly between her legs. Slowly, as the ice flannel numbed her intimately, she breathed a bit easier.

"Yessah," she said.

"I've opened the sitting room door. The DVD will be finished soon."

"Yessah."

"You've done well today. He was happy."

Sam cocked his head and waited for a few more moments. Then, he shrugged and went into the kitchen. He poured himself a glass of orange juice and stood by the kitchen sink, staring unseeing at the window above it. Mrs Richards walked past. At the last moment, she shot a glance at the window and turned away, disappointed when she saw Sam.

Sam downed the orange juice and left the glass by the sink. He had to find a way of getting Eyo out of the flat, to another location where she could service the clients without interruption and without arousing interest. At the moment, he was providing Eyo's services to only a few select and handpicked people, but it was only a matter of time before news of what he was offering would spread and he would be bombarded with offers. Besides, he wasn't altogether comfortable with the idea of turning his home into a brothel. Space was an issue, which was why Eyo's services were performed in the bathroom. There were four regular clients, each of whom came twice a week at prearranged times. And they were starting to grumble about how uncomfortable the bathroom floor was, despite the fact that Sam made sure he laid the softest blankets he could find, on the floor.

The toddlers Eyo babysat were an issue as well. Right now, they were down to four, Rachel having decided not to avail herself of Lola's nanny service anymore, to Lola's intense annoyance.

"Imagine that! She got us started on this babysitting thing and then, all of a sudden, she decides that she's not comfortable with Eyo looking after her son. Who does she think she is?"

"Four is the perfect number because it is manageable. Any more and there will an accident or something that Eyo wouldn't be responsible for," Sam had told her. Thankfully, she had seen sense.

In the morning, when the toddlers were dropped off at the flat, he made sure they were settled in and popped a cartoon DVD in the player. When his clients called his mobile to let him know they were waiting outside his front door, he would leave the sitting room, close the door behind him and let them in, straight into the bathroom where Eyo would be waiting. As soon as he closed the bathroom door behind him, he would go back to the sitting room, shut the door behind him and keep a close eye on the clock. He also made sure the television volume was at just manageably loud levels. When the men's time was up, he would first ensure that the sitting room door was shut behind him before going to the bathroom and knocking discreetly on the door. Sometimes, the men asked for overtime, which he gave entirely at his discretion. Not that he liked doing that, at least not in his home. If they were based in another location, like a room he'd rented out specifically for that purpose, then yes, he would grant them as much overtime as they wanted, but not just yet.

The plan was working so far. But being a wise man, he knew it was only a matter of time before it unravelled, which was why he had to figure out a way to get Eyo somewhere else to perform her services with ease. There was also the small matter of what to do with the toddlers she was babysitting, while she was out of the house performing these services.

Sam sighed and poured himself another glass of orange juice from the fridge. So many decisions. He looked at his watch, which showed it was quarter past three p.m. It was time to pick up his children from school. Ever since her twelfth birthday, Tolu had been campaigning to walk home from school herself, but Lola had refused, citing the growing number of reported evil-doers lurking around schools, looking for lone children like her and Joshua to pounce on. The more Sam thought about it, the more he was convinced that Tolu had a point. She was twelve, incredibly bright and with an attitude guaranteed to scare off even the most dedicated evil-doer who would dare think about coming near Joshua and her. But at the same time, if they walked home themselves, it meant that they could come at an inopportune moment, like when Eyo was busy with a client.

He heard the bathroom door open and close. Eyo came out, her face closed. She appeared distant. Mechanically, she went across the corridor and into the kitchen, emptying the ice cubes inside the kitchen sink. Then she wrung the flannel and spread it on the edge of the sink. When she finished, she left the kitchen. Not once, in the fifteen seconds she spent in the kitchen did she acknowledge Sam, standing a few feet away from her. Soon, he heard the sitting room door open and the welcoming cries of "Eyo!" that came after. A few moments later, he left the flat to pick up his children, making sure Eyo was locked in with the toddlers. He had already called the mothers. None of them were coming to pick their children before he got back from the school.

Eyo picked up one of the toddlers and put him on her lap, clenching her pelvis tightly to stem the throbbing aches and cramps between her legs. She played with the toddler's hair absent-mindedly. One hand went to her temple and caressed it lightly, carefully. She also had a dull ache inside her head. There were three children on the floor, surrounded by toys. From the smell that suddenly permeated the air, one of the children needed changing. Eyo put the child on her lap back on the floor and got off the sofa. She went to the suspect, knelt down and turned the child over in her lap. The smell said it all.

"Euww!" she said, making noises at the child.

Eyo felt faint as she felt something push down her vagina. The child laughed, distracting her momentarily, and then an unexpected pang of pain shot through Eyo. She remembered Sade smiling at her like that a long time ago. She put the child back on the floor and stood up. She gave a loud cry, staring in horror at the mangled, bloody blob on the wooden sitting room floor, which had come from her vagina and slid down her legs.

Just then, the front door lock turned and Joshua came bounding into the sitting room. He ran back out into the corridor.

"Dad!" he shouted. "Eyo's blood is on the floor!"

Fifteen

"I'm telling you, there is something not quite right about it , but nobody is listening to me. I first called you three months ago and you keep telling me to write an official letter. Why don't you just come here and see for yourself what's been going on?"

"Mrs Richards, we can't go barging into someone's home just because a girl wearing a scarf and wig looks out of a window."

"That is not what I'm saying. I've seen two strange men go inside the flat today. There was one yesterday and another one the day before that. I'm telling you, something is not right."

The man on the other end of the phone looked at the heaving paperwork on his desk. He had four house visits to make that day, each requiring copious amounts of bureaucratic follow-up. Three of them resulted from telephone calls just like this, from so-called concerned neighbours calling social services about their neighbour's children. In reality, they were just looking for ways to get rid of people they didn't like on their street or estate. The man sighed in defeat. He had to go and see the child the woman was talking about. They had a legal obligation to do so. It would probably come to nothing but would generate enough paperwork to sink a ship and waste enough of his time to ensure that the children who really needed his attention weren't seen today.

"Where did you say you lived?"

Mrs Richards told him.

Sixteen

Larry put back the covers on Eyo. "She had a miscarriage," he said.

Lola blinked and shook her head, as if to clear out the wax in her ears. "Pardon?"

"You heard me." Larry straightened the covers on the bed. "Look, I don't know what you guys are doing, but from now on, don't call me or come to my house. Ever. By law, I should report everything I've seen on this girl today, but I wouldn't because I've already put myself at professional risk by coming here. Here," he shoved some pills into Lola's hands. "Give her this when she wakes up, which should be in about two to three hours. She should take these other pills every day for the next two weeks. She should also be in hospital."

"We can't. She doesn't have papers," Lola said.

"You should've thought of that before doing this," Larry said through clenched teeth. He gathered his belongings and let himself out. When he left, a silence descended on the flat. The children were spending an impromptu night with Lola's sister. Sam and Lola went into the sitting room. They both sat on opposite ends of the sofa.

"Well, she couldn't have gotten pregnant by herself. Not unless there was an additional chapter to the Immaculate Conception," Lola said.

"I don't know what you're talking about," Sam said.

Lola got up and stood in front of her husband. "Look at me," she commanded him.

Sam ignored her.

"I said, 'Look at me!'" she insisted.

When Sam looked up, she slapped him. "Get rid of her! I don't want to see her in this flat when my children come back tomorrow."

She left the sitting room and a minute later, Sam heard the bedroom door lock. He sat still on the sofa, looking at the wall in front of him. Then he made a telephone call. "There's a package coming your way," he said when the person picked up the phone. "You won't be disappointed."

On the end of the telephone, Stella, who was known as Big Madame, hung up the telephone and waited.

*   *   *

Eyo felt somebody lift her. She heard the door open and then felt a blast of cold air on her face. She moaned. The ground beneath her felt shaky, making her queasy. She heard a ping and then the sound of a machine door closing. She tried to shift, to make herself more comfortable.

"Keep still or else I'll drop you," she heard a man who sounded very much like Sam say. She tried opening her eyes and shut them quickly when the moving space around her started moving towards her.

She felt nauseous. She breathed in deeply, then turned to the side, wincing when pain shot up her insides. She heard another ping and cold air hit her. She inhaled deeply, welcoming it. The nausea cleared a little. She heard a door open and then she was spread out on what felt like a lengthy cushion. It was warm. She heard the door close, and then, another one opened and closed in front of her it seemed. There was the sound of an ignition being turned and then they were moving. She wished they could stop. The rolling movement was making her feel nauseous again. Something heaved in her stomach, Eyo turned to the side and hurled her insides out.

"No! Not in the car!"

The movement stopped and she heard a door open. There was a squeak of something winding down. The car door shut again, but it was better this time because she could feel the wind on her face.

They started moving again. She must have dozed off because, when she opened her eyes, they had stopped moving and Sam was leaning over her. He had some pills in his hand and a bottle of water.

"Take this," he said.

Eyo shook her head.

"Don't make things difficult!" Sam said angrily, forcing the pills and water down her throat.

She didn't remember anything after that. The next time Eyo opened her eyes, there was a woman standing over her.

"Welcome to The House, Eyo. I am Big Madame," the woman said.

The darkness enveloped Eyo again.

Seventeen

Mrs Richards pretended she didn't know the man that just went past her kitchen window. But she went to her front door and pressed her ears against it. She heard her neighbour's doorbell ring and a minute later, she heard Lola's voice.

"Yes?"

"Reg Parkham, Social Services," Mrs Richards heard the man say.

"And?"

"We have reason to believe that we may be of help to your fami…"

Mrs Richards heard Lola's front door shut firmly. A moment later, she heard Lola's doorbell again.

"Can I help you?"

This time, it was a man that opened the door. Inwardly, Reg cursed the vagaries of his job. "I hope you can. I'm from Social Services. We're just doing an assessment of families' needs in the local area and we have reason to believe that we may be of use to you."

"Thanks, but we're fine," the man said, closing the door. Reg put his foot in the doorway and stepped forward.

"I don't think you understand, sir. I believe we may be of use to your family." This time, Reg spoke firmly, looking straight into Sam's eyes. He flashed Sam his ID card: *Safeguarding*

Children Board, it said across it. Sam stepped back and allowed Reg inside the flat. He didn't bother asking him to take off his coat, taking him straight inside the sitting room. In the kitchen, Lola ignored the two of them, choosing to bang pots and pans to make her displeasure known.

Reg sat on the proffered sofa and Sam sat on the chair opposite the computer. Reg did a quick assessment. It was a typical family room, dotted with photos of family events. He noted the photos of the two children on the walls and on top of the television. None of them resembled the skinny girl with the terrible wig and headscarf the neighbour described.

"Those your kids?"

"Yes."

Reg brought out a folder from his rucksack. "And what about Eyo?"

"Eyo?"

"Yes, Eyo."

Sam paused. "I don't know why you're here or who's been telling you stuff. Not that it's anyone's business, but Eyo was my niece on holiday, who's now gone back to Nigeria."

"Right. And Sade?"

"Sade was her twin sister. She's gone back to Nigeria as well."

"Mind if I take a look around the flat?"

"Help yourself," Sam said.

Reg shut his folder and put it back in his bag. He stood up and followed Sam around the flat, his eyes missing nothing. The tour ended with them in the hallway.

In the kitchen, Lola shot the two of them poisonous looks and slammed a pot on the cooker.

"Thank you very much for your time," Reg said.

"No problem," Sam said, letting him out.

When Reg went past the flat of Mrs Richards, he looked up at her kitchen window and there she was. He gave her a slight shrug and carried on walking. In her flat, Mrs Richards went to her sitting room and sat down, thinking.

Back in the office, Reg filed his report and concluded it with the following words: *no further action necessary.*

African
Lolita

Eighteen

Eyo tried not to shift while the man was talking. She had been sitting on his lap for an hour. He stroked her hair and back, talking softly, not that she really understood what he was saying. The man tapped his left leg lightly on the floor. That was the signal. She got off his lap and knelt down. He was already naked. Eyo lowered her head and got to work. The man's breathing got heavier, his hand pressing hard on her head, forcing her head down even lower.

A is for a-p-p-l-e. B is for b-r-e-a-d. C is for c-a-t. D is for d-o-g.

In her mind's eye, she could picture Tolu standing over her imperiously, her voice impatient whenever she got something wrong.

"Eyo, you're not listening!"

In that flat, her life had been good, even though she hadn't known it. Her eye caught the man's belt, still in his trousers wrapped around his knees. She didn't like spelling 'belt'.

Suddenly, the man lifted Eyo up and put her back on his naked lap, so that she was straddling him. He brought his head down on her naked chest. A few moments later, he erupted, his shoulders shaking. Silently, Eyo waited to be dismissed. The man's left leg shifted and she disengaged herself from him. She turned away while he got dressed. There was the sound of coins clattering on the dressing table. A moment later, he walked past her and left the room.

She was alone. She moved the chair they used back towards the dressing table and ironed out the creases on the bed. She squatted and cleaned herself using the wipes she took from the dressing table drawers. When she finished, she stood up and peeked through the drawn curtains. It was dark outside. She had no idea if that was because it was night-time or daybreak. She thought it was night-time because the man was wearing a suit, which meant that he came straight from work. Or a bar. A faint smell of alcohol had lingered around him when he came. At least he hadn't hurt her.

Eyo moved away from the curtains when she heard footsteps coming towards the room. The door opened and a woman came in. She was about five-foot-eight, light-skinned, slim and extremely attractive. She pursed her lips when she saw Eyo standing a few feet away from the window. She didn't know what it was about windows and Eyo. No matter what she was told or how many beatings she got, she couldn't keep away from them.

"Eyo, how many times have I told you to keep away from the windows?"

"Sorry, Big Madame," Eyo said.

Big Madame ran a professional eye around the room. She gave a small sound of satisfaction at what she saw. Her eyes landed on the coins on the dressing table.

"He left you some money."

Eyo didn't answer. They went through this every time clients left tips. The first time, she had been stupid. She had taken the loose change and hidden it in her pocket. The next day, she was summoned to Big Madame's office, the evidence of her 'stealing' on the table.

"You don't steal from me Eyo," Big Madame had said. "Everything here is mine. Your clothes, whatever the clients give you. Everything is mine. Understand?"

Eyo had nodded in understanding. She shared a room with a Nigerian girl who was a few years older than her. Their routine was regimented. They were locked in for naps at certain hours of the day and they ate separately from the other working girls. Sometimes, they were taken to the other houses, always in the middle of the night, and they would stay there until Big Madame decided that they should come back to this one. Big Madame decided when they should eat, sleep, watch television or do anything. Eyo hated her.

Big Madame went to take the coins off the table. She pocketed them.

"You've done well today, Eyo," she said. "Mr Lau was very happy."

Eyo didn't answer. She did that often. People would be talking to her and she would be still, silent, sometimes even sulky. It used to annoy Big Madame no end in the beginning but not anymore. This was one of the reasons why she was the most popular 'special' girl. She did what needed doing without direction. And, she did it well. Almost too well. Sam's boasts had not been unfounded.

Big Madame drew in a big breath. There was work to be done. No point in standing around here doing nothing. "Time for your nap," she said.

"Yes, Big Madame."

Eyo followed her out of the room and up a flight of stairs. They walked down a short corridor, past the bathroom and stopped in front of the door next to it. Big Madame took out a bunch of keys and opened the door to the room of the 'special children'. It was more like a dormitory, with a bunk bed, small dressing table and wardrobe. The other girl, Nkem, was already in bed. She turned a blank face to the door when Eyo came in. Big Madame pushed Eyo gently into the room and locked the door after her. Eyo clambered up the bunk bed. She didn't like heights, but she had chosen to sleep on the top deck because it's what Lanre would've done. He was a brave boy. Adventurous. Unlike her who was scared of everything. He was the reason she had forced herself to climb up the bed and lie on it her first night here, trying hard not to look down the side and imagine her brains splattered on the beige carpet. Just as he would've shouted, *Eyo, look! I'm on top of the bed!* so she had whispered to herself, *Lanre, I'm on the top bed*, when she clambered up, heart palpitating. And she liked it, she had decided. Underneath her bed, Nkem shifted. She spoke to Eyo in pidgin English.

"You *dey* fine?"

Eyo turned her head on the pillow and traced her hand on the wall. She was trying to write "pillow" with an imaginary pen. She wondered if it was spelt as it sounded: *peelow*.

"Yes, Nkem. It was Mr Lau."

"He okay."

Eyo gave up trying to spell. She was tired; her nipples tingled. Mr Lau's grinding was painful, to say the least. And there was the migraine, constantly, wearing her down. Sometimes, all she wanted to do was lie down somewhere and never get up again. An image of her mother cooking in the darkened corridor and chatting to Mama Fola flashed across her mind. She blinked away the tears that rose in her eyes, irritated with herself.

She started tracing her finger on the wall again. This time, she tried spelling her name. She thought it was spelt a-y-o, but she wasn't sure. Nkem wasn't much help being a complete illiterate herself.

Nkem yawned. A few moments later, she was asleep. In less than an hour, Big Madame would come and wake them up. They would have a light dinner and if they 'behaved', she sometimes allowed them to watch cartoons. Nkem loved *Tom and Jerry*. She would laugh at each episode, as if she'd never seen it before, although she'd probably seen it at least a million times. Nkem was already at the house when Eyo arrived. They both didn't talk much about what they did, preferring to relegate it to the dark corner of their minds where it lay buried and, if both of them had their way, would stay buried.

Eyo yawned and her finger fell away from the wall. The last image that went through her mind before she fell asleep was of her street in Ajegunle at dusk. Her father and the landlord were sitting languidly on the benches outside their face-me-I-face-you: her father lazily watching her approach the building; the landlord keenly observing Lanre scampering impatiently and telling her to hurry up so he could get his football from their room.

Eyo fell asleep.

*   *   *

Eyo heard the keys in her sleep before the door opened. She opened her eyes just as Big Madame came in. "Rise and shine, the two of you. It's Friday, a busy night," she said.

Big Madame went to the wardrobe and took out their working outfits for the night. The look had to be just right. Clients didn't like the children looking too young or too old. Pubescent was the preferred look.

Eyo and Nkem stretched and yawned simultaneously. They both got off the beds and waited while Big Madame laid their clothes on their beds. Afterwards, they followed her out of the room into the bathroom next door. Big Madame waited while they brushed and showered. When they finished, she herded them back to the bedroom and watched while they got dressed. With brusque movements, she applied some make-up to their faces. Again, the look was natural and untouched because that was how clients preferred it. Personally, she didn't know who the clients thought they were fooling. Their demands for natural-looking, untouched children was at odds with their sexual preference but–hey!–each to their own. Big Madame stood back and surveyed her handiwork critically. *Perfect*, she thought.

"Dinner is Nigerian pepper soup, with bread," she said.

Her two protégées nodded subserviently.

"Come along then," Big Madame said. She gestured to the door and they followed her, Big Madame locking the bedroom door carefully behind her.

The dining room was downstairs, at the back of the house, with an open doorway leading directly to the kitchen. Like all the rooms in the house, its curtains were drawn. The only natural light came from a small window high up on the kitchen wall, almost touching the ceiling, next to the extractor fan. The cook, a Sierra Leonean woman, was perspiring heavily in the kitchen. The dining table had a seating capacity for eight people, although it was currently laid out for four. Big Madame took her seat at the head of the table and Nkem and Eyo sat on either side of her. That was the way she preferred it.

They heard noises and the dining room door opened. A woman came in, clutching a worn-looking bag. She looked slightly anxious. Big Madame gestured to her to sit down. The woman did.

"Girls," she said, "this is Bola, my good friend."

"Welcome," Nkem and Eyo said at the same time.

Bola nodded and started eating. They all ate in silence. Big Madame didn't like people talking at mealtimes, unless it was instigated by her. Eyo stole glances at Bola. The woman could be any age, and from the way she wolfed down the soup and bread, probably welcomed the meal. Eyo could tell she was desperate to talk to Big Madame about something from the way she would look up expectantly at her, open her mouth and shut it again. Big Madame didn't need to say much. She was the only person Eyo knew who could say a lot from her facial expressions without actually modifying her face.

Eyo's bowl was empty, the bread finished as was Nkem's food. They both waited to be dismissed. Big Madame clapped and the cook came in to clear the dishes. Big Madame nodded at Eyo and Nkem. They both got up and followed the cook out of the dining room. When they left, Bola gave a sigh of relief.

"Stella, *na* you be *dis* Big Madame? Is this you?" Bola's voice was disbelieving.

Stella wiped her mouth delicately with a napkin and put it back on the table. "My dear, what can I say?" she said with a coy smile.

"Thank you for this. I'll never forget it," Bola said.

"You're my friend."

Bola played with her bread. "We're friends, aren't we?" She stared into space for a few moments. "It's just so difficult and Italy…"

"Forget Italy. You're here now. How are your husband and children?"

Bola put the bread back on the side plate. "Very well. I spoke to them last week." She sighed, then gathered herself. "They're well," she repeated.

Stella watched the array of emotions flit across Bola's features. She reached out and patted her friend's arm.

"Bola, it's okay."

Bola picked up a spoon. As she bent over the soup bowl to start eating, tears poured her cheeks.

"Yes," she said.

Nineteen

"I have a daughter about your age," Bola said.

Eyo said nothing. They were downstairs, on the sofa in the lounge for special clients. Only Nkem and Eyo were allowed to wait for clients in that room, usually under the watchful eye of Big Madame. She didn't usually allow them to mingle with the older women, but she made exceptions with Bola. She always made exceptions when it came to Bola.

"She's in secondary school now. See." Bola took out a passport photo from inside her bra and showed Eyo.

Eyo gave the picture a cursory glance and gave it back to her. Bola tucked it back into her bra. She should've known better than to expect a word from Eyo. The girl didn't speak; everybody knew that.

The door opened and Nkem came inside. She went to a corner and sat on the floor, staring unseeing at the blank television screen. There was a murmur of voices outside the room: Stella's and a man's. They heard receding steps, the front door opened and closed, and then Stella entered the room. She gestured to Eyo to follow her, and Eyo did.

Bola stole a few looks at Nkem. She was still sitting on the floor, only this time, she had turned to her side, her back to Bola. Bola knew better than to try talking to her. She sighed heavily. She knew it wasn't *her* business, but Nkem and Eyo had no *business* being in this house.

"Bola, I'm telling you this and I won't tell you again. Some things will not be discussed between us," Stella had told her.

"But they are both so young."

"Bola, you can talk, leaving your husband and children in Nigeria to come to Europe to do this, so you could earn some money and send it home. I didn't question your decision, so don't question what I do."

"But Stella…"

"Big Madame." Stella's voice had turned icy.

Bola had caught her friend's warning tone and heeded it. She had a lot to be grateful to Stella for. If it wasn't for her, she would still be in Turin servicing up to ten men a night at five euros a go. Some of the girls even charged lower prices as competition was fierce. Not surprising as the streets were awash with Nigerian women just like her, at night.

"Bola."

It was Stella, calling her on the other side of the door. Bola shook her head, as if to shake away her thoughts. She stole another look at Nkem and got up. She waited until she got to the door before unclasping her belt. The dressing gown parted, revealing the scanty underwear underneath. Her stilettos were by the door. She slid her feet into them. Puckering her lips, she breathed in and opened the door. She had a customer.

Twenty

Friday was usually their busiest night but today had been slow. Big Madame was annoyed. Eyo could tell by the way she'd pursed her lips and shoved them into the bedroom.

"Stella, it's not their fault. Leave them alone," Bola said.

Nkem and Eyo both held their breaths, wondering what Big Madame would say. Her temper was legendary. She didn't like being contradicted. Everyone knew that. Everyone but Bola, it seemed. Eyo thought Big Madame secretly liked Bola being around. She could see that she trusted her because she allowed her to do many things she used to do herself. Like allowing her in the special room and accompanying Big Madame on their daily routine: nap time, bedtime, television time and other times.

Big Madame shot Bola a poisonous look, which she ignored.

"Goodnight, girls," Bola said gaily.

"Goodnight," Nkem and Eyo said.

Big Madame turned out the lights and she left the room with Bola in tow, locking the door behind them.

In the dark bedroom, Nkem spoke. "Do you think we will ever go back to Nigeria?" she asked Eyo.

Eyo could hear the uncertainty and fear in her voice. She wished she couldn't. It made her fearful and she didn't like it, after all, she was meant to be a robot, devoid of feeling. She didn't even know if she wanted to go back to Nigeria. How could she tell Mama what happened to her? Where would she start? She'd always told her that as the eldest child and a woman, she had to endure. If she went back to Nigeria the way she was now, barely knowing how to read and write, Mama would be disappointed. And angry. She would think that she'd wasted Uncle Femi's money.

Eyo! Carry me!

It was Sade in their room in Jungle City, bouncing up and down on the sleeping mat, her pudgy arms outstretched to Eyo. Eyo clamped her mind down on the images, reminding herself once again that she was a human robot.

Watch the water, Eyo! I said, 'Watch the water!'

Eyo put her hands over her ears to block out her mother's voice, as clear as the day she left Nigeria. In the uukaay, she had water at her fingertips, but she thought she'd never felt more unclean in her life.

Below her, Nkem too was thinking. She knew she would never go back to Nigeria. She belonged to Big Madame. Her father had sold her. If her mother was alive, she knew she wouldn't be in the uukaay. She would still be in her village, happy and away from men who hurt her here in the uukaay every day. Even better, she would be away from Big Madame.

It was her stepmother. The woman hadn't wanted any reminders of her husband's first wife around, especially a girl. So she found a way to dispatch Nkem for good and convinced her father that it was in Nkem's best interest. Nkem liked to think that her father wouldn't have gone ahead with selling her if he had known what Big Madame did. But that would've been a lie because everybody knew what she did for a living. Big Madame didn't talk about it but she didn't deny it either. Not that anyone cared. She lived in the UK and went back to the village in Nigeria every Christmas, with money, jewellery and all sorts. Her house was the biggest in the village with three cars, which she changed every two years. Her siblings went to the best private school in the state and her father never failed to remind everyone about his wealthy daughter in England. And that was what mattered to everyone. The fact that Stella was rich. They all knew how she made money in England and they didn't care. Poverty and hunger did that to people.

Every time Stella went back to the village everybody went to her house. They all wanted to know if she could help them go to the uukaay "to work". No one asked about the jobs they would do once they got there. Sometimes, she took a girl with her back to England. Sometimes she didn't. She brought Nkem back with her to England on one of her journeys to the village. Nkem only found out she'd been sold when she overheard her stepmother arguing with her father that four hundred thousand naira was too low a sale price for Nkem. That he should've bargained harder and higher.

That was three years ago. She was eleven then. One day, when she was old enough, she would be like Big Madame. She would go back to her village and parade her wealth in front of her stepmother and father.

See, she would say, when she got out of the gleaming car that would bring her to the village. *See what you will never get.* And she would drive away to the biggest hotel in the neighbouring town and wait for her father to come and beg her forgiveness. She would forgive him, but only on condition that he chased her stepmother and her children out of the house. That was Nkem's favourite part of the daydream: standing outside her father's house, watching in glee while he tossed them out on the street.

She couldn't wait for that day, but for now, she consoled herself with thoughts of her mother. She imagined she was in heaven, watching over her, with God. Even though she'd been eight when she died, Nkem remembered her mother's faith. She used to punctuate every sentence with, "Nothing is impossible with God. Remember that even when it seems impossible, God can change situations in the blink of an eye, just like that." And she would snap her finger to illustrate her point.

Nkem wondered what her mother was making of God now, with her daughter holed up in a European brothel. She stopped crying, now irritated with herself. She should be more like Eyo. The girl never cried about anything. She didn't even seem to feel anything. Sometimes, Nkem wondered if she was even human.

"Nkem, I don't think we should talk about Nigeria." Eyo's voice was soft.

It broke into Nkem's thoughts, but she heard the catch in it. They were both silent, each lost in their thoughts.

"Big Madame says that even if something happens to us and we die, nobody would notice because nobody knows where we are. In any case, we don't exist anywhere in the uukaay." Eyo's voice was a monotone. "But I wouldn't die here," she added fiercely. Resolutely. A sudden, clear image of her mother by her roadside food stall flooding her mind. It was the clearest image she'd had in a very long time. "I wouldn't," she repeated as if reassuring herself.

"Neither will I," Nkem said.

*   *   *

Bola tried to stifle a yawn. She stole a look at the clock on the wall. Five more minutes to go. The humping toad on top of her clenched his teeth and finally thundered to a halt, shaking like a leaf. He collapsed on top of her, his back slick with sweat. Bola waited for a few moments before disengaging herself. The toad fell to her left side. He wasn't bad-looking. He was about six-foot-one, a bit on the pudgy side, with brown hair, brown eyes and a shy demeanour.

"Marry me," he said.

"If I did, you wouldn't respect me as much," she said.

The toad laughed and started playing with her breasts. He bent over one and clasped his mouth over a nipple. Bola shot another look at the clock: three more minutes, although with the way things were going, he'd probably ask for overtime. She was scheduled to call her husband in Nigeria in ten minutes. She forced herself to remain calm and bid the irritation to go away.

The toad unleashed her nipple and raised his head. "Let's spend the day together," he said.

"If you saw me in the morning, you'd probably run away," Bola quipped.

"I'm serious."

"So am I. Come on, it's time to go." Bola got off the bed. The toad watched her get dressed.

"I'll be back tomorrow," he said.

"I'm sure," Bola replied.

When he finally left, Bola had a quick shower before calling her husband. She didn't like talking to him while still unclean. When she finished, she went to Stella's office. The room was lined with books and folders on wealth management and trading laws. Bola often thought that there were enough secrets and money traded in this room to bring down the movers and shakers of the British economy, many of whom were Stella's clients. Bola sometimes wished that she had her friend's business acumen. Stella understood three things: sex, money and power. Here, in this office, she traded in all three with her customary discretion and understated style.

Seated behind the table, Stella looked at her friend. She could always tell when Bola had spoken to her family in Nigeria. She became subdued and extremely irritable.

"How are your daughters?" she asked.

"Very well. You were right. That skirt went down a treat with Sola," Bola said.

Stella shut down the computer and put her hands on the table.

"I've been meaning to talk to you about Mark," she said.

"The toad?" Bola sat on the chair across the desk.

"Yes, the toad." Stella paused for a few moments. "He's getting attached to you," she said.

"What do you care? He comes every night and you make money off him. Isn't that the point?" Bola asked waspishly.

Stella let it slide. She knew she was thinking of her family in Nigeria.

"Ordinarily, I wouldn't care, but this is not an ordinary attachment. It's something more. Be careful, that's all."

"Stella, leave me alone."

Stella picked up a folder and started thumbing through it. There was something else she wanted to tell Bola but decided against it. She'd heard reports from reliable sources that Bola's husband had been fooling around with not one but several women. Bola wouldn't be the first woman in Nigeria to leave a husband and children to come to Europe and make money from sex work. As far as Stella was concerned, prostitution was an economic enterprise and was nothing to be ashamed of. But she did have issues with men who, instead of making the illegal, arduous journey to Europe themselves, sent their wives instead. And she had particular issue with Bola's husband because he was the most spineless of them all. Bola was worth a million of him.

This year was her tenth in Europe, the Promised Land. She remembered her journey here very well. She was in Nigeria, her last day of secondary school. She had just turned onto the dirt path that led to her house when she was approached by a man. He asked her if she wanted to go to Europe to work.

What kind of work? she'd asked him. She knew the guy. Everyone in the village did. Rumours flew around about what he did; some said he was a drug dealer. Others said he took women to Europe "to work." There were other rumours, but none that anybody could verify. One thing was true though: He had money.

What kind of job do you think? the man had asked, looking directly into her eyes.

Stella had thought hard for all of one minute. Her father was a bully who ruled his home with his fists. She was eighteen, the oldest in a family of six. Her mother sold her meagre farm products in the local market, the proceeds of which her father poured down his gullet in the local bar each night. The way she looked at it, her future in the village looked about as appealing as her current life. That night, she left her village with the man. She also lost her virginity to him, figuring she'd better get some practice. She'd always been practical that way.

Two weeks later, she arrived in Turin, Italy, with a false passport, birth certificate and a debt of thirty thousand US dollars, which was the man's fee for bringing her to Europe. She paid off her debt in eighteen months and moved on to Amsterdam for economic reasons. Then, the streets were still relatively devoid of Nigerian prostitutes. While there, she struck a deal with a Nigerian legal resident: ten thousand US dollars in return for a marriage to him to secure her legal papers in the country. It took another three years, but she eventually received her legal residency papers.

She applied for a European Union passport and two weeks after it came in the post, she packed up and headed straight for the UK. It never occurred to her to settle down in London. She didn't like the city. It was too crowded, too noisy and, besides, she was bound to have fierce competition with the kind of services she wanted to offer. One of her regular customers in Amsterdam lived in the UK. It was he who suggested that she set up her business services in Leeds. So when he called her about a package a few years later, promising her that she "wouldn't be disappointed", she'd taken the "package" in.

And Sam was right; Eyo had not been a disappointment. Wilful, yes, but definitely not a disappointment in terms of satisfying the clients. Stella didn't ask her where she got her skills from. She wasn't interested in the past. She preferred the here and now, and the future, because she was a long-term planner. The fabulous life she lived now—and on her own terms—was the result of all the planning she did ten y,ears ago when she had said 'yes' to that man in her village.

Sometimes, however, she still looked round and found it hard to believe that she was a successful businesswoman, which is how she viewed herself. She had no patience for people who refused to see the wealth of opportunities sex offered to those willing to use it to their advantage. Take her father. The same man who used to spend his evenings using his wife and their children as punching bags now kowtowed to her every time she went home to Nigeria.

The first time she went home–five years after she had left–she brought money and gifts for every member of her family. That same night, her father tried to hit her mother. Stella had thrown herself in front of her and told her father in icy tones that if he ever hit either her mother or her siblings again, there would be repercussions. She neglected to explain what she meant by "repercussions". Her father had looked into her eyes and known that she had meant what she said. He never hit her mother nor her siblings again, understanding that the lifestyle his daughter's earnings from Europe accorded him was dependent on his treatment of his wife and children. That was the kind of power sex and money offered, Stella mused.

Stella didn't mix business with pleasure. She had never been that sentimental. She had a number she called to fulfil her physical needs, and whatever bouts of loneliness she experienced had now been alleviated by Bola's presence in the house. She trusted her completely. They were childhood friends and she was the only one she had told about her plans when she left the village that night, ten years ago. So when she received the telephone call three months ago from a hysterical Bola in Turin, saying she couldn't take the street work anymore, Stella had pulled out all the stops to get her to the UK. It had cost her a lot of money, paying off the agents who brought Bola to Italy and getting the false documents, but she hadn't cared. Her friend was worth it.

And now, across the table, Bola looked at the clock on the wall, above Stella's head. *Tick tock, tick, tock*, just like her life in Europe. "Stella, he's my husband. Besides, my children are with him. There is nothing I can do except this: provide for them."

They knew each other too well. Stella was sure the same sources had told Bola about her wandering husband. She reached out to open the small fridge underneath her table. She pulled out two ice cream tubs and put them on the table. Next, she took out two spoons from her table drawer and dangled them tantalisingly in front of Bola. Bola laughed and drew herself closer. Stella offered her a spoon and shoved the tub of Häagen-Dazs across the table.

"Ready?" Stella asked, her tub opened, spoon hovering over it.

"You know I'll win," Bola said. "I always do."

They both started eating. Bola did win the eating competition, but only because Stella took her time finishing hers so her friend could win.

Twenty-one

It was time to go. Eyo followed Big Madame silently down the corridor, down the stairs and out of the front door. The car was already outside, its engine running quietly. By its door was Bola, a grim look on her face. Eyo couldn't see Big Madame's face, but she imagined the haughty look she would've given her friend in return. Last night, she'd heard them both shouting at each other behind the closed doors of the office, which was right next to the special lounge.

"Stella, they are children. Let them go!"

"Bola, I've told you to stay out of my business."

And then the doorbell had rung and Big Madame went to get it. And from the looks of things tonight, they still hadn't made up. Today, mealtimes in the dining room had been arctic. Eyo and Nkem wolfed down their food in their haste to be dismissed.

"Oh!"

It was Nkem behind her. She had missed a step and tumbled into Eyo. The girl was notoriously clumsy. Eyo stole a look up and down the street. It was dark and quiet with the odd light on in the houses. Which meant it was early morning. She heard a dog bark. Directly in front of her was Bola, an imploring look on her face. As if she could read Eyo's mind and knew what was going to happen next. If Eyo reached out, she could touch the car handle and open the car. She would get in with Nkem and Big Madame and they would be taken to another house—it was always a different one—where they would stay as long as Big Madame wanted them to do so. Then they would be brought back here under the cover of darkness, until Big Madame moved them. Again.

If she touched the car handle.

So Eyo didn't. She reached out as if to turn the car handle but tore down the street instead, with Bola behind her, her voice a strangled pitch.

"Eyo! Nooo!"

Eyo ran, not knowing where she was running to, but that fact seemingly not as important as whom she was running from. She felt the autumn wind in her hair, her heart thundering in her ears. She could hear footsteps behind her and a man, probably the driver—she didn't know his name, as Big Madame didn't encourage them to be familiar with one another—panting heavily behind her. She was at a junction. There was a traffic light in front of her, its light on green. The road was devoid of cars, but just then, a car came hurtling down at great speed, with loud music blaring. She could just about make out someone's head behind the windscreen, bobbing in tune to the music. It was a young man, Eyo saw.

She heard someone else's footsteps behind her. The person said her name quietly, firmly, as if reprimanding a wayward teenager. That was all Eyo needed. She hated that voice. She heard it in her sleep. Her waking moments were also filled with that voice. It told her when to bathe, when to use the toilet, when to eat and how to dress. The voice wanted to consume and brand her and make her bend to its will, but she refused. She was Eyo, an illiterate girl from Jungle City, who had battled area boys, drug addicts and a sick father on a daily basis.

Eyo hurled herself in front of the speeding car. The last thing she heard before the blackness came was someone, presumably the young driver, screaming, "Oh my God!"

✳   ✳   ✳

The driver carried Eyo and staggered into the house. Big Madame opened the door impatiently and quickly shut it behind them.

"Take her to the special lounge, until I decide what to do with her. Now!" she commanded. The driver hurried down the corridor. In the special lounge, he laid Eyo out on the sofa and covered her with a blanket. She was unconscious. Blood was pouring out of a gash on her forehead. Bola ran into the room.

"What happened?" she asked. When she saw Eyo's bloodied forehead, she ran out and came back in with some cotton wool that she held against Eyo's forehead to stem the blood.

"She threw herself in front of a moving car," the driver said before leaving. Big Madame did not like him hanging around any more than necessary. He met Nkem in the corridor. The girl looked like she was in a trance.

"Nkem! Come in here!" Bola's voice was sharp. Nkem bolted inside.

"Sit," Bola commanded.

Nkem sat on the floor. They both looked at Eyo. At the blood escaping from the now soaked cotton wool and her body flopped on the sofa, at an awkward angle. She was still unmoving.

Outside the lounge, it was business as usual. None of the other working girls had come out to investigate the source of the commotion. Big Madame had trained them well. They knew their place.

In the office, Big Madame was thinking. She did not like traitors. That was why she rewarded loyalty so handsomely. She had a million decisions to make, but only one was of paramount importance: what to do about Eyo. The girl made her look bad by running away and flinging herself in front of a moving car. Like a mad woman. Big Madame was furious. She made a call.

"There was an incident fifteen minutes ago. It might've been captured on CCTV," she said. She also named the road.

The Chief Constable of Yorkshire Constabulary thought for a few moments before speaking. Then he remembered the road.

"Don't worry too much about it. Those cameras aren't working and haven't done so for a few months. Funding's just been approved to get them back up again. Is Eyo okay?"

"I didn't say it was Eyo," Big Madame replied.

"You wouldn't have called me otherwise," the Chief Constable said before hanging up.

Big Madame heaved a silent sigh of relief, then she dialled another number, summoning a doctor, one of their regulars, to the house. A hospital was out of the question. There would've been too many questions.

Big Madame came to a decision. She would let Eyo stay. She wouldn't punish her–not that she didn't deserve it–because she didn't think she could stomach a sermon from Bola. Besides, Eyo was very popular with clients. Replacing her wouldn't be impossible, but there was no need for that just yet. At the same time, she felt she ought to start looking, just in case. There was no telling what Eyo might do next. Big Madame got up and smoothed her skirt, a gift from a satisfied client of Eyo's. Yes, Eyo would stay.

*　　　*　　　*

"Eyo, are you awake?"

Eyo kept her eyelids shut.

"I know you can hear me. You were very fortunate that nothing happened to you out there. Just a few concussions. But let me tell you now: If you pull that kind of stunt again, the consequences will be grave."

Eyo turned her back to Big Madame, wincing at the splitting pain that went through her skull, and faced the window. The heavy curtains were firmly pulled together, masking the natural light. She had no idea what time of day it was. Bola signalled to Big Madame. *Let me take care of it*, her eyes said. Big Madame left the bedroom.

Bola watched Eyo for a few minutes, marvelling at the fact that she was still alive. Stella had filled her in on what the driver omitted to tell her: Eyo had landed on the bonnet when she threw herself in front of the car. The shock made the young driver brake so suddenly that Eyo was flung off the bonnet and back onto the road, the car coming to a screeching halt moments away from her still body. It had taken quite some time to convince the driver that they didn't need his details and, yes, Eyo was fine. They would take care of the rest.

They had the doctor's prognosis. "A few concussions but nothing major. In fact, nothing short of a miracle," he concluded.

Bola's daughter in Nigeria, Sola, was exactly the same age as Eyo. The thought of her having sex, much less anyone paying to have sex with her, made Bola feel ill. She had chosen to come to Europe to do sex work. Eyo hadn't and neither had Nkem. Stella said it was just business, that she was meeting a particular demand, but that didn't make it right. Stella might have refused to tell her where or how she got the girls, but Bola knew that no child in their right mind would've chosen this kind of life.

Bola reached out and stroked Eyo's hair. Her braids needed redoing, she noted. Tears fell from Eyo's shut eyelids, her thin body started shaking.

"Mama."

One word, but it was all Bola needed. She sat on the edge of the bed and gathered Eyo in her arms, weeping silently.

*   *   *

The tightening in Eyo's chest was like a black hole, a deep shapeless void that threatened to engulf her, unless she screamed and got it out. And so she started screaming. Ear-piercing screams that chilled the heart of the person holding her. When she finished screaming, she wailed like an animal, and when she finished doing that, she wept for a long time, with wracking sobs that convulsed her thin body so hard she had to lift up her head from Bola's chest for air. When she finished sobbing, she became still and fell back on the bed, spent. Bola gave her some tissues to blow her nose. Eyo took them gratefully. They both smiled at each other, Eyo tentatively, like someone testing her smiling muscles to confirm they still existed.

"I'm sorry about your shirt," Eyo said in a low voice. Bola had to lean closer to hear what she said.

"This?" Bola looked down at her T-shirt. It was drenched in snot and Eyo's tears. "That's why they invented washing machines."

Eyo's face was swollen, her eyes like slits. She yawned and her stomach growled. The crying had tired her out, Bola could see. "Let me get you some food from the kitchen," she said, smiling brightly.

"Big Madame doesn't like."

"You leave Stella to me," Bola said firmly walking to the door. When she came back a few minutes later with a steaming bowl of Nigerian pepper soup, Eyo was fast asleep. Bola put the tray by the bedside table and watched her. She looked about ten years old while she was sleeping.

The door opened and someone came inside the room.

"She's going back to work tomorrow. We'll move her back to the bedroom she shares with Nkem tonight, so you can have your bedroom back," Stella said.

"It's okay. She's only spent one night. I'll survive," Bola said.

"No. She goes back toni…"

Bola shot her friend a warning look.

"I don't know why you're mad at me. I didn't ask her to throw herself in front of a moving car. And as for all that screaming, what if we had clients?" Stella asked irritably.

"You're right. I shouldn't meddle in your affairs. Business is business," Bola said.

Big Madame didn't like emotion. She dealt in facts: sex and money. There was logic to the two; it was called business. She gave her friend an annoyed look. "You know I don't like it when you get all emotional like this," she said.

"Stella," Bola said, suddenly weary, "Not tonight. I'm tired."

"Fine." Stella's voice was clipped. She turned a dismissive glance to Eyo on the bed and left. Bola sat on the edge of the bed, her eyes on Eyo, tears streaming down her cheeks.

Twenty-two

There was a popular Nigerian church song that Eyo used to sing with her brother when they were out on the streets selling ice water. Lanre loved it and danced to it every time they sang it. Eyo used to ask him playfully if he knew how ridiculous he looked, dancing with one hand on his tray to keep it on his head and the other hand making funny moves.

Bola was singing and dancing to that song today. Eyo hated it. Nkem clapped, laughed and joined Bola. Lying on her bed, Eyo turned her face to the wall, determined to clamp down on the images threatening to overwhelm her: Mama singing the song as she dressed Lanre and Sade before going to church; Mama Fola singing it as she did her laundry in the outback.

Eyo turned to watch Bola and Nkem. The two of them were now facing each other and dancing Nigerian style, shaking their shoulders and dropping to the floor in fluid movements. Eyo felt a pull. She wanted to join them. Just then, the bedroom door opened and Big Madame came inside. She took in the scene with one acid glance. Nkem scurried to her bed and threw the duvet over her face. Eyo faced the wall. Bola laughed and wiped her moist forehead.

"Stella, these girls. They think they can outdan…"

"Bola, they're meant to be having a nap." Big Madame's voice was cool.

"I know, but you know me and music…"

She didn't finish. Big Madame had walked out of the room. Bola followed her and watched as she locked the girls inside.

"Heaven forbid something like a fire breaks out and those girls are locked in there."

Big Madame didn't answer. She continued downstairs to her office in stony silence, with Bola following her. When she got there, she sat at her desk.

"You're getting too attached to these girls. I don't like it," she said.

"I talk to them. They're human beings."

"They're not your children."

"I never said they were."

Big Madame put her hands on the table. "You won't take them to bed anymore. I'll carry on doing it myself," she said, fixing unwavering eyes on Bola.

"Fine."

"Fine."

Bola stormed out of the office. Who did she think she was, talking to her like that? Just because she had money. Bola stalked down the corridor, mimicking Stella's walk. *Yes, I'm Stella. I have money and I own everybody, not only in this house but in other houses all over Leeds as well. That's why they call me Big Madame.*

She paused when she got inside her bedroom. She and Stella were the only ones in the house with their own bedrooms. Everybody else shared. They were also the only ones with their own keys. Apart from the girls–Nkem and Eyo–whom she kept under lock and key, Stella forbade anybody from locking their bedrooms. She didn't give anybody their bedroom keys either. Stella was not averse to walking in during a client's visit, if the client was running overtime, to demand payment. If the client insisted on paying after service, Stella would wait right there in the room until they were finished to pick up payment. Bola wondered how the girls could work with clients in front of Stella. But then, knowing Stella, she probably would sit on the chair and make notes on the girls' performance, while she waited for them to finish.

Her friend's mechanical attitude to sex astounded Bola. Nonetheless, if Stella ever appeared in the room while she, Bola, was with a client, she would kill her. Not that Stella would anyway. Even she knew her boundaries.

Stella. Her faithful friend, the one who bailed her out of the street trenches of Italy and brought her to the UK at great financial cost. Not that Stella ever talked about it. Every time Bola brought it up, Stella would say firmly, *That was in the past; this is now.* She had never asked for repayment and, theoretically speaking, Bola could wake up and leave anytime she wanted. But where could she go? She was an illegal immigrant and despite Stella's assurances that her papers were the best money could buy so she could "go out there and do stuff", Bola knew it was only a matter of time before the mighty arm of the immigration services would catch up with her. So she preferred working at The House. Her living expenses were minimal as she had free accommodation and food. She gave Stella half of what she earned because she believed it was the right thing to do. She didn't want to be a financial liability on her friend.

Her friend. The same one who locked Eyo and Nkem–young children–in their bedroom each night. The same one who hired them out to men with "special sexual preferences" every day and rotated them around various locations in Leeds to satisfy their burgeoning clientele. This same friend was her best and most loyal friend. And on one particular issue, her most loyal and best friend was right: Nkem and Eyo weren't her children. But did that make what they were doing in this house right? A house. Bola almost laughed to herself as she sat on the bed. Who was she kidding? This wasn't a house. This was a brothel and she was a prostitute, earning money to support her family in Nigeria. Only now, it seemed she was also supporting her husband's mistresses as well.

Stella had never liked Michael, Bola's husband. But then, Stella always did think that nobody was good enough for her best friend. Bola had married young because her parents didn't have money. Michael was a university graduate—or so he led her parents to think—almost ten years older than she was. She found out a few years after they'd been married that his university diploma was a fake.

After ten years of married life and most of them on the breadline, there was never any question of who was going to Europe to find work. Just as there had never been any question of whose meagre earnings as a shop cashier would support their family. Bola knew that. However, she used to pretend otherwise to herself because it made her feel like she had choices. Michael tried; Bola knew. But it was hard, almost impossible for someone with a university qualification to get a job in Nigeria, much less a barely literate man spouting a fake one. She *had* to come to Europe. She didn't have a choice.

Her vibrating mobile intruded on her thoughts. It was a text from Stella. *Mark's on his way*, it said. *And you couldn't tell me this in person?* Bola wanted to stomp down to the office to ask her. Instead, she grimaced. Her most loyal client was proving to be an albatross. His visits to the house or, more specifically, to her were now twice daily. He popped in on his way to work and on his way back. In the mornings he liked to talk while she pretended to listen. And in the evenings he wanted the full girlfriend treatment. Only she wasn't his girlfriend. She was a hooker he was paying for.

"We could be so much more than this," he had said to her this morning, as she wandered around the room in her underwear. "Think about it, you and me, a couple" he said, placing a kiss on her lips.

Bola fought the impulse to gag. Sex was one thing but full-on kissing was something she endeavoured not to do, but it was part of 'The Girlfriend' package, so she bore it. This morning, he also gave her a lingerie set: bra, French knickers, stockings–the full works. All red and frilly. Bola had looked at the label and sucked in her breath. *It must have set him back quite a few quid*, she thought. She pasted a smile on her face.

"I want you to wear it when I come this evening," Mark said.

She had nodded. And now, he was on his way. Bola started preparing.

*   *   *

"Bola?"

Bola looked up and sideways from the magazine she was reading and looked back down again, hating what she saw. They were sitting side by side on the sofa in the special lounge, awaiting clients. Eyo was wearing a blue dress, complete with bow, shoes and stockings. It was a look more befitting an eight-year-old, not someone on the cusp of puberty. That meant she was expecting Mr Lau. He was very specific about what he liked to see Eyo wearing. Eyo also had the dress in pink and white. Bola hated them all.

"Yes?"

"Can you read?"

Bola looked long and hard at Eyo. There was an unspoken request in Eyo's eyes.

"Yes," Bola spoke quietly, answering her request.

Eyo reached out and touched her arm. She held on to it, her hold strangely childlike, not the touch of a seasoned child sex worker. Bola knew the difference. She was, after all, a mother.

"It was my Papa that used to do it to me," Eyo said conversationally, as if she was talking about the weather,

Suddenly, Bola understood many things. Why Eyo was popular with the 'special clients'. They always told Stella that she knew what needed doing and did it well, without fuss and without guidance. That was why they were willing to pay way above premium price for her services instead of Nkem's. It all made sense to Bola now. She reached out and drew Eyo closer to her. In the distance, the doorbell rang. They heard a man's voice. Eyo froze. Bola tried drawing her closer but Eyo shrank away. Again, Bola understood. Eyo, the human had gone, replaced by the detached sex worker. A moment later, the door opened. They heard Big Madame's voice.

"Eyo, Mr Lau is here," she said.

Eyo got up and left the room with Big Madame. Behind her, Bola threw the magazine she was reading on the floor.

Twenty-three

Jacqueline Wilson. Eyo traced the author's name on the book cover with one finger. She liked her books. Bola sometimes read them out to her. She sent them by the bucket load to her daughters in Nigeria. "I even read them myself sometimes," Bola said.

They heard the door open. Bola took the book from Eyo and shoved it under the sofa. It was Nkem, popping her head around the door.

"Eyo, Big Madame wants to speak to you," she said and disappeared behind the door.

Eyo got off the sofa and headed for the door but not before flashing Bola a smile. *She should smile more often*, Bola thought, waving her away good-naturedly.

Eyo's initial confidence quelled as she approached the office door. She hadn't spoken to Big Madame since the car incident almost three weeks ago, which wasn't so hard when one thought about it. There were four other girls in the house. They were adults sharing two to a room. Two of them were Nigerians and the other two were from Ghana and Sierra Leone respectively. Their bedrooms were upstairs on the second floor, while Eyo and Nkem shared a room on the first floor. Bola and Big Madame's bedrooms were on the ground floor, where the special lounge, office, kitchen, visitors' lavatory, the other girls' waiting room and, of course, the client service rooms were. The House was a maze of rooms, corridors and interconnecting doors that Eyo only found out about when she saw Big Madame doing something, such as walking through a connecting door or something.

Eyo and Nkem were kept separate from the adult women. They ate with Big Madame. They had different client waiting rooms, different bathrooms, lounges and everything else. Big Madame ran The House in such a way that Eyo and Nkem and the adult women rarely, if ever, saw each other. In all the time she'd been at the house, Eyo didn't think she'd ever heard the adult women having a conversation with Big Madame. No one did, except Bola. The same thing applied to the other houses she and Nkem were circulated around. The women did as they were told and that was it. Big Madame preferred it that way. Eyo wasn't sure, but she thought the women probably preferred it that way as well. Emotional bonds complicated matters.

And now, Eyo raised her hand to knock on the door, but it was opened from the inside by Big Madame. She entered and waited by the door, awaiting instructions. Big Madame went to sit behind the desk. She placed her hands lightly on the table and surveyed Eyo's face for a full minute. Eyo met her eyes unflinchingly. Inwardly, Big Madame thought, *She's like a camel, unwilling to be broken.*

"I have decided not to punish you for the stunt you pulled three weeks ago. But if you ever think, much less do something like that again, the consequences will not be good." Big Madame turned her attention to the document in front of her. "Dismissed," she said.

Eyo left the office and went back to the special room. Bola looked up.

"You okay?" she asked her.

Eyo nodded as she joined her on the sofa. Bola retrieved the Jacqueline Wilson book from its hiding place under the sofa. "I think it's time we got back to this," she said.

Eyo giggled, a trilling sound that somehow pained Bola. Eyo settled back on the sofa and rested her head on Bola's arm. Bola patted her gently and started reading.

*   *   *

Bola stretched languorously and yawned. She loved Sunday mornings. In Nigeria, after church, her family would either receive visitors or go and visit people themselves. She preferred the latter as it meant they didn't have to spend money on food for other people. There was a knock on the door. Bola yawned again before telling the person to come in. She knew who it was anyway. Only one person in The House 'visited' other people's bedrooms. Stella came in and perched herself on the edge of Bola's bed.

"I don't suppose you know what the time is?" Stella said, not really expecting an answer.

Bola shrugged and pulled the duvet up to her chin. Stella made herself more comfortable on the bed. "Mark wants to spend the whole weekend with you. He specifically requested The Girlfriend package," she said carefully, watching her friend's face.

Bola grimaced. "What did you say?"

"I told him everything was negotiable."

Bola shrugged.

"Do you want me to do something about him?" Stella asked, her eyes still on Bola.

"What do you mean?"

"You must know that he has developed a very strong attachment to you."

"So?"

"I'm just saying, that's all."

"Why do you care anyway? He's paying, isn't he?"

"Ordinarily, I wouldn't care, but I care about you, so I have to make sure you're okay with it. But just so you know, it can complicate matters," Stella replied.

"What do you mean?"

"You know, they develop strong attachments, fancy themselves in love and, all of a sudden, they see themselves as supermen come to rescue their damsels from *this* life." Stella waved her hand airily around the room, when she said 'this life'.

"Let him. We all need someone to make us feel superhuman and if I have that effect on Mark, what can I do except to be thankful for such a unique gift?" Bola said, lowering her eyes coquettishly.

Stella threw a pillow at her and they both laughed for a few moments. Then Stella spoke, "There's something else."

Bola groaned theatrically.

"It's Eyo." Stella's eyes settled on Bola. She noticed how Bola averted her gaze when she mentioned the girl's name.

"What about Eyo?" Bola's voice had become studiously detached.

"You're getting too attached to that girl. It's not healthy."

"Whatever."

Stella placed her hand on Bola's arm gently. "I'm just saying, that's all."

"Well, you've said it. Now leave it."

Stella tickled Bola's arm. "Guess who I had here last night?" she said.

It was an olive branch and Bola reached out to take it. "One of your rent boys?"

Stella nodded. "Not just anyone," she said.

"Not Turbo Man?!"

Stella attempted a coy smile and the two of them collapsed on the bed in raucous laughter.

In their bedroom, Eyo and Nkem waited for Big Madame to unlock their door, so they could bathe.

"Eyo?"

"Yes, Nkem."

"That night when I saw you run down the street. I really wanted Big Madame to catch you. Does that mean I'm a bad person?"

Eyo took her time before answering. "No."

"I just didn't want to be left alone here in this house," Nkem said.

"I understand."

There was a companionable silence before Nkem spoke again. "I see Bola likes you."

Her tone of voice made Eyo pause. It reminded her of her days in Jungle City when Mama's friends would come round and when they left, Mama would call her aside. "You heard the tone in that woman's voice? If ever you hear that tone in your friends' voices, I want you to take heed because you never know what they're up to."

Maybe it was Ajegunle that made people naturally suspicious of one another. Or maybe Mama was just naturally inclined that way, but whatever it was, Eyo recognised that tone in Nkem's voice and, just like Mama had warned her many lifetimes ago, she took heed.

"Nkem, she likes the two of us."

"No." Nkem's voice was emphatic. "She likes you."

On the top deck, Eyo was tracing some English words on the wall. "You can think what you like," she said.

Nkem tried to stem the tide of jealousy that overcame her. First, her mother dies in childbirth. Then her own father sells her to a European brothel madam. It didn't matter what she did or where she was, she would never be good enough. And clearly, she wasn't even good at sex work because she'd been upstaged by an upstart from nowhere. Eyo had been in The House for a year at the very least. There were no clocks in the house and they only went out at night when they were moved to the other houses, so it was difficult to say. Clients always asked for Eyo, and they protested vehemently whenever Big Madame fobbed Nkem onto them, as if she, Nkem, had suddenly become second-hand goods she couldn't wait to get rid of. As if that wasn't bad enough, it seemed that Big Madame even had a grudging respect for the upstart. And look at Bola! The woman got all dewy-eyed every time she was with Eyo.

It was Eyo. She got all the attention. And Nkem got nothing. It always happened that way.

It wasn't fair. Or right.

Twenty-four

It was Tuesday night, which was usually rather slow. Bola and Eyo were in their favourite position, on the sofa in the special lounge.

Eyo sometimes wondered what time it was. In the house, night and day merged into each other with numbing tedium, broken only by the constant ringing of the doorbell and coded knocks on the door.

"How old do you think I am?" she asked Bola.

Bola wondered if Eyo knew her English was infinitely better than she believed. There was even a tinge of an English accent when she spoke.

"I think you're probably about thirteen or fourteen now. That makes you a teenager," Bola told her.

"What's a teenager?"

"It's when someone crosses over to become a young adult."

"I've been an adult for a long time."

"Well, if it makes you feel any better, I'm the most childish adult I've ever known," Bola said.

Eyo smiled just as Bola had hoped she would. "My Mama would've liked you. She was very funny," she said.

Is. Bola wanted to correct her. *Is, Eyo. Is. Your Mama is still in Nigeria and you will...will what? See her again?* As if she,

Bola, knew that for sure. Irritated with herself, Bola changed the topic quickly.

"So, you are going to read the Jacqueline Wilson book by yourself? Well done!"

Eyo smiled shyly.

"Tell you what: I'll register at the library and start bringing you her books to read. Would you like that?"

Eyo's wide smile gave Bola the answer she wanted.

The next day, during her afternoon nap time, Eyo thought about the Jacqueline Wilson book. It wouldn't be easy reading it. But she would endure, just like her mother and Mama Fola had cautioned her because enduring was everything. Eyo was a slow reader, her fingers followed each line of text like a faithful convert. Sometimes, when she didn't understand what she was reading, the inclination to give up would overwhelm her, then she would remember the reason why Mama sent her to England and she would struggle on, determined. If she was really stuck, she would go and look for Bola to help her. If there was a lull in business, they would head for the special lounge. Every time they heard the door open, Bola would grab the book from Eyo's hands and either shove it under the sofa or pretend to read it herself.

Eyo estimated that the Jacqueline Wilson book would take about a month to finish. If Big Madame did not find out and kill her first. That was another thing Bola was teaching her: dates. She tried teaching her to read the time once, but Eyo had struggled with it, so she stuck with the calendar month. Not that it made a difference to Eyo because she couldn't tell the time nor date in the house. There were no clocks or calendars in the rooms she and Nkem used: their bedroom, bathroom, dining room, kitchen, special room. Nothing. The windows were covered with heavy curtains which were always drawn and the bathroom had an extractor fan, not a window. Big Madame wondered why she was always drawn to the window. Was it really so surprising in light of the shadows she lived in?

Eyo drew a blank over her mind. She hated it when she started thinking of anything, much less Big Madame. She decided to turn her mind to happier things. Like Bola. She liked her. Bola reminded her of Mama Fola back in Ajegunle. Her memories were not as sharp as they used to be, but once in a while, they came back with such ferocity. She would feel a sharp pain in her heart, like someone had taken a real knife and plunged it in there. As much as she physically hurt from what the men did to her every day, Eyo thought she preferred that to the pain she felt whenever she thought of Mama and her life in Ajegunle. That was why she played the robot game in The House. Robots did as they were told. They didn't have any feelings and contrary to what Tolu had told her long ago, they weren't stupid. It was because she played the robot in this house that she'd been able to survive as long as she had. She did as Big Madame wanted, all the while wondering how and when she would be able to escape. Exactly what she would do if she left the house she wasn't sure. *Anything was better than being here*, she thought.

At least she could read. Well, a bit. She was still a bit slow but she was getting better. Mama would be proud of her. That was the reason she was sent to the UK–not uukaay, Bola had told her–and she was very proud of herself for doing it.

The key turned in the lock and the bedroom door opened. It was Big Madame, coming to wake them up from their afternoon nap. Eyo clambered down from the top bunk and allowed herself to be herded to the bathroom.

"What's the matter with you?" Big Madame asked Nkem sharply. The girl was lagging behind Eyo, shooting her malevolent looks. If Eyo noticed, she didn't show it. She was bent over the sink, spitting out the remains of the toothpaste in her mouth.

"Nothing," Nkem mumbled, stung. She didn't want to get on Big Madame's bad side. She wanted things to go back to the way they were before Eyo came. She wanted to be the only girl offering 'special services' to the clients. She wanted Eyo to be gone so she could reclaim the feelings of love and physical affection she got from clients as the only special services girl. It was the only sense she'd had of being wanted since her mother had passed away. And Eyo had taken it away. What's more, Nkem didn't think that Eyo knew, much less valued, what she had taken away from her. It grated sorely on Nkem.

She went to the bath and sat on the side, her legs reaching across to the wall on the other side. Big Madame ran the water and handed her a lathered sponge. Nkem started cleansing herself. Big Madame watched the two of them, her eyes missing nothing.

Eyo finished at the sink and swapped places with Nkem. When they both finished, they were herded downstairs to the dining room. Dinner was potatoes with a fiery Nigerian tomato sauce and beef. They all started eating in silence. Bola's laughter reached them before the door handle turned. Almost involuntarily, Nkem found herself looking at Eyo. As expected, the girl kept her eyes on her plate. Nkem brimmed over with intense resentment.

"Is this a house of entertainment or a morgue?" Bola asked as she eased herself into a chair.

Big Madame gave her friend a warning look. The cook bustled out of the kitchen and served Bola. Bola ignored Stella and turned to Nkem. "So, what's the plan for tonight then, girls? The usual?"

Nkem didn't answer. Eyo continued eating. She could've been the only person in the room for all the attention she paid them. Back in their home in Ajegunle, meat hadn't been a regular accompaniment with their meals. One of the things Femi had promised her on the plane was the fact that she could eat all the meat she wanted in the UK because it was so cheap. Eyo pushed the beef around her plate for a few moments. She didn't want it. Here she was, eating meat, and her family in Ajegunle probably hadn't tasted it this year. She pushed her plate away. It wasn't right.

"You will finish your dinner." Big Madame's voice cut into her thoughts.

"I don't want it." Eyo's voice was clear.

"You will finish your dinner," Big Madame repeated.

Nkem looked from Eyo to Big Madame and back to Eyo. Bola looked down at her plate, willing Eyo not to be difficult. Eyo saw her mother's roadside food stall, the way she would carefully measure every plate and, at the end of each day, wrap everything up so nothing was wasted. She would not be happy about Eyo wasting food. She breathed in, drew the plate back towards her and started eating again. It went to her stomach and sat there, at the bottom, like lead. It was as if it was reminding Eyo of how evil she was eating like a queen while her mother and siblings had nothing but *ogi*.

At the other end of the table, Bola sighed inwardly in relief. She had wanted an easy night. Nkem moved her empty plate to the side. She had eaten every morsel. Big Madame didn't even look at her.

"Just another day in the UK," Bola said to nobody in particular.

*   *   *

Sometimes, Bola thought she was fond of Mark. Like today. He was fully dressed and stretched out on the bed. She was sitting on the chair, facing the dressing table and looking into the mirror. She looked for telltale signs of hard living on her forehead and eyes and decided that there were none. She smiled at herself in the mirror. On the bed, Mark smiled with her. He patted the space next to him. Bola went to lie on it and Mark drew her close so they were spooning. He sighed in contentment.

"Marry me," he said.

"Yes," Bola said.

When Mark left, Bola called Michael, her husband in Nigeria. She told him about Mark's proposal and her response. Michael agreed with her.

"Well, this is what we have been working towards all along: a European passport, even if he took his time asking for your hand in marriage. A few more years of this and then you can leave him. But not before you get the passport. Remember: The passport is the thing."

Bola hung up. He was right. The passport was the thing. Without it, she would be just another illegal immigrant in England, constantly looking over her shoulder, fearing every knock on the door and everybody on the street. Without the passport, she wouldn't be able to have all the things that legal residents took for granted, like having your real name and not someone else's.

Without the passport, she wouldn't be able to give her children the kind of life they deserved: a life in the UK where they would have access to the best education and opportunities in life that she never had.

That didn't make her a bad person. It made her a good mother. However, she couldn't help but wish that her husband had told her to rescind Mark's proposal and come back to Nigeria. It would have shown her that he still cared a little for her.

Twenty-five

Stella reached out for the light switch. Just before she turned it off, plunging the room into darkness, she spoke.

"Bola will be leaving us soon. She's getting married."

She left the room, locking them in for the night.

Nkem tried smiling, but she couldn't. She didn't want Bola to get married. If Bola got married, the halls would be quiet once again. The special lounge would mourn her absence with its deafening silence. She would go through the whole day, weeks and even months without somebody hugging and reassuring her that things would work out okay. No matter that neither Bola nor Nkem believed it themselves. Nkem liked hearing it because she could at least pretend that there would indeed come a day when she would leave the house and do things she supposed other people took for granted. Like having friends. Wearing clothes she wanted to wear, not ones that had been picked out to fulfil men's desires. She would like to wake up in a room that let in the sunlight and walk around the streets in broad daylight. But above all else, she would like to read. To make something of herself and prove to her father, stepmother, Big Madame and everyone else that she was just as good as anybody. All she needed was a chance to prove it.

A tear fell down Nkem's cheek. She brushed it away and stared resolutely at the bed above her, willing Eyo to say or do something, *anything*. But the top bunk remained silent. Nkem thought then of how much she hated Eyo.

*   *   *

Bola pushed down a flash of irritation when Mark bent over to give her a goodbye kiss. His lips always felt clammy on hers. He was a good person, she knew. He called her his "guardian angel, the one who rescued me from the dark pit of loneliness." When he said that, Bola would refrain from telling him anybody could've easily done what she did for him, for a fee. And she did tell him, once.

"No," Mark had said. "At least you cared. The other girls hadn't."

Did she care? Bola didn't know. Sometimes she thought she did. Other times, she was convinced that it was only a matter of time before God struck her down for her callousness. Although she wasn't the first married woman in Nigeria to come to Europe as a sex worker, she didn't think others took it as far as she did: marrying a British passport holder under false pretences. Just so she would be a British passport holder herself.

Stella said she wasn't the first. "Didn't your time in Italy teach you anything?" she'd asked her.

"What if he finds out that I'm already married?"

"Bola, listen to me. How will he find out?"

Bola had thought about it. Stella was right. There was indeed no way that Mark would ever find out. The chances of him going to Nigeria were non-existent. She hadn't told Mark too much of herself and he'd been content not to pry, maybe because he in turn was scared of what he would find out. What he did know was this: She was an orphan and she had a brother in Nigeria that she didn't get along with. Her parents passed away in a car accident when she was eighteen and she came to

Europe shortly thereafter for a crack at a better life. Whenever he tried to dig deeper, Bola would feign anger or pretend to withdraw, claiming, "I'm an African. I've had a hard life. The kind Europeans could never imagine." And Mark would leave her alone.

"Hellooo?"

Bola looked up. Mark was looking at her with concern. Bola realised that he had been talking to her.

"Are you okay?"

"Of course!" Bola gave a short laugh. "I just realised that I don't have a clue how to arrange a wedding in England. Things are done differently in Africa, you know."

"Well, we could do it the African way, if you want," Mark said.

"No. The English way is best," Bola said emphatically.

"You sure?" Now he was looking at her as if *he* wasn't sure.

Bola pushed his head down towards her lips. "I've never been more sure of anything else in my life," she said.

"Good," Mark said. "Registry it is then. I'll let my parents know."

Bola turned her face sharply to the side and Mark missed her lips.

"Parents?"

"Yes, my parents," he said. "Why? Is there a problem?"

"I don't know. How about the fact that I'm a prostitute?"

"Stop saying that," Mark said quietly.

"You can cloak it any way you want, but it's true. How are you going to explain that to your parents?"

She pushed him away from her and went to sit on the chair facing the dresser. She should've known it was too easy!

Mark came to stand behind her, resting his hands on her shoulders. "Bola, I've told them about you. I said we met at a singles event."

"It's just that you've never mentioned them until now. And anyway, they'll find out. They always do." Bola's voice was flat.

"I've never mentioned them because I haven't felt the need to. As for them finding out about this," he waved his hand around the room, "I think it's highly unlikely. But if they do, well then, we'll simply deal with it when the time comes."

"I don't like secrets."

"Well, what do you suggest? That I tell them? It's down to you. If you want to tell them about your past, fine. We'll do that. If not, then that's equally okay."

He was so reasonable and kind; Bola wanted to hit him. She sighed. "Fine," she said.

"Fine what?"

"Fine, we won't tell them anything."

"Thank you." Mark kissed the top of her head and left.

Bola looked at herself in the mirror, then took a deep breath. Everything was going to be all right. Of course it was.

* * *

Everybody was watching her, wondering what she would do because Bola was getting married. Eyo wondered what they expected her to do. So what if Bola was leaving? As if she cared. And that was what hurt. The fact was that she did care and it made her angry. Robots weren't supposed to care about anything. If she did as she was told: have sex with all the men that came to the house and went about her business like a robot, like she used to do before, she wouldn't be feeling this way. Like this ball of pain in her chest that was a little like when she boarded the plane with Uncle Femi and it circled the runway and eventually took flight, soaring into the sky and literally leaving her heart in Ajegunle. That was what she felt like now.

Big Madame and Lola were right. She would die in the UK. In this house, and in all likelihood, with a man between her legs and Big Madame watching with her beady eyes to check that she'd serviced the client properly. Nobody would look for her or mourn her because she didn't exist on record anywhere in the UK. Because she was a nobody.

Eyo turned the door handle of Bola's room and sighed in relief when it turned. Big Madame and Bola were in the office, a few doors down the corridor, from where she could hear them talking. She knew she shouldn't be in Bola's room. She should be in the special lounge with Nkem, awaiting Mr Lau. But she'd told Big Madame she needed the toilet. Under normal circumstances, Big Madame or Bola always escorted them to the toilet but not on this occasion.

Eyo stepped into Bola's room and walked to the window. She parted the curtains and, with heart pounding, she opened the windows as far as she could. Then she climbed onto the windowsill. She was about to hurl herself through it when a voice stopped her in her tracks.

"What," the voice said, "do you think you're doing?"

Twenty-six

It was Bola. She closed the door quickly behind her and ran to the window. She pulled Eyo back and turned her around to face her, anger in her voice. "What do you think you're doing?"

Eyo didn't answer. Bola slapped her and repeated her question.

"I don't know. I just wanted to look out of the window and, the next thing I know, I was climbing the windowsill and…" Eyo faltered.

The door opened and Big Madame came in. She took in the opened window, swaying curtains, Eyo's tears and Bola's heavy breathing at a glance. Her expression didn't change. But Eyo saw her eyes. Something passed in them. Something that, in true Big Madame style, was impossible to pin down.

"Eyo, Mr Lau is here," Big Madame said. Without pausing, she added, "This is not the toilet."

The last sentence was a statement.

"I will go to Mr Lau," Eyo said, facing Big Madame with clear eyes. She went through the open door and walked out without a backward glance.

"Nothing happened," Bola answered her friend's unspoken question.

"But of course," Big Madame said. She smiled and left the room.

Bola went to close the window. Her mobile phone vibrated. It was a text from Michael. *Not long to go now,* it said. *Remember: The red's the thing!* She deleted it. Then she wondered how a red passport no more than twelve and a half centimetres in length could exert so much power over one's life. Somehow, it just didn't seem right.

*   *   *

Back in her office, Big Madame rested her hands on the table. After a few minutes, she got up and went to stand outside one of the two rooms for special clients. Not that she needed to. Mr Lau's grunts could be heard all the way down the corridor and beyond. She peeped through the spyhole in the door and watched him and Eyo who was going about her duties with mechanical precision, her face its usual expressionless state. Big Madame stepped back from the door and went back to her office. She placed her hands on the table again. The doorbell rang. Two short rings and then a long one. Mark's special ring. She heard Bola open the front door, Mark's voice, the door closed and then footsteps in the direction of Bola's bedroom.

Big Madame checked her watch. Mr Lau had requested extra time with Eyo tonight.

Eyo. Big Madame didn't think she had ever met anyone who intrigued and infuriated her in equal measure.

*   *   *

Bola stifled a grimace when Mark joined her on the bed, then berated herself. She should get used to him invading her space.

After all, that is what married people do: get in each other's faces all the time. She should know, being a married woman herself.

Mark lay next to her, wrapping his arms around her so they were spooning. He planted a kiss on the curve of her neck and sighed contentedly. He wished they were already married, not getting married in a month.

"You all set to meet my parents tonight?"

"They'll hate me." Bola's voice was a monotone.

"No, they'll love you, just as much as they love me."

"Won't they think it's a bit strange that you're marrying a girl that they've never met, who is fifteen years younger than you are?"

"I'm forty-five, Bola. At this stage in their lives, they're just happy to see me settle down."

"Do they know about your 'visitations' to certain women?"

Mark flipped her over and started pulling off her underwear. "Stop worrying. We're getting married and that's that."

The red's the thing. Her husband's text flashed through her mind. *It was the only thing,* Bola thought.

*   *   *

Mr Lau was finished. Eyo slid out from under him and rolled off the bed. She went to stand by the window. The urge to draw the curtains apart and stick her head out of the window was almost overpowering, but she resisted. It wasn't the time. Back in Jungle City, she had hated the smell of rotting garbage and faeces playing host to mosquitoes and other disease carriers so much that she had preferred staying indoors where the smell was marginally better. *What wouldn't she give to breathe that disease-ridden air again?* she thought to herself.

She sensed her mind drifting towards Mama, Sade and Lanre and clamped down on it. Their images deserved better. They belonged to another time long ago, when she would dredge up their memories and caress them to give her hope. They belonged to the time before Uncle Femi brought her to the UK and, quite possibly, the time before her father started touching her and… Eyo shook her head a little, irritated with herself. Why was she thinking of her father now?

There was a noise from the bed. Mr Lau was getting up. He motioned to Eyo. She went to him. She knew the drill so well she could perform it in her sleep. Mr Lau went to sit on the chair. She sat on his lap and stroked his hair, while he stroked her back contentedly. Then he started talking to her. Eyo sat quietly, nodding occasionally. Her body language was that of a keen listener. In reality, she was thinking of Jungle City, the smell of the abattoir on Malu Road, the entryway into Jungle City, and the howl of the harmattan winds as it blanketed Lagos and its inhabitants with its peculiar brownish tinge. Sometimes, she would sit in front of their face-me-I-face-you, with Sade playing at her feet and Lanre playing football, and watch the winds dance rings around people's ankles, infiltrating their already dry skin and cracked heels, layering them in fine harmattan dust.

Harmattan was her favourite season. It changed people's appearances, turning sweat-slicked bodies into grey mirages of their former selves, as the dry season sapped their skin of moisture. Sometimes, they looked like walking zombies with their cracked lips and dry, white skins. That was why Mama coated them in shea butter and slathered their lips with petroleum jelly every morning, before they left to pound the streets with their trays of ice water. When they got back from their daily hawk, they would be covered in dust, their lips dry and skin indistinguishable from other victims of the weather.

"Look at you," Mama would say scrubbing Lanre vigorously with the raffia sponge, her ears impervious to his yelps. "If I didn't know better, I would swear you deliberately roll around in dust just to annoy me."

"Yes, Mama," Lanre would say.

"'Yes, Mama,'" Olufunmi mimicked him. "You think I don't know that you're going to try and sneak off and play football as soon as I finish bathing you? It's seven p.m. I don't know who you think will want to play with you at this time of the night. And if you think I'll let you waste my hard-earned water on you, just so you can 'play football', you've got another thing coming."

Mr Lau was still talking. Eyo caught some words. *Pictures. Computer. Work. Stress.* None of them meant anything to her. She wished he would shut up and let her think. The door opened and Big Madame came in. Eyo clambered down from Mr Lau's lap. It was time for her next client.

*　　　*　　　*

Bola fingered her hair nervously as they waited for the front door to open.

"Stop fiddling!"

"It's all right for you. They're *your* parents," Bola said.

Mark gave her a look, which she ignored.

The door opened and a sprightly woman in her sixties stepped into the porch. She gave Mark a big smile and held out her arms to Bola.

"Welcome," she said with a beaming smile.

A few weeks after that, at breakfast, Big Madame made an announcement.

"Bola moved out in the middle of the night. She's now living with Mark." She picked up her fork and continued eating her scrambled eggs.

Eyo looked down at her plate and thought, *Bola would've said something.* Perhaps she wanted to, but Big Madame prevented her from doing so. Not that Eyo believed that. If Bola had wanted to tell her she was leaving, she would've told her, regardless of what Big Madame thought.

Nkem played with the eggs on her plate. She thought to herself, *I will never laugh again.*

Twenty-seven

Eyo was familiar with fear. It was the feeling she got every time she walked home to Jungle City, knowing that her father would be there waiting for her. It was the sickening feeling she got whenever Papa said he would happily turn his affections to Sade if Eyo did not cooperate with his demands. It took a while, but, gradually, the fear turned into a dark hole. All she did was turn it inwards and shove it all the way deep inside her, where it would never see the light of day. When she did that, she found herself strangely energised and inwardly stronger.

The same thing happened when Sam started his nocturnal visits. At first, she fought back, but the only thing she got back in return was a severe beating. Then, she started fearing him, but that didn't get her anywhere either. Until Tolu told her about robots. She hadn't known it then, but what she had been doing by shoving her fear inwards and downwards and locking it there was robotic. Tolu might have taught her the alphabet, but her explanation of robots gave her the skill she needed to survive, and for that, Eyo would always be grateful to her.

Today, Eyo was not feeling fear. Neither was she feeling her familiar, deadened, robotic self. Today, she felt oddly exultant. Indeed, she felt that she had stepped out of her own skin and was now observing herself from somebody else's body. If there was one thing she had learnt from Bola, it was this: That hope kept one alive. If being a robot helped her get through each day at The House, hope–inadvertently stimulated by Bola–kept her alive. Bola had given her a hope of many *what-ifs*? What if she could get out of The House? What if she made it back to Nigeria? Bola, by teaching her how to vaguely read and bringing the whiff of a life of freedom lived by the millions of Leeds residents into The House, had given her more than a reason to hope. She had given Eyo a reason to live. She had also given Eyo perhaps the only tool she needed to flee The House: the fighting hope of freedom.

Eyo smiled to herself when she thought of her plan to leave The House for good. Never to come back.

*   *   *

Nkem burrowed herself deep into the duvet. Up, on the deck above her, Eyo was silent; her mind busy. Outside, the street was still, the late winter afternoon punctuated by the occasional bark of a dog and the plaintive mewling of a cat. Once in a while, a car would come zooming down and they would hear its door open, a smattering of conversation as the car owner spoke to their passenger or called out to the inhabitants of their home to help with the shopping.

Soon, Eyo thought, she would be one of those people on the outside. She would no longer be an indoor shadow, forced to come out for airing when the rest of the world was asleep. She would be a person. Like the girls she saw on television, going shopping with friends–perhaps with Bola?–giggling or going to school. Yes, school. That would be the first thing she would do once she got out. She would go to the police and ask them to take her to school. No, she couldn't go to the police. Big Madame would find out. She knew everyone and had spies everywhere. No, she had to think of something else.

Bola. Yes, Bola would help. She was her friend. *But maybe Bola wouldn't want to help her.* Maybe Mark wouldn't let her. Maybe she should just go back to Jungle City. Eyo almost laughed at herself. No, she couldn't just go back to Jungle City. Mama would be happy to see her. No, she wouldn't. Eyo imagined her sad, disappointed smile.

"All that money your uncle spent…"

She imagined her brother's and sister's downcast faces. In particular, Sade's baleful glare, her accusing voice.

"You were supposed to stay there and then send for us."

Thinking of her sister made her think of her father, which she didn't want to. She veered from one extreme: the absolute certainty that Sade was safe from their father, to the other: that she wasn't. Papa was no different from Sam and all the men who walked through the front door of this house every day. The only difference was that he was her father.

He used to say there were two Nigerias: one for the rich and one for the poor. They belonged to the latter and that was just the way it was. That was why there was no point in sending her to school. After all, she would only end up being a maid or–God willing–a market stall holder. He preferred the latter because it meant that she had her own business. In any case, there was no point in sending her to school because she was a girl. Now, Eyo wanted to tell him that it was precisely because she was a girl that he had sent her to the UK to work and make money for him.

Eyo turned over to face the wall as her mind ran over her last few moments in Ajegunle. It seemed so long ago and then, sometimes, it felt like it was yesterday. However long ago it was, whenever she thought of her life then, it was like watching it through the eyes of someone else. Eyo then thought to herself that she would do anything to go back to that life, even if it had Papa in it.

*   *   *

On the bottom deck, Nkem vowed to herself that she wouldn't break the silence. Big Madame would be coming any minute now to get them prepared for tonight's work. She told herself that she didn't need to talk to Eyo. She didn't like the girl. A few minutes later, she conceded defeat, hating herself for it.

"So, are you going to be Bola's bridesmaid?"

Her question hung in the air. For a moment, it seemed like Eyo wouldn't answer, then Nkem heard her sigh.

"Nkem, I'm not discussing this with you," Eyo said.

"I forgot. You're everybody's favourite. You don't need to talk to the likes of us."

There was a resounding silence from the top deck. Nkem tried again.

"I wonder what you will do with yourself now that Bola has moved in with Mark."

Eyo did not respond. Nkem tried again.

"I know about the reading."

On her bed, Eyo turned to face the wall. Perhaps it was best that Bola had left the way she did. It made it cleaner and less awkward. Still, Eyo wished that she had said goodbye. She would've liked to have hugged her and thanked her properly, the way Mama told her to thank people who've helped her.

"Remember, Eyo. God sees everything and there's one thing He abhors more than anything else in the world in children: bad manners. As for the landlord, I don't expect you to be rude to him because I don't expect you to talk to him. If he tries to talk to you, walk away. If he tries to touch you, scream as you're walking away. You hear?"

Eyo had nodded and they had both laughed, knowing full well that she had no intention of not being rude to the landlord.

Eyo wondered if Bola had taken the Jacqueline Wilson books with her. All of a sudden, hope rose within her. *Bola would come back for me. She wouldn't leave me here.* And then just as suddenly as it came, it died. *Big Madame would never allow it.*

"Nkem, I think you should leave me alone."

"'Nkem, I think you should leave me alone,'" Nkem mimicked Eyo. "Don't worry. Your secret is safe with me. For now."

There were footsteps coming down the corridor and then the jangling of keys outside their room. The bedroom door opened and Big Madame came in silently, keys dangling in her hand. It had taken Bola to come to the house for Nkem to realise how much Big Madame ruled over them all by silence. She hated it.

When Bola was with them, mischief and, by default, noise was always round the corner. It was just the way she was. Take their afternoon naps for instance. She would open the door and jump on them in their beds. Or she would stand by the bunk bed and let out a yell to wake them up. Sometimes, she would come in, carrying a portable radio, turn up the volume to the highest level and then switch it on. Other times, she would run into the room and scream, *Boo!* at the top of her voice. And it didn't matter wherever she was in the house; you could hear her. Nkem had heard her tell Big Madame on more than a few occasions that the house was like a morgue and *I've been sent by the good Lord to resurrect it.*

Nkem was finding it hard to adjust to the way things were before Bola burst into their lives. The house's deafening silence. The repetition and tedium of clients, the rotation of the houses and Big Madame herself. By virtue of whom she was, Bola had brought a restless hope and hunger for something outside the walls of the house, only Nkem didn't recognise it. Because she couldn't recognise it, she couldn't put a name to it. Not knowing why she chafed inside and the longing to be free of The House where she had accepted her lot before Bola came made Nkem agitated and angry.

"Time to get up," Big Madame said. She didn't so much talk to them as give orders.

Eyo clambered down from the bed and made her way to the bathroom. Nkem followed her in silence. Big Madame followed the two of them, pleased. This was what she liked: silence and obedience. She loved her friend dearly, but the year or so Bola had spent with them in the house had threatened to overthrow her regime, something she had taken years to establish. Bola's moving in with Mark had given Stella back the reins to the house. Order had been reimposed and Bola's chaotic presence a distant memory. Or soon-to-be distant memory in Nkem's case.

It was clear that the girl was having problems adjusting to Bola's absence. Not that Big Madame was concerned. In time, Nkem would revert back to her normal self because she was a simpleton, lacking the creativity and drive to take charge of her own life. Big Madame had recognised this trait in her all those years ago in the village, which was why she brought her to the UK. She knew that Nkem would give her little or no trouble. Whatever spirit she had in her was broken within the first few weeks of her landing in the UK. No, she wasn't worried about Nkem. And she wasn't duly concerned with Eyo either. She had the means to keep her in her place.

They had dinner, although Eyo still found it hard to equate the abundance of food she was offered to the slim pickings her family were undoubtedly eating in Jungle City. That's why she never asked for seconds. Nkem had no such compunction, often having second helpings. Big Madame encouraged her because she liked her girls looking healthy. However, if she felt that any of them were putting on weight, she swiftly cut down their food intake and made them eat nothing but fruit for days on end.

Big Madame folded her hands on the table. A sure sign that she wanted to talk. Eyo looked straight ahead.

"Bola asked me to pass her regards to you two. Her wedding's in two weeks."

Nkem nodded and started eating again. Big Madame didn't have to look at Eyo to know that she wasn't even looking her way. The doorbell rang. It was Friday. The rush had begun.

*   *   *

Mr Lau stroked Eyo's plaits, the ordinariness of the act bringing much calm to the storm raging within him. He had been escorted out of his office building earlier that morning, flanked by two security guards. He found himself at The House, with Big Madame opening the door, but had no recollection of the journey there.

She hadn't said a word. That was why she was the best in the business. She opened the door and let him in, as if it was a regular visit and not an eleven a.m. one on a Monday. In all his years of being a regular at The House, Mr Lau could not recall ever visiting on a Monday.

"Eyo will be with you in a few moments."

That was all Big Madame said before waving him inside. He had followed her without looking back. It was now lunchtime, a few hours later. He was sitting on the chair, while Eyo sat on his lap, still dressed. His upper body was slanted towards her, his head on her chest. She twirled his hair around her fingers in that particular way she knew he liked and massaged his temples lightly. Mr Lau felt his problems evaporate.

Eyo stopped kneading his temples and gracefully got off his lap. She let her dress fall away from her in a practised movement and took Mr Lau's hand. She attempted to lead him to the bed.

"No, I've told you this a million times already. Not today. Put your dress back on and sit on my lap again."

"Sorry, sir."

Eyo climbed back on his lap and start twirling his hair around her fingers again. They didn't say much for the next ten minutes until Eyo spoke.

"If I was in your house, I would be able to do this for you all the time."

Mr Lau lifted up his head from her chest. "Big Madame would never allow it," he said.

Eyo continued twirling his hair. "You're right. In this house, with all the men coming in and asking Big Madame for me, it's much better for me to be with all of them than to be with you alone, who hasn't asked. And the price these men ask for me keeps on increasing. Who knows when next you'll come and not find me," Eyo replied, her voice bland.

"Hmm," was all Mr Lau said.

Later, on his way out, he approached Big Madame.

"I have a proposition for you," he said.

Big Madame listened, her hands folded on the table. When Mr Lau finished, she thanked him politely and told him that she would consider his offer. Then she went back to the office to think.

Twenty-eight

Johnny tore up the M1 in his car, like a man possessed. When he got to The House, Big Madame led him inside and into the special lounge. On the sofa was an unconscious girl. She looked about fourteen years old.

"How old is she?" Johnny asked.

Big Madame raised an eyebrow. Johnny grinned.

"What did you give her?"

"Diazepam, so you're good for a few hours," Big Madame answered.

"How many?"

"Enough for you to leave with her right now and stop asking me questions."

The girl was thin, with skinny arms. Her long lashes framed her cheeks. Johnny bent over and lifted her from the sofa. He carried her to the car.

"Free?" he said, as he dropped her in the back seat.

"That's the only word you Nigerians understand," Big Madame said as she stood in the doorway, watching him, a strange smile on her face.

Johnny got into the driver's seat and started the car. He waved to Big Madame as he drove away, but she had already closed the door.

*   *   *

"Look at you, looking like a blushing bride. If I didn't know better, I would think you were one indeed," Stella teased her friend.

Bola laughed. "Married life is good. Mark is okay," she said. Her eyes clouded briefly, and she seemed to shake herself physically before turning to Stella.

"Sometimes, I think I'm the most evil person on earth. There are times when he touches me and I'm filled with loathing for myself and for him. And then other times, I feel quite tender towards him…"

"The way a dog owner feels towards his dog," Stella completed, affecting an understanding look. Bola took one look at her face and they both burst out laughing.

"You're mad," she said.

"Maybe," Stella said. "But I made you laugh and that's all that matters."

Bola looked around the office. "You really helped me out. There's no way I could've done this without you," she said. She reached over the table and clasped her friend's hand in hers. "Thanks."

Stella returned the clasp and, with her free hand, reached out for the Häagen-Dazs in her fridge.

"No, wait. How about we get Nkem and Eyo in here? I'm sure they would like some," Bola said.

"Bola, I'm not going to do this with you again. Your life here is over."

"I don't know what prompted the speech. I'm just asking if the girls could have ice cream with us."

"You knew there was no way that I would say yes."

"Maybe, but that doesn't mean that I shouldn't try. Which reminds me: I need to talk to you about Eyo."

"I thought you would. She's gone."

"Gone where?" Bola looked around the office as if expecting Eyo to emerge from somewhere.

"She's no longer here."

A sickening comprehension dawned on Bola. "You didn't…" she said, her voice faint.

"She's no longer with us. That's all you need to know." Stella's voice was firm.

"You knew I was going to come for her."

"I suspected you might try something like that, yes."

"Why, Stella? You knew I was coming for her and yet you did this."

Stella folded her hands on the table. "It's all done and dusted now."

"Where is she?"

"She's gone. She went late last night. That's all you need to know."

"Stella, why?" Bola's voice had taken on a sorrowful plea. "Why Eyo? You knew that after my wedding I would come and get her. You knew. That's why you've done what you've done." Bola's shoulders slumped.

Stella assessed her friend coolly. "She put Mr Lau up to bid for her. He was to be her ticket to freedom." Stella sneered the last word. "He didn't tell me, but I knew she was behind it. She had to be taught a lesson. She wouldn't have stopped at

Mr Lau. She would've found a way to destroy everything I've worked for. The girl's clever, or had you forgotten?"

"Where is she?" Bola's voice was louder this time. There was a hint of anger in it.

Stella's voice became brisk. "I don't know. London. Amsterdam. Madrid." She gave a graceful shrug.

Bola sat back on the chair, deflated. When she spoke, it was a whimper. "Dear Jesus, I'm so sorry."

Twenty-nine

Eyo opened her eyes. She felt groggy, as if she had just emerged from a long, deep sleep. She looked around. She was in a strange bed, in a strange room with a strange man unbuckling his belt. She didn't show any surprise, merely a resignation to her fate.

Or so Johnny thought. As a rule, he liked to break in new girls himself, to test them out and iron out any difficulties that might ensue. By the end of the first week, any spiritedness left in the women would have been broken by his fists and his particular brand of sexual gratification. With that thought in mind, he spent the next three days with Eyo, without cause for concern. He was so pleased with her that he called Big Madame and rained effusive thanks down the telephone for her 'gift'.

"You will soon learn," was all she said before hanging up on him. It was another twenty-four hours before he understood what she meant.

They were in a small, functional one-bedroom flat off the bustling Stroud Green Road in Finsbury Park, north London. On the bed, Eyo was silent, her eyes following his every move as he dressed and prepared her for her first client. Her silence was not unusual. In fact, she'd barely said more than ten words to him in the three days he'd been with her.

The client went into the bedroom. Johnny waited in the corridor and put his ear to the closed door. In no time it seemed, he heard the customer's restrained grunt. He went to the poky sitting room, sat down on the tired sofa and quickly stood up again when he heard a scream coming from the bedroom. He hesitated for a few moments, then ran into the bedroom when it became clear that the scream was from the client, not Eyo. When he got inside, the man was holding his privates with one hand and attempting to lunge at Eyo who was lying on the bed, an expressionless look on her face, with his other hand. Johnny threw himself in front of the client.

"You think it's funny? I'll kill you, you little s…" the man screamed in painful anger, before he could finish.

What happened next seemed to happen in slow motion. Eyo flew off the bed, sidestepped Johnny and lunged herself, all thin arms and legs, at the punter, kicking him and screaming in Yoruba at the same time.

"Olosi! Oloriburuku! Ware! Paa me! Paa me o! Stupid, evil man! Kill me! Kill me!"

That was the first time Johnny heard her speak Yoruba. He pulled her off the man, gave her a hard slap and flung her back on the bed. She curled up in the foetal position and went silent, her body heaving. He hurried the punter out of the room, apologising profusely, and locked Eyo inside. Later, when he went back to the bedroom, the only screams that could be heard were Eyo's.

The owner of the shop downstairs heard the muffled screams and shook his head. He wasn't sure what went on in the flat above, but he didn't want to know and neither was he interested. One of the things he liked about England was the fact that people kept to themselves. Back home in Angola, people were nosy. He flipped the magazine he was looking at to the next page and yawned.

Eyo and Johnny did not make much headway with the second client either. This time, Johnny waited in the corridor, with his ears firmly cocked to the bedroom. After about five minutes, the client came out shaking his head. He met Johnny in the corridor and demanded his money back.

"She's just sitting on the bed. It's like I'm not there," he said.

Johnny gave him back his money and escorted him out of the flat. This time, he didn't bother apologising to the client. He went to the bedroom with barely restrained violence, which he sexually unleashed on Eyo. He did not leave the room for the next two days except to go to the toilet and receive the takeaway food he ordered on the telephone. The third day, he received a visitor. The visitor ran his hands over Eyo's battered body, taking note of the swollen eyes and cut lips. He also checked her intimately.

"I think you need to lay off for a while. She has severe lacerations in her privates. How old did you say she was?"

Johnny shrugged. "Fourteen?"

The visitor held some medication towards Johnny. "This should do it. She needs at least a week to heal and rest. Her body has gone through severe emotional and physical trauma."

"I've got a business to run," Johnny said.

"You won't have any business to run if she doesn't rest," his visitor said wryly.

"This government does you a great disservice by not making you a permanent resident doctor of the United Kingdom," Johnny said in mock solemnity as he reached out to take the medication from him.

"If they did, people like you wouldn't have anywhere to go for such specialised service," his visitor retorted. The smile didn't reach his eyes though. He glanced at Eyo sleeping on the bed and stood up.

"What did you give her?" he asked.

"A spoonful of herbs in a hot infusion I forced her to drink." Johnny laughed at his own joke and stopped when he saw the look on his visitor's face. "If I hadn't, there is no way you would've been able to touch her. Trust me; she's an animal."

"Still…" The visitor looked at Eyo again before letting himself out.

A week later, Eyo received her third London client. This time, the man came out of the room with a slight look of awe and a satisfied smile on his face. But Johnny wasn't convinced. He had learnt that with Eyo, things weren't always what they seemed. And in the next eighteen months, he was proved right.

Jungle
Girl

Thirty

Johnny peered through the keyhole and entered the room without knocking. Inside the bolt-hole was a narrow bed against the wall and a forlorn-looking chair by a rickety chest of drawers. It was difficult to tell the colour of the walls, but they looked greyish. The air was thick with the smell of sweat, secreted bodily fluids and stale cigarettes. Neglect ricocheted around the room, aided by the January wind coming through the thin curtains and opened window.

Inside the room, a lady was sitting on the edge of the bed, looking into the unseen distance.

"Come on out. The night's still young."

"At least give me a minute. I've just finished with one punter. Give me a break," the woman replied.

"You don't have a minute. You've been out there for two hours and you've only had one customer. Either you get back there immediately or I drag you out myself."

The lady sighed, adjusted the strips of clothing she was wearing and walked past Johnny, a sneer on her face. He ignored her. They both walked out of the room, down the narrow corridor, each step guaranteeing a squeal of protest from the creaking floorboards under the threadbare carpet. The corridor occasionally resonated with the sexual sounds associated with that particular establishment.

They came to the end of the corridor and turned right, through a set of doors and a narrow flight of stairs. On the landing, they saw a lady injecting herself in the arm. Johnny looked away in distaste. The stairs led them to a small reception which was manned by a bored-looking man. His eyes were fixed on the television a few feet above him. He nodded to the two of them as they made their way to the front door and out into the dark, bracing cold.

They walked for a few minutes without saying anything. Then Johnny slowed down and slinked in the doorway of a side street. The woman went to stand on the adjoining street, joining some other women on the pavement. She shivered slightly before striking a provocative pose. She didn't have to wait long. A man soon approached her.

"How old are you?" he asked.

"Thirteen," she replied.

The man paused. "You're not thirteen," he said.

"And you're wasting my time," the woman replied.

Johnny took a menacing step towards her. She didn't see him, but she heard his footsteps. The man quickly walked away. Johnny walked to her and shook her angrily.

"Eyo, I'm warning you. I don't want any drama tonight."

"My name is Jungle, not Eyo," the woman said.

Johnny ignored her and slunk back into the shadows of the side street. He had five girls to watch over and there he was, wasting his time on just one. She always did that to him. He lit up a cigarette and inhaled deeply. He heard the other women making catcalls to men and some women as they walked past them. The lady who preferred to be called Jungle stood sulkily, ignoring everything around her. A few of the women tried engaging her in conversation, but she scowled at them. They soon left her alone. A van pulled up in front of Johnny and a man and a woman got out. They started taking things out of the van. Johnny ignored them and kept on smoking his cigarette.

"And how are you doing today, Johnny?" the woman asked him.

"Business is a bit slow. When will you take off your nun's habit and embrace your true calling?"

"When you step inside the church and embrace the Lord," the woman replied.

The woman and the man worked quickly, setting up a folding table with hot beverages, snacks and a few chairs. A couple of jumpers were placed over the back of one chair. The man and the woman went out into the main street where the women were soliciting. There were a few catcalls from the women when they saw them.

"Hey, Father Stephen! Give us a fatherly kiss!"

"Sister Mary, let me show you how to get some!"

Father Stephen and Sister Mary took in the catcalls good-naturedly. They went up to each woman, taking a few moments to talk to them.

"Sharon, there's a spare jumper out there for you. Or would you rather I brought you a cup of tea?"

"Stephanie, here's the cough syrup you asked for."

Not all the women responded. When she saw Sister Mary coming towards her, Jungle turned her face abruptly towards the dimly lit road opposite. If she craned her neck far enough, she could see the lights from the King's Cross Station. A car slowed to a crawl in front of her and she lifted up her minuscule skirt. Sister Mary averted her eyes. Jungle wasn't wearing any underwear. The car moved on. Johnny tore down the pavement furiously. Jungle pretended that she didn't see or hear him. Johnny came right up to her face, pushing Sister Mary impatiently to the side. Sister Mary put a restraining hand on his arm.

"No, Johnny," she said.

"Stay out of it, Sister," he replied.

Father Stephen hurried to where they were standing. "Is everything okay here?" he asked.

"Yes. Eyo and I are just going to have a little chat," Johnny said, dragging Jungle away in the direction of the hotel they had just vacated.

"My name is Jungle, not Eyo!"

"Johnny…" Father Stephen ran after them.

"Stay out of it, Father!" Johnny called out to him. They rounded a corner and disappeared from sight.

Sister Mary turned her attention back to the other women on the pavement. She had just enough compassion and harsh realism to enable her to get through the hours she spent pounding these pavements on their behalf. In the beginning, she thought she would be Jesus' hands and feet, showing them another way. She had been so naive. Turned out that she was the one who learned from the girls she felt called to serve. Over a period of some years, she had been spat at and threatened by them and their pimps. She had seen a number of the girls die from drug overdose. One had been killed by a punter, and several had almost died from severe assaults by both their punters and their pimps.

Between herself, Father Stephen and God Himself, they'd managed to get some of the women off the streets and safely squirrelled away in places where they would never be found by those looking for them. But it wasn't enough. In the last five years, they'd seen an influx of Eastern European and West African women, most of them young ladies plus the odd child, flood the back streets of King's Cross and Camden, the two areas their parish covered. It was a pandemic with a tragic cost, usually the lives of the women tied up in it.

Sister Mary shook her head and brought her attention back to the young girl in front of her. She was high. Sister Mary could see it in her eyes.

"Oh, Daisy, what are we going to do with you?" she said softly, as if speaking to herself.

Daisy looked back at her with glassy eyes.

*   *   *

An hour later, Jungle was back on the street. She winced when she stuck out a leg in an attempt at a sexy pose. The movement had sent shots of pain up her hip. Johnny never hit her face because visible bruises were bad for business. However, there were plenty of other, less visible places on her body that he made bruising use of. She would pay him back for this and every beating, Jungle swore to herself. A car crawled to a halt in front of her. She leaned into the driver's window. A moment later, she got inside the car and it drove off.

Father Stephen watched the car drive off. He said a few inward prayers to God to keep her safe. Jungle was not the youngest sex worker on the streets, but she was one of the youngest. She appeared on his and Sister Mary's radar about two years ago, but they were no closer to knowing her than they were the first day she appeared on the street, with Johnny lurking behind her, watching her every step.

Jungle hadn't repulsed their attempts to be friendly. Her attitude was something far worse: complete indifference to their ministrations. When they attempted to speak to her, she would ignore them. Sometimes, she would start walking away when she saw them coming. At other times, she would simply stand there and blank them out. Indeed, for the most part, Jungle kept to herself. From what Father Stephen could see, she maintained a detached relationship with the rest of the girls on the patch. He knew she wasn't a drug addict because the other women said so and Johnny himself confirmed it. He also knew that she had been brought over to the UK from Nigeria. As to how she came in contact with Johnny, he didn't know. And Johnny wasn't saying. Still, he and Sister Mary persevered in talking to her and letting her know that they were available.

Sometimes, Father Stephen thought it was a waste of time.

Thirty-one

"Here. I bought you some chips." Johnny held the steaming takeaway towards Jungle. She turned up her nose in distaste.

"You look sick. Not good for business," Johnny said. He took a lone chip from the packet and popped it inside his mouth.

"Well, you've started eating it, so you might as well finish it," Jungle said, looking away.

Truth be told, the smell of vinegar was overpowering and made her feel ill. She got off the bed and grabbed the jacket hanging over the back of the only chair in the room. "I'm going out," she said.

"No, you're not." Johnny shoved her back onto the bed and held out the steaming packet of chips towards her. "I won't ask you again," he said.

Jungle hesitated, then she saw the look on his face. She seemed to change her mind about refusing his offer. A knowing smile appeared on her face. She undressed slowly. Johnny tossed the chips on the bedside table.

"And afterwards, you'll eat the chips. Except this time, they'll be cold," he said.

Jungle muttered an expletive. Johnny responded with a triumphant smile as he unbuttoned his belt.

*　　　*　　　*

Jungle felt a slight rustle near her ear and tried to brush it away, but it remained. The rustle became louder and she felt something warm on her stomach. She opened her eyes and turned her head to the side. The vinegar-sodden chips were still on the bedside table, the smell even worse now that they were cold. She resisted the urge to tip them over the floor because it would be a pointless exercise; Johnny would only make her eat them, even off the floor. His arm weighed down on her, right across her stomach, his mouth breathing into her ear. She flung his arm to the side and rolled out of bed. She walked across the studio flat to the kitchenette and made herself a hot chocolate, taking care to make as much noise as possible. She heard Johnny turn over.

"Eyo, you continue with that noise and I swear…" he said.

Jungle resisted the urge to fling the scalding hot chocolate in his face. She wasn't Eyo. Eyo was the ignoramus who came to this country five years ago, full of hope. That girl was dead and she would remain buried. Every time Johnny called her that name, he resurrected her, making the subsequent burials more difficult but not impossible. One day, he would stop calling her that name completely and Eyo would remain dead and buried forever. Which suited her fine.

Jungle got dressed quickly.

"You're eating the chips."

Jungle didn't bother to look up from tying her calf-length boots. Not even when she heard Johnny reach out across the bed and throw the packet of cold chips at her. They scattered all over the floor of the flat.

"No," Jungle said.

She sensed rather than saw Johnny jump out of bed. He strode across the room and grabbed her ear, the pain forcing her to the ground. He twisted her ear, forcing her head down towards the floor. Tears stung her eyes, but Jungle refused to cry. She wouldn't give him the satisfaction.

"Why do you do this?" Johnny asked. He sounded like he genuinely wanted to know.

Jungle tried angling her head to look up at him. "Why should I make it easy for you?" she sputtered.

Johnny gave her a shove and she collapsed on the floor.

"You will eat the chips," he said.

*   *   *

Sometimes Jungle got on the bus and went on long walks. Her favourite walk was from Camden Town to Finsbury Park, a long straight road that took just under an hour, sometimes more. She didn't have any money for the bus because Johnny took everything from her. En route to the park itself, she never failed to stop at Finsbury Park Station and sit at the bus stop, the one under the bridge, and look across the road to the church on the right and the mosque to the left, the two of them, like their comrades all over the world, trying to entice people to their cause. The view reminded Jungle of a particular building of worship in another country and a life she wished she didn't remember.

When she left the bus stop, she would walk the five minutes to the park and sit on the grass. If it was a sunny day, she would lie back and enjoy the sun. Sometimes, she turned tricks in the park and had even built up a select but steady clientele from the scores of young North African illegal residents haunting Blackstock Road, just across the park. She didn't mind them too much. She just didn't like it when they cried and told her about the families they'd left behind in pursuit of the European dream. Sometimes, they would try to dig for information about her life, but she never gave them any. She wasn't interested in their stories. And as far as she was concerned, she'd earned the right to keep *her* life story to herself.

Finsbury Park wasn't too different from the jungle she came from. The glue sniffers were there, just as they were in Jungle City. The mentally ill roamed the park, just as they roamed about in Jungle City. And just as in Jungle City, Sundays and Fridays unleashed a gathering of the faithful onto the streets, all of them sated on saintly belief. She hadn't understood her father's mild disdain of the saintly when she was in Jungle City, but almost six years and three thousand miles later, she believed that she understood it well. Even better than he did.

Mama would be ashamed of her. She had turned into a heathen.

Jungle did not have a Mama, she reminded herself. Eyo did, but she was dead. A shadow fell on Jungle's face.

"Jungle?"

Jungle opened her eyes. It was one of her Algerian clients. She patted the space next to her and the man sat down.

"*Ees* good weather?"

"Yes."

They both sat down in companionable silence.

"In Algeria, the sun hot hot," the man said.

Jungle nodded and didn't say anything. She didn't have to. The man just wanted company. Quite a few of them were like that: lonely, sexually frustrated and angry. They were angry with themselves for believing the European dream would be as easy as those who went back home to Algeria from Europe made it out to be. They were frustrated with the Home Office for not believing their asylum claims and driving them underground. And again, angry at themselves for preferring to stay in a country as illegal immigrants without any means of financial or social support, rather than to return home and face the shame of failure. They were also angry and frustrated at not achieving what everyone else who went to Europe seemed to achieve: success.

Jungle and the man chatted for a while about nothing in particular. Then, Jungle started the long walk back to Camden. She still had a few hours to kill before the night–and work–started.

*   *   *

"Eyo!"

Johnny could barely contain his excitement as he entered the studio flat. He was holding something in his right hand, which he hid behind him.

"Don't call me that name," Jungle said automatically. She was sitting on the bed, watching a daytime soap.

Johnny approached the bed and thrust out something at her. It was a rectangular box wrapped in gaudy paper. She took it from him and opened it. It was a brand new Barbie doll. Jungle threw it across the room, turned off the television and threw the duvet over her head.

"Eyo!"

"How many times do I have to tell you? Stop calling me that name. My name is Jungle. Call me Jungle. It's not hard. J-u-n-g-l-e. See? I've spelt it out for you." Her muffled voice was a snarl.

"Eyo…"

Jungle turned her back to him. She felt the bed dip, and Johnny gently lifted the duvet off her face.

"I thought you would like it," he said.

"You thought wrong. Besides, I don't know whatever gave you the stupid idea that I liked stupid Barbie dolls," she said.

"Because every time we walked past stupid shops with stupid Barbies in it, you would keep on looking at the stupid dolls and stop listening to a stupid word that I say."

"That's because you're stupid," Jungle said. But her voice was softer, with a hint of a smile in it.

Johnny leaned over her and kissed her fully on the lips. Jungle wrapped her arms around his neck and drew him to her. Johnny thought he heard a sniff from Jungle and inwardly shook himself. It was a ridiculous idea. Jungle never cried.

A few hours later, Johnny climbed out of bed and took the few steps across the room to get to the kitchenette. He popped some bread in the toaster and turned on the kettle.

"Chuck that stuff away. The smell's making me sick," Jungle moaned, half asleep, from the bed. "That noisy kettle isn't helping either," she said.

Johnny spooned some chocolate granules into a mug and took out the butter from the fridge. Five minutes later, he laid the results of his endeavours on the bedside table. Jungle turned her face away.

"Do we have to go through this all the time?" Johnny asked.

"Do *you* have to go through this all the time?"

Johnny sat on the bed and turned Jungle back to him. "Eat up. It's Friday night. Busiest time of the week," he told her.

Jungle sat up and reached out for the hot chocolate. Johnny took it out of her reach.

"Not until you eat the two pieces of toast," he said, shaking his head at her, as if she was five.

"Then you'll be waiting a long time," Jungle replied.

She turned her back to him again and flicked on the television to the opening strains of *Coronation Street.* Johnny took the hot chocolate and poured it down the kitchen sink. Jungle ignored him, as he knew she would. He took his jacket from behind the door.

"I'll be back in ten minutes. I want you to be ready," he said.

He went to the cupboard and slipped the remaining packets of hot chocolate into his jacket pocket. He then rummaged through Jungle's jacket until he found her flat keys. He slipped those in his pocket as well. He left the flat but not before locking her in.

"Ten minutes," he said, before disappearing.

Jungle threw the side plate of toast at the door and, with a determined shake of her head, turned her attention back to the television.

∗ ∗ ∗

Jungle gasped. Something was tightening around her neck. She opened her eyes. It was Johnny. He had a wild look in his eyes and his hands were squeezing her neck. Jungle tried clawing his hands off, but Johnny only squeezed harder.

"Where is it?" he screamed at her.

Jungle started flailing about on the bed. Her throat felt dry. She could feel the blood rushing to her eyes.

"Johnny, I promise you, I don't know what you're talking about," she gasped out.

"You're lying! I know you're hiding money from me. Where is it? I won't ask you again!"

Jungle felt herself being pushed up the bed and against the wall. He was finally going to kill her this time. She knew it.

"Johnny…"

All of a sudden, he released her. Jungle flopped back on the bed and gulped in some air. Through hazy eyes, she saw Johnny opening and slamming shut the cupboards in the kitchenette.

"You're hiding something from me. I know you are," he shouted.

Jungle rolled herself into the foetal position, her back to him. "I'm not," she said, her voice dull.

Johnny went under the kitchen sink and fiddled with the U-bend. He held it up triumphantly and looked inside it; it was empty. He looked behind the television and under its stand, then he turned out the contents of the wardrobe and chest of drawers in the studio flat. Next, he went to a door that led to the bathroom. Jungle could hear him tipping things over and jerking open the bathroom cabinet. A few minutes later, he came back out, went to the bed and started speaking to Jungle.

"I'm sorry. You know that I hate you hiding things from me," he said.

"Yes, Johnny, I know," Jungle said, her voice dead. She started shivering.

"Come on. Get back to bed. I didn't mean to wake you. It's my temper. I just can't see straight when I think of you hiding things from me. It drives me crazy. I can't think, and then I do stupid things."

All the time he was talking, he rearranged the bed, put Jungle under the duvet and then finally covered her with it. He got in bed with her and ran his hands tenderly through her plaits.

"It's you. You make me do this to you," he said.

Thirty-two

The other girls didn't like being on the streets much, but Jungle didn't mind. She liked the cold wind in the freezing winters. The air felt crisper and cleaner. She liked the sultry nights in summer because they reminded her of the humid Nigerian nights she once knew. She didn't even mind being outdoors when it rained because it made her feel better, knowing it was the same rain that fell on her family in Nigeria. She corrected herself. Eyo had a family in Nigeria. Jungle didn't.

She leaned against the lamp post and shivered slightly, adjusting the hot pants she wore. From the corner of her eye, she saw Father Stephen and his sidekick disembark from the van. She turned her gaze back to the road. A car sidled to a halt in front of her. Jungle bent over and leaned into the car, through the open window. There were four men in the car, which reeked of alcohol. They leered at her. Jungle drew back at once.

"My friend's getting married next weekend. How about a little something to remind him of what he'll be missing once he gets hitched?" the driver said.

Jungle shook her head and withdrew farther on the pavement.

"Think you're too good for us, don't you?"

She didn't answer. She looked across the road to where Johnny was loitering with the other women. He saw her face and attempted to cross the street.

"Never mind. We're off to Gatwick. Going to Romania. The women are better and cheaper, or so we've been told," the driver said. He drove off to the cheers of his friends.

Johnny had crossed the street. "What?" His voice was impatient.

"Nothing."

"You made me run across the street for nothing. You think it's a joke?" His voice had risen. He slapped her.

Jungle slapped him back and then kicked him in the ankle for added measure. Johnny started slapping her around the head. People walked past them without giving them a second look. Jungle didn't fight back. She figured that if he knocked her head around long enough, it would burst open and she would finally be left alone. She would be free.

"You like it when I do this, don't you?" Johnny was now shaking her. "Half of the stuff I let you get away with, none of the other girls would dare try. Drives me nuts."

He shook his head in disgust, gave her a final shake and ran back across the road. Jungle saw drug addict Daisy go up to him and caress his face. *Well, she can have him,* Jungle thought.

She rubbed her head to steady it. It felt rather woozy after Johnny's shaking and hitting. Another car pulled up. Jungle puckered her lips and went to the car, drawing her minuscule top lower down her chest as she leaned into the car window.

"How old are you?" the driver asked.

"As young as you need me to be and as old as is needed," she said. "Thirteen," she added when she saw that he was still waiting for an answer.

"No, you're not," he said driving off.

Jungle straightened her top and walked the few steps back to the pavement. Johnny had moved her to the street when she started getting fewer specialised clients. They were complaining of being cheated, of getting an adult when they clearly stated they wanted somebody younger. Her first night on the streets had been a shock. She wasn't used to soliciting for favours, although she had ended up getting a fair amount of punters. There were other things she wasn't used to: the amount of drug-addicted women working the streets. Johnny had drugged her once, when he first brought her to London; she hadn't liked it. She hated the feeling of not being in control and had sworn to herself that she would never allow herself to be that vulnerable again.

Jungle wrapped her arms around her body. She could hear Father Stephen advancing. She stared straight ahead at the road opposite her. She couldn't see Johnny, or Daisy for that matter.

She didn't care. In fact, all the women on the street could have him for all she cared. Not that what she cared mattered. Johnny owned them all—yes, all the girls on this particular strip of the back streets of King's Cross.

A couple walked past. The girl had long blonde hair which she flicked when she walked past Jungle, but not before giving her a disapproving look. She sighed and pulled her boyfriend closer to her, laying her head on his shoulder as they walked down the pavement. Jungle ignored them. *Stupid people*, she thought.

"You alright, Jungle?" It was Father Stephen. "It's just that you looked rather peaky just then. Here, I've brought you some hot chocolate."

Father Stephen stretched the cup towards her. Jungle hesitated before taking the cup. She took a sip from it and kept her eyes fixed on the road opposite. She hoped the police would find Daisy the drug addict and Johnny in the midst of their sexual endeavours and they would be jailed for gross public indecency or whatever they would charge them with. *That would teach 'em!*

A group of about five girls walked past them, their arms linked. They were wearing identical Friday night uniforms: tiny skirts, minuscule tops, tottering heels and garish makeup. They were singing loudly and brashly.

"Pervert!" one of them called out to Father Stephen as they walked past, taking up the width of the pavement. Jungle retreated farther on the pavement. She knew what was coming next.

"And you should be ashamed of yourself! Tart!" another one called out to her.

Father Stephen watched Jungle's face. It was expressionless. She took another sip from the mug and held it out to him. Father Stephen shook his head.

"It's for you," he said. "You need it," he added, noting her thin frame.

Jungle saw a car slow down in front of her and walked back up to the edge of the pavement, striking a provocative pose. Father Stephen busied himself by looking at his watch. He hoped to strike a nonchalant demeanour that would scare off the punter and allow him and Jungle to talk. This was the most she had ever spoken to him in the eighteen months since he first saw her on the street.

"I'm lost. How do I get to the Strand?"

He heard Jungle give the driver directions and then he drove away. He watched her for a few moments, debating whether or not to talk.

"If you want to talk to me or Sister Mary about anything, anything at all, this is where we are." He told her the address of the church and the sanctuary they ran for women. "It's right there, just behind the British Library. Seven minutes walk, tops," he said.

Jungle listened, her face still expressionless. Silently, she downed the rest of the hot chocolate and handed the mug back to him.

"Thank you, Father," she said.

He had been dismissed. But Father Stephen was happy. He turned back to the other girls on the pavement and started talking to them. Across the road, Jungle saw Johnny and Daisy emerge from a darkened side street. Daisy had a huge grin on her face. A car slowed down in front of Jungle. She leaned towards the car window. A few moments later, she got in and the car sped off.

*　　　*　　　*

Sundays were her favourite days. She walked to Finsbury Park and stayed there for hours, observing everything and everyone. Sometimes, Johnny joined her, although she would have preferred that he didn't. When he was around her, she couldn't think. He filled her head, her mind and everything around her so that she couldn't see or do anything else. In the park, she could think about the days she went trawling around Lagos to sell ice water in plastic water bags, with Lanre. She wondered how she could have been so happy in her ignorance then and not known it.

"*Kilo se?* What's wrong with you?" Johnny asked her.

Jungle wrapped her jacket around her body more snugly and settled more comfortably against the bark of the tree.

"Why don't you like speaking to me in Yoruba?"

"I don't know what you're talking about." A closed look had come on Jungle's face.

Johnny tried to kiss her, but she pushed him away. "Why don't you go to Daisy the addict?" she taunted.

"Jealous?"

Jungle gave him an 'as-if' look. She stood up and dusted her jeans. They were so tight; it seemed that they were moulded to her body. Johnny had bought them for that very purpose. She adjusted her jumper and the scarf around her neck.

"I'm walking back," she said.

"No, we're not. We're getting the bus." Johnny stood up as well.

"Johnny, please. I would prefer to walk."

"And I said we were taking the bus. Now quit your whingeing and let's go."

They left the park and crossed the street to the bus stop opposite the park. Jungle sat down in the bus shelter, while Johnny paced up and down. He couldn't be still in one place. His energy drove her nuts.

"Johnny, sit down," Jungle said.

"Shut up," Johnny replied.

The other people in the bus shelter pretended they didn't hear them. A bus soon came and they got on. It was one of the new bendy buses. Jungle secretly hoped for the day when she could run up and down the bus when it was empty and shriek in delight as it wound its way through London. She would feel like a child–free.

They found an empty double seat by the window and sat down. Johnny put his hand on Jungle's thigh and started caressing it. His movements became more sensual. It was one of his 'things': doing things in public that would humiliate her and draw a response from anyone watching. Jungle thought about shaking his hand off but changed her mind. It would only make it worse. She just wanted to go home, lie down and not have to think. She wished Johnny would go to another girl today. He owned about five other girls. *Surely, he could give me a break today and just leave me alone?* That was all she wanted today: a clear head. With Johnny around, it would be unattainable.

Johnny's hands were dangerously close to her privates. She hoped he wouldn't unzip her jeans and put his hands inside her underwear, in full view of everyone on the bus. It was just the kind of thing he would do. She decided to ignore him and looked out of the window. She didn't want to see the look of disgust on people's faces, when he finally did whatever humiliating act he was surely planning.

"Eyo?" It was a lady's voice.

Jungle looked up. It was Tolu.

Thirty-three

"I don't know what you're talking about," Jungle said.

She grabbed Johnny's hand and got up. Johnny looked from Jungle to the lady, and back again at Jungle.

"Wait a minute," he said. He tried cutting his hands loose from Jungle's but failed. The bus stopped. They were in front of Finsbury Park Station.

"Eyo? It's me, Tolu! Don't you remember? From…"

Jungle pushed past her and more or less jumped out of the bus, dragging Johnny with her. The bus drove away with the lady inside, still looking at Jungle, a perplexed expression on her face.

"I told you I didn't want to take the bus!" Jungle screamed. She yanked her hand off Johnny's and stomped off in the direction of Camden Town, angry tears stinging her eyes.

Johnny ran after her. "What's wrong with you?"

Jungle didn't answer. She was stomping up the road, like a woman possessed. "You! Everything! I didn't ask to come here to this stupid country. I didn't know. They didn't tell me. What are you looking at?!" she snarled at a female passer-by who dared to look at her.

The lady quickly walked on. Johnny grabbed hold of Jungle's hand and pulled her towards him. She snatched it away and carried on walking furiously ahead. She spotted a bench outside a discount shop and slumped on it, her anger dissipated. Johnny joined her.

"Who was that girl?" he asked.

"I don't know what you're talking about," she replied, her face taking on the expressionless look he knew so well.

Jungle folded her arms and looked towards Camden. She wanted to keep on walking, preferably alone. She needed to think. And she did that best without Johnny with her.

"Did you live with them when you first came to the country?" Johnny guessed.

Jungle gave him a disparaging look, as Johnny knew she would. She zealously guarded every bit of information about her life before she met him. In fact, she plainly refused to make any allusions to it. He used to try to talk to her about her life with Big Madame, but he was always met with resounding silence. Like now.

"You're mad," Johnny said, shaking his head.

"Now that you know that, why don't you run to Daisy and leave me alone," Jungle replied, her eyes in the direction of Camden.

"Fine. Be like that," Johnny said.

He got up and strode off in the direction of the bus stop. Jungle watched him, despising him with every fibre of her being. It was because of people like him that she was trapped in the UK, in no-man's-land. She didn't exist in the eyes of the state, and if anything were to happen to her, nobody would notice or care, as Johnny—and Big Madame, Lola and Sam before him—remind her. She was an illegal immigrant. She was invisible. And dispensable. She would die a prostitute in the UK, unmourned and unnoticed. Mama would never find out what happened to her.

She hadn't thought about Tolu and her family in a long time. She hadn't wanted to. Thinking about them gave her a not unfamiliar feeling of powerlessness. When she came to the country all those years ago, she had been in the power of Tolu's parents. They had done with her as they'd wished, knowing nobody cared and nobody would come looking for her. Tolu's mother–Jungle refused to say her name–used her the way one would use an old rag. Her husband, just like her own father, took from her what wasn't in their power to take. Big Madame was no better, taking from Jungle and selling what wasn't hers to sell. They were all alike–taking, taking, taking, with no thought for the person they were demolishing and killing with each bit of her body they sold.

Jungle wondered about Bola and clamped her mind shut. She didn't like to think about her. If she did, she would start entertaining thoughts of Bola coming to rescue her from Johnny, which was really stupid. She was sure that Bola had better things to do with the new power her red passport gave her than coming down to London and looking for a stupid, illegal, teenage sex worker.

She hated them all. She hated the power they'd all had over her life and she still did. She did not own an item of clothing she paid for herself. Johnny bought everything. Even her sanitary towels. The studio flat she–they–lived in was Johnny's. He had three others in Camden where he kept the other girls and rotated which ones he stayed in, although he spent a lot of his time in Jungle's.

Every bit of money she made on the streets of King's Cross and as a hired-out sex worker–he sometimes sent her to private homes–went to him. She didn't own a mobile phone and Johnny wouldn't buy her one. Besides, who would she call? And she had forgotten the little she'd learned about reading and writing. It was no more than she deserved, selling herself like the degraded person she was. She didn't deserve better. Johnny always told her that and she believed him.

As an illegal, she didn't have access to medical care. Jungle thought back to *that* day when she had an argument with Johnny. She had felt some cramps in her intimates but hadn't taken much notice until they became so bad; she collapsed on the floor. Johnny didn't do anything, until he saw the blood between her legs, staining the flat's beige carpet. That was when he called his Ethiopian doctor—an illegal himself—to come over to the studio flat. The man had come and forced her to drink something—she didn't know what. The next thing she knew, she had opened her eyes and was on the bed. Johnny was sitting on the only other piece of furniture in the room, a sofa, chortling to himself. He spoke to her without taking his eyes off the television.

"You had a miscarriage. I told him to take care of it for good. You won't be carrying no babies again," he said.

Jungle had turned her face away. She had known that she was pregnant but hadn't said anything to Johnny. Secretly, she had harboured a fantasy of having a baby, someone of her own to love. That was why she stopped taking the pills, pretending to take them every day in front of Johnny. Instead, she would place them under her tongue and spit them out in the toilet afterwards. She had seen herself washing the baby, singing Yoruba songs. Her mother and Mama Fola were somewhere in the background, teasing her and telling her how badly she was spoiling her baby.

It was a foolish dream. She knew that. Still, she had dared to hope and, like before, it hadn't gotten her anywhere. Perhaps it was for the best. Knowing Johnny, even if he had allowed her to carry the baby to term, he would've sold it off to the highest bidder. He once told her that there was a high demand in the European market for African babies.

What kind of life could she have offered the child anyway? Jungle wondered. A life of no recognition and subject to the powers of people like Johnny and Big Madame. And babies got sick. She would've had to enlist the help of the Ethiopian doctor, and she didn't want that. He was too closely associated with Johnny and her present life. Sometimes, Jungle felt as if she was a thousand years old. She felt as if she'd lived a thousand lifetimes and the next thousand yawned before her, like a chasm.

Jungle now stood up and started walking slowly back to Camden Town. She felt pressed in by her thoughts. She wished she could get away from them. They made her feel agitated and vulnerable, and she didn't like that.

The Finsbury Park church opened its doors, and the faithful spilled out. Some were chatting and laughing in Yoruba. Jungle made her way through the crowd, an aged teenager in the midst of a thousand lifetimes.

When she got back to the studio flat, she let herself in. Johnny was waiting for her, in the middle of the flat, a strange expression on his face. He was holding some money in his hands. They were rolled bills. *Her* rolled bills. Comprehension dawned on Jungle. It was the money she'd secreted away from her North African punters at Finsbury Park.

"What is this?"

His voice was strange. Jungle heard something like the crashing of the ocean waves in her ears. Blood rose to her face and she felt hot.

"Johnny, please. Let me explain."

Johnny threw the money on the bed and walked to her. "No," he said, giving her a blow and dragging her by her plaits across the room. "Let *me* explain."

Thirty-four

He was finally going to kill her. She knew it. She could see it in his eyes.

"Why are you hiding things from me?" he screamed at her as he dragged her across the room by her plaits.

"Johnny, please."

Jungle tried to wrench herself free from his grasp. She thought he would wrench the hair off her scalp. It certainly felt like it.

"Shut up!"

Johnny dragged her to the wall and smashed her head against it. Jungle passed out. When she came to, she was naked. Her hands were tied above her head and attached to the headboard. Her feet were bound in the same way to the bedstead. Johnny was making himself a cup of tea. She watched him, fearfully.

"I know you're awake," Johnny said, without turning around.

He finished making the tea and walked back to the bed. He sat on the chair. Jungle watched him, the way a mouse watched its predator.

"I'm not going to ask you again. Where did you get the money from?"

Jungle turned her face and body away from him, tears falling down her cheeks. She didn't want him to see her crying. He would think he had won.

There was a knock on the door. Johnny put the tea by the bedside table and let in two men, one of whom was carrying something that looked like camera equipment; the other, lighting stuff. Jungle watched them, her heart beating wildly. They began setting up the equipment, fumbling with the lights and cameras. Nobody paid her any attention. When they finished, Johnny laid a beige spread on the floor, right in the middle of all the cameras and lights, and came to the bed.

"I told you never to lie to me," he said. He gestured to the men, who started unbuckling their belts.

On the bed, Jungle started kicking furiously, trying to break free from the rope that tied her. Johnny produced a syringe from somewhere on his person.

"Daisy has used this. You know she's not particular about who she shares her syringes with. I trust you to behave, otherwise who knows which part of your body the syringe will end up in."

Jungle wanted to tell him to go to hell, but she didn't. He knew how much she feared syringes or anything that made her feel vulnerable. Gently, almost tenderly, he started untying her, talking to her conversationally.

"You're going to show these men a good time and I want you to look like you're enjoying it," he said. He reached out his hand towards her and Jungle shrank back.

By now, the two men were completely naked. She could see them just over Johnny's shoulder. The studio flat was dark. The only lights in the room came from the lights focused on the beige rug in the middle of the room.

Johnny reached out for the syringe and Jungle quickly got off the bed, a dull ache in her head. Like a conductor directing an orchestra, Johnny led her to the beige rug and went behind one of the cameras. The two men came to join her. One stood behind her and the other one stood in front of her.

"Smile," Johnny said, bending over and looking into the camera.

*   *   *

Jungle walked up and down the pavement gingerly, trying hard not to limp. The other girls on the patch ignored her. Johnny had given them serious warnings. He was in a bad mood tonight and they risked getting a beating themselves if they showed any sign of caring for Jungle.

Across the road, Daisy the drug addict made exaggerated movements, caressing Johnny's jaw whenever she thought Jungle was looking her way and walking seductively every time a car drove past. She wanted to show Johnny how hard she was working. Unlike Jungle who never did anything and caused him nothing but trouble.

Jungle's feet were throbbing. The five-inch heels weren't helping either. She reached out and leaned lightly on the lamp post, ignoring the people who went past her.

She was alive. She couldn't believe it. Whenever she thought of the two men and what happened on the beige carpet, she would freeze and start shaking. And they had brought in a dog.

Jungle shut her mind down and put it on autopilot. She wouldn't think about what took place in that studio flat over the past three days. She wouldn't. Tonight was her first night out. She wasn't going to think about anything except ignoring the shooting pain in her ankles, ribs and the dull ache in her head.

She had been foolish. She should not have hidden the money in the flat. She didn't have any friends or anyone she could trust with it, so it had seemed like the most logical thing to do. She should have known better. She knew Johnny was obsessed with the idea of any of the girls, especially Jungle, hiding things from him.

The money had been hidden under the bed, in a torn supermarket plastic bag, under a loose, creaking floorboard covered by the same mouldy beige carpet that covered the rest of the flat. It was or had been the perfect hiding place. She had two thousand pounds sterling in that bag. She didn't know how many men she had slept with in the course of her job, but the money represented the men she had chosen to have sex with to do something with her life. It had taken her almost two years to save up that money. Two years of frequenting Finsbury Park and servicing frustrated North African men.

She thought that if she had five thousand pounds sterling she would have enough to get away. She didn't know where she would go, but she would be away from King's Cross, Johnny, Sam and his family, Big Madame or anyone who knew her. She had even entertained notions of going somewhere called the Nigerian High Commission. She didn't know where it was or what they did, but some of the Nigerian girls who whispered to her when they walked past her in King's Cross sometimes mentioned it. She reckoned they would help her. Maybe even take her back to Jungle City. Except she wouldn't tell Mama if she went back. She would wait a while, find a way, *any* way, to make money in Lagos. When she was sure she had enough, she would appear and Mama would be proud of her for having done well in the UK, for having *endured* and not brought shame to the family.

That was the plan. Until Johnny found the money.

"What you offering?"

The voice intruded in her thoughts. It was a middle-aged man. She could tell he was Nigerian from his accent. She leaned into his car window, trying hard not to wince at the shooting pains in her side and feet.

"Depends on what you want," she said, giving him a practised smile.

"Where are you from?" the man asked her in Yoruba.

Jungle didn't blink. "I don't know what you're talking about," she said.

"I want a proper Nigerian girl. Somebody who understands what a Nigerian man needs," the man was still speaking in Yoruba, looking at her intently.

Jungle drew back from the car. She didn't much like being with Nigerian men. They always tried speaking to her in Yoruba. If that didn't get a response from her, they would start talking about how Christianity or Islam could save her from the streets. And inevitably, they would start talking about how much they hated the UK and couldn't wait to go back to Nigeria. Jungle would listen with feigned interest. But the minute their time was up, she would leave. She never hung around for more than necessary and she never spoke to them in Yoruba.

"Where are you going? I thought you were one of us. Come, get in," the man said.

Jungle tried sauntering back to the car, clenching her lips in pain. They agreed on a price and she got in the car. Father Stephen followed them in his van, cursing himself for his foolishness.

*   *   *

Father Stephen stood up when Jungle came into the reception. The hotel receptionist ignored him. Everybody in certain hotels in King's Cross knew him and his work with sex workers. Most tolerated him. Others, such as now, ignored him.

Jungle stopped when she saw him. She didn't know how, but she knew he had been waiting for her. She sank wearily, slowly and painfully into a seat. Without taking his eyes off the television screen, the receptionist spoke.

"I don't want any trouble from Johnny tonight. He said that he wants you back out there immediately," he said.

"Calm down. She's leaving soon," Father Stephen said. He went to where Jungle was seated and stood beside her.

The receptionist wasn't finished. "In and out. That's what Johnny said. If he finds out that you've been hanging about here instead of going straight back on the road…"

"Oh, put a sock in it," Father Stephen said.

"Just saying, that's all."

Father Stephen gave an exasperated sigh and turned his attention back to Jungle. She had taken her shoes off and was rubbing her feet. He could see the dark rings around her ankles and some welts on her legs. She leant back on the chair, her eyes closed. She looked fourteen and exhausted. He noted her thin arms; they were also covered in bruises.

Father Stephen crouched down close to her. He knew not to touch her. She would've shrunk from him. If she didn't scratch his eyes out first.

"Jungle, let me get Sister Mary and the other Religious Sisters to help you. You're not well," he said.

It was the first time in a long while that anybody had offered to help her. Jungle thought of many things to say, but in the end, she just sank her head into her hands and wept. By her side, Father Stephen waited. When she finished weeping, she gathered herself and walked out of the hotel, a little of her original hauteur restored in her gait. She did not give Father Stephen a backward glance.

*   *   *

Late that night, Johnny came back to the studio flat with Jungle. He made tender and passionate love to her. And just before falling asleep in her arms, he whispered in her ear and told her how much he loved her. She made him do the things he did. He had to teach her a lesson when she misbehaved because, if he didn't, she would continue hiding things from him and make him look like a fool. He promised her the latest Barbie, complete with accessories. He then kissed her slowly, lingeringly and told her again how much he loved her and couldn't imagine his life without her.

Jungle listened to him with tears in her eyes, which he wiped off. Finally, he slept, his head on her chest. As he slept, Jungle traced his face with her finger and tears fell down her cheeks again. Then she crept off the bed, out of the studio flat and into the garden.

When she came back into the flat, she was holding a cricket bat she'd shoplifted from a sports store earlier that day. She advanced towards the bed with it in her hands. She lifted up her hands and brought the bat down hard on Johnny's face. And she didn't stop.

Thirty-five

Ten years ago, a new family started attending Mass in Father Stephen's community church. There were the father, mother and two boys aged ten and eight. The boys were unusually quiet. Post-Mass, they did not run around the church like the other children, tearing down the place and generally getting under people's feet. They did not fraternise with other children either, preferring each other's company. In his dealings with them, Father Stephen found them exceptionally well behaved, with a less-than-healthy attachment to their mother. They weren't particularly enamoured with their father either, he noted. They lowered their eyes when he spoke to them and flinched every time he came near them. They didn't seem to seek his affection or welcome it when he gave it to them.

Father Stephen had been in the business of serving people long enough to recognise the classic symptoms of abuse. At first, he did nothing. He discussed the matter with one or two trusted friends and advisors. He was told that these were precarious times for the Roman Catholic Church. They didn't tell him what not to do, but they did caution him to be careful. These were young boys. Any involvement with them and their parents, however well meant, was bound to be misinterpreted by certain people.

And so Father Stephen waited and watched. Then, one Sunday, he saw the mother come to Mass alone, with bruises on her face. By the time he battled his way through the post-Mass pleasantries with other worshippers, she was gone. He paid a visit to their house later that week, but no one came to the door. He did, however, notice the slight twitching of the window curtains upstairs. The next Sunday, the mother was back, alone again. Warning bells were beginning to ring loudly and persistently in Father Stephen's ears. This time, after Mass celebrations, he rushed to the front of the church, brushing off attempts by other worshippers to engage him in conversation. He caught her just as she was about to board the bus and managed to persuade her to wait for the next one instead.

"I was round yours the other day," Father Stephen said.

She couldn't meet his eye. "You must've just missed us going to the shops. We're usually home," she said.

He saw her bite her lip. *She had said too much*, he could hear her thinking.

"If you and the boys need anything, just give us the word," he said, looking straight into her eyes. He saw shame there. Shame that he knew her secret. The bus came and she hastily got on it.

A week after that, he was summoned to his superior's office. There was a charge against him, his superior said. A man had accused him of inappropriate behaviour with his children. Two boys aged ten and eight.

Father Stephen had looked at his superior in holy disbelief. *This is a joke*, he said.

I'm afraid not, his superior replied.

It's that family I told you about. It's the father, isn't it? Father Stephen said.

His superior had nodded.

What now? Father Stephen asked.

There has to be a formal investigation. You'll be suspended from duty, while it's taking place. And all contact with children is forbidden from the moment you leave this office, his superior said. *I'm so sorry. You know how things are, with all these lawsuits against the Church.*

Father Stephen had left the room, a walking zombie. He could not remember a time when he had not wanted to be a priest and serve God by serving people. That someone he barely knew could have power over him by such evil insinuations pained him deeply. He wasn't stupid. He knew the recent sex scandals had affected the Catholic Church badly, but he'd somehow felt himself inoculated from them because of his work in the community and the trust his congregation had in him. Moreover, he knew himself. To serve God by serving humanity had always been his innermost desire. And doing what he did, he saw the good, the bad and the depraved in people, God's creation. Yet he chose to continue serving people because, by doing that, he truly believed that he was serving God.

In the end, it came to nothing. The father withdrew his charge and the family packed up and left the neighbourhood. It was agreed by all that it would be best if Father Stephen served in another parish, far, far away from Manchester, where he was. He chose King's Cross because he was told that the kind of people he felt called to serve were there. The episode with the family had been unpleasant, but it confirmed to him where he felt most useful: among the sexually vulnerable, innocent victims of other people's lust and depravity and those who lived and worked on the sexual fringes of society. And so down to King's Cross he came. And had been ever since.

Like Sister Mary, he counted their successes, but he remembered their failures more: the anonymous girls who overdosed and died in crack houses, their bodies interned at the state mortuary. As a matter of course, he conducted the funerals, reasoning that, in death, they would get the dignity they didn't have in life.

He grieved over the teenage girls he saw on the streets, many of them runaways from broken families and at the mercy of their pimps. Lately, he had begun to see a new, worrying trend. Young men, some not more than twenty-one, modelling themselves on the American pimps they'd seen in music videos and the lifestyles of their favourite hip-hop entertainers. These young men set themselves up as businessmen, declaring with relish that they were in the business of sex. In the neighbouring housing estates of King's Cross, Camden Town and Islington, they strutted about with expensive watches, whose names Father Stephen couldn't pronounce and hadn't heard of, and shiny silver jewellery on their persons, which they called bling. He called it crass.

Jungle stood out for a number of reasons. She was not a drug addict. Most street prostitutes were. That she was a teenager was obvious. Even more obvious was the fact that she was one of the Home Office's invisibles. Father Stephen knew a bit of Johnny's history, the bits he told when he partook of far too much alcohol. He was in his thirties, one of the hundreds of children abandoned in the UK by their Nigerian parents in the seventies and early eighties.

Johnny never made any references to family or friends to speak of. He had associates, but that was it. He traded in illegal West African prostitutes, a lot of whom he passed on to his associates in Amsterdam, Madrid and Turin. The women he traded in tended to be practising prostitutes in West Africa. Those who claimed that they had no notion of the work they were coming to do in the UK were soon disabused of their noble ideas of working as waitresses or studying.

Jungle was the youngest and, as far as Father Stephen could see, the only one among Johnny's girls for whom Johnny had–what other human beings might have called–vague feelings. That their relationship was destructive, he had no doubt. He had seen evidence of it himself. Where it was leading, at least for Jungle, was, in Father Stephen's eyes, clear. Sooner or later, something or other was going to break in their relationship. And in the aftermath, Jungle would need someone there for her. He, Father Stephen, together with the Religious Sisters, were determined to be there when it happened.

*   *   *

Father Stephen heard the banging and turned over, determined to convince himself that the banging was in his dream. All he had to do was wake up for a few seconds, make himself more comfortable on the bed and he would be back in dreamland– no getting out of bed necessary. Then he thought he heard Jungle's voice and, in a flash, he was out of bed. He peeped out of his window and there she was, banging on the Sanctuary's front door and crying like a madwoman.

He was out of his room and at the front door in seconds. He let her in and she fell into his arms, crying.

"I think I've killed him," she said.

Father Stephen led her into the kitchen and sat her down. He called Sister Mary on his mobile and she joined them from the Religious Sisters' quarters across the courtyard, a few moments later. She was just about adequately dressed. He made them both cups of steaming hot chocolate. Jungle was shivering. There was a large cut on the right side of her lip and bloodstains on her bare arms. Father Stephen managed to get the studio flat address from her, left her with Sister Mary and raced down in the car to Camden Town.

The studio flat door was still open. Father Stephen let himself in. Johnny was sprawled on the floor, unconscious, blood dripping from a huge gash on his forehead. The studio flat was in disarray. The bedding and the mattress were half on the floor. Further evidence of a scuffle could be seen in the sheared pieces of Jungle's clothing he saw on the floor.

Johnny groaned and his head rolled to the side. Father Stephen paused for a while, undecided. He didn't want to call the police. Jungle might get in trouble. He dialled nine-nine-nine and waited for the ambulance to come. When it did, barely five minutes later, he got inside the ambulance with Johnny and they sped away to the Royal Free Hospital. At the hospital, he declared himself Johnny's parish priest and then waited while they wheeled him away. While waiting for the doctor's prognosis, he made a call to the Sanctuary. Sister Mary told him that Jungle had fallen into exhausted sleep. He told her that Johnny was alive. He couldn't tell her any more than that.

"Father, what shall we do?" Sister Mary's question was a loaded one.

"We'll take it one day at a time. That's what we'll do," Father Stephen said.

Sister Mary knew him well. That was his way of saying that he didn't have a clue.

*   *   *

The throbbing pain in Johnny's head brought him from the abyss of a comforting, dreamless sleep back into the land of the living. His throat also hurt. He tried opening his eyes and had to close them again as the harsh overhead hospital lights seared them. He spied Father Stephen sleeping in an uncomfortable-looking chair by his bed. The events of everything that brought him to the hospital started flooding back to Johnny.

"Water," he whispered through painful, cracked lips.

Father Stephen got up immediately and called for a nurse. She came and fussed over Johnny and gave him a small glass of water, which he downed quickly.

"Easy now," the nurse said. "Don't want to do too much just yet." But she took the glass from him and scurried away, presumably, to get him a refill.

"She's not getting away with it," Johnny said in the silence that followed.

"Try to have a good night's rest. Well, what's left of the night anyway and I'll be back in the morning," Father Stephen replied.

"She's not getting away with it," Johnny repeated. He then closed his eyes and ignored Father Stephen who watched him with something akin to intense dislike and morbid fascination.

"Johnny…"

Johnny screwed his eyes tight and attempted to move his head away from the Father, with limited success. He couldn't stop the groan of pain that escaped his lips.

"I'll be back in a few hours, Johnny," Father Stephen said and he left the hospital. He walked back to the Sanctuary, one question raging through his mind. *What should I do, Lord? What should I do about Jungle?*

Thirty-six

When Nike left law school, she had radical ideas about how she would change the world as a human rights lawyer. She saw herself as the female equivalent of Kofi Annan but with more powers. She had wild fantasies of herself disembarking from planes in the remotest and most dangerous parts of the world, surrounded by nodding acolytes and desperate people, all with their arms outstretched towards her, begging for help. She had visions of herself walking into international criminal tribunals and seeing her legal nemeses quavering in fear.

Yes, Nike had many dreams. What she got in return was a job as children's safeguarding officer in the local council and unofficial social worker to the underage sex workers and older women that Father Stephen and Sister Mary came in contact with through their outreach work in King's Cross.

She called him Father look-into-my-eyes. He had the knack of making her do what he wanted by telling her to think of the bountiful rewards her Father in heaven had stored up for her. When she would reply, increasingly sharply these days, that she would rather have her treasures on earth, Father Stephen would laugh and tell her to trust God.

It drove Nike mad. It drove her husband, who was the more religious of the two of them, even madder. Still, they kept on giving in. Presumably, because the lure of eternal heavenly riches was too much for either of them to resist.

When her mobile went off at six a.m. on a Monday morning, Nike ignored it and turned over. She knew who it was because she'd set the person a special ringtone. Her husband yawned and spoke sleepily.

"That's Father Stephen," he said.

Nike put the duvet over her head. The mobile rang again, demanding to be picked up. Nike lifted her head from underneath the duvet and groaned. She grabbed the phone from the bedside table.

"Father Stephen…" she started, intending to give him a verbal dressing-down.

"Nike, I need you at the Sanctuary. It's bad. It's that Nigerian girl I told you about–Jungle."

"Father, is she alive?"

A dead body was the only reason she would head to the Sanctuary at that time of the morning, she told herself.

"Nike." Father Stephen's voice rang with religious authority. "I want you to be at the Sanctuary within the hour."

Nike was immediately contrite. "Yes, Father."

"I'll drop you off," her husband offered when he saw her face.

When they got to the Sanctuary, they were shown to the kitchen. There was an extremely thin girl sitting at the table, nursing what seemed to be a mug of hot chocolate. Her eyes were clear, but her face bore the marks of a rather recent beating. She was wearing an oversized hooded grey sweatshirt with grey tracksuit bottoms.

"Hello. I'm Nike," she held out her hands, taking the seat next to her. Jungle did not take the proffered hand.

"I'm not going back," she said.

"Jungle…" Father Stephen went round to where she was sitting and stood next to her.

Not too close, Nike saw, which was good. But then, this was Father Stephen; he knew his stuff.

"My name is not Jungle," the girl said.

Father Stephen and Nike looked at each other. Nike signalled to Father Stephen and Sister Mary to leave the room. They left. Nike moved her chair a bit closer to the girl.

"I'm here to help you and nobody is going to make you do what you don't want to do."

The girl started crying.

*   *   *

"So?" Father Stephen and Sister Mary crowded anxiously around Nike, when she came out of the kitchen.

"Nothing," Nike said.

"That's all you've got? You've been there for an hour!"

Sister Mary shot Father Stephen a look that told him to restrain himself. Nike signalled to them to move away from the kitchen door. The three of them moved closer to the front door.

"Well, I couldn't really say nor do anything. She just cried and kept saying that she wasn't going back. That if anybody tried to make her do anything she didn't want to do, she would kill them all."

There was a silence.

"And she spoke in Yoruba throughout," Nike added. "Just as well that I understood."

"Strange. Well, that's a first," Father Stephen said. "What do we do now?" He looked at his watch and sighed. "I've got to go to the hospital. The guy she tried to batter to death is still there. It's more than likely he'll be discharged today. If that is the case, he's coming here. He knows she's here."

"That's her pimp?" Nike asked.

Father Stephen and Sister Mary nodded.

"Do the police know about this incident?"

"Of course not. I didn't report it. Actually, it's a bit complicated. She's an illegal. I didn't know what would've happened to her if I had called the police," Father Stephen replied.

"You don't make it easy, do you, Father?" Nike said. "Tell you what, we'll leave things as they are and I'll come back later today to talk to her. The police can't do anything anyway. She's under sixteen. That makes her a child and a minor. That fact alone takes precedence over her immigration status. In any case, let's wait and see if the pimp does or says anything. If he decides to press charges…"

At this, Sister Mary snorted. Nike carried on speaking.

"It could well happen. We must be prepared. If he decides to lodge a formal charge of assault against her, there's nothing we can do. Is there any way I can get some information about this girl, anything at all?"

Nike saw the look on both their faces and sighed in defeat. It was going to be a long day. She bid them goodbye and walked out into the biting February air. Father Stephen and Sister Mary tiptoed to the kitchen door and opened it an inch. They peered through the opening. Jungle was staring into space.

*   *   *

Johnny looked better. His two days of enforced stay at the hospital clearly helped, Father Stephen noted. Even the swelling on his face had gone down. He drew up a chair by Johnny's bed, happy to sit until Johnny decided to talk to him.

"She's mine. As soon as I leave this dump, I'm going round there and I'm going to get her."

"She's not yours. She doesn't belong to you."

Johnny gave Father Stephen a pitying smile. "Nobody does this," he pointed to his face, bruises and the bandage around his temple, "and gets away with it. *Nobody.*"

"Let it go," Father Stephen said.

"I think you should mind your own business. You know what? I think you want her for yourself," Johnny sneered.

A wave of revulsion came over Father Stephen. "She's under sixteen. I could report you for statutory rape."

At this Johnny smirked, or as possible as it was for him to smirk with his bruises. "Prove it. I doubt she knows her own age and let's not forget, she's an illegal. How can you report someone that doesn't exist?"

"Of course she knows her age."

Johnny tried getting up from the bed. From his chair, Father Stephen watched him for a few moments before going to him. Johnny motioned for him to plump his pillows. He sank back in evident relief when Father Stephen finished.

"She came here on a false passport, using a false name. She was illiterate, and even now she can barely read. And what I know of where she comes from, birth certificates are not exactly de rigueur. So tell me, *Father*, how do you report someone has been raped when, technically, they do not exist in the eyes of the law? Let's see: You don't know the person's age, real name and, hmmm, let me think… How does Jungle feel about you reporting this statutory rape thing that you want to report?"

Father Stephen looked at him with intense dislike.

"Perhaps *I* should take her to the police. After all, *she* was the one who assaulted me with a baton," Johnny continued.

Father Stephen made movements to leave.

"When you see her, tell her I said it's not over. I'm coming over there to get her and I will give her a taste of her own medicine. She can't hide from me. She knows that."

Johnny's voice bounced on the priest's receding back. Father Stephen was thinking, *Lord, speak. What should I do?* When he got back to the Sanctuary, Nike was waiting for him.

"Any progress?" he asked her.

Nike shook her head. "She wouldn't talk. Or eat."

Father Stephen nodded wearily. Somehow, he hadn't thought that Jungle would make it easy.

*   *   *

She could still hear her mother's voice as if it was yesterday.

Don't say or do anything that would bring shame on me and your father. Going to London is a big deal. Not everyone gets to go. Behave yourself and don't bring shame on Uncle Femi or the family.

Jungle thought of the videos she'd taken part in with Johnny directing, sometimes taking part in himself. She thought of the last video with the two men and the… She couldn't even bring herself to say it, and she felt an intense revulsion for herself. She let the cold shower run over her head and stood there, thinking it was no more than she deserved. Next, she took the sponge and scrubbed herself raw, hoping to capture some essence of the cleanliness she had when she left Nigeria to come to the UK.

"Jungle, you've been in the shower for thirty minutes. Are you okay?" It was Sister Mary.

She came out of the shower, shivering, and wrapped the towel around her. She opened the bathroom door. Sister Mary took one look at her and held out her arms. Jungle shivered and went into them. She wept.

*   *   *

Jungle reached out for the door handle. It was time to leave. She didn't belong in the Sanctuary. It was for good, clean people, not degraded people like her. She wished she could've said goodbye to Sister Mary and Father Stephen, but she thought they wouldn't understand. It wasn't her fault. She had to go back to Johnny. She needed him. He was the only one who understood her. She knew he wouldn't be happy when he saw her and would definitely punish her, but she didn't mind. In time, he would forgive her for what she had done. He always did.

She shivered at the draught that came in through the bottom of the front door. Her hand hovered over the door handle and stopped, when she heard Sister Mary's voice behind her.

"Jungle, do you think that this is the life your mother envisaged for you in the UK? If you do, then go back to Johnny and we will pretend the events of the last few days never happened. But if you believe that your life in the UK as it's happened wasn't what she wanted, then Father Stephen, I, and other people will do everything we can to make it right for you."

Jungle stopped. She didn't like the Sister's familiar use of her mother's name. *She's my Mama, not yours!* she wanted to scream at her. But she didn't. Instead, she hovered by the door. On the other side of that door, she knew, was Johnny. On the other side was Big Madame, Mr Lau, Sam, Papa and everybody who'd taken from her what wasn't theirs to take and sold it to other people, who'd then bought it without further thought as to where their product came from.

On the other side was Johnny who made her laugh and bought her Barbie dolls because he knew that she liked them.

On this side were Father Stephen and Sister Mary, who tried to speak to her for almost two years and never gave up, even when she ignored them all that time.

On the other side was Johnny who dressed her wounds tenderly after beating her and always asked her brokenly, *Why do you make me do this to you?*

On this side of the door were Father Stephen and Sister Mary, who only asked if there was anything at all *they* could do for her. Everybody else had taken from her. In comparison, they wanted to give to her.

On the other side of the door was Johnny who made sure her insides were so damaged that she suffered from crippling stomach cramps and intense migraines. He also took out her womb without her permission because she got pregnant against his wishes.

On the other side was Johnny who she would never see again, if she stayed on this side of the door.

Johnny. Her lover, who filmed her with other men and women because he fancied himself an amateur porn director. He also made her have sex with two men and an animal and, later, made her watch the video to punish her.

Johnny, her boyfriend, who made sure she ate by cooking for her and forcing her to eat, even against her wishes.

She would never see him again. Jungle turned away from the front door, ran past Sister Mary into the study-cum-bedroom she'd been given and lay down, staring at the ceiling. When she got up from the bed an hour later, it was as if she'd been sleeping for a long time and was now awake with a renewed sense of purpose and sadness. The poster of the Madonna and Child on the bedroom wall did little to lift her emotions.

Where were you, she asked the poster, *when all these things were happening to me?* She didn't receive an answer, but she did hear a gentle knock on the door. She told the person to come in. No one had ever asked her permission to enter a room she was in, and here she was, giving permission to somebody to enter a room that wasn't even hers.

Sister Mary came in with a bowl of soup. "I think you'll like this. It's Nigerian pepper soup. I made it myself."

Eyo looked at her.

"I worked in Benin, Nigeria, for a few years. We nuns get around, you know," Sister Mary said with a twinkle in her eyes.

Eyo took the bowl from her and started eating. Sister Mary sat on the edge of the bed and watched her intently.

"Jungle, it will be all right," she said.

"My name is Eyo. Jungle is dead," Eyo replied. She continued eating and, when she finished, she gave the empty bowl back to Sister Mary and went under the duvet. She slept immediately.

When she woke up, she summoned Sister Mary and told her she was ready to talk.

*   *   *

Nike was a social worker and something of an immigration expert. It came with the job. Being Nigerian also helped, as a large percentage of her clients were Nigerians. However, Jungle's case had her professionally stumped.

These were the facts Nike managed to piece together: Jungle, aka Eyo, was brought to the UK some years ago by somebody. She was barely literate. She had some idea of her age but was not sure. She was brought to the UK, using a false passport—that much was certain. To do what, Nike was not sure, but she narrowed it down to two things: being a maid or a sex worker, with or without her knowledge. At some point, she was abandoned in the UK and the girl decided to revert to the oldest trade in the world to make money. Knowing she needed protection of some kind, she put herself under Johnny's guidance. Which brought Nike to another question: How did Jungle meet Johnny?

Nike sighed. If only Jungle would talk. There were so many gaps that needed to be filled. Nike wasn't scared of Johnny. She came across dozens of men like him in her work. No, she wasn't scared of Johnny.

As a Nigeria-born social worker, Nike took her work rather personally. Perhaps because most of the children she saw were from her part of the world, and she, maybe more than her colleagues, saw it as a personal duty to get justice for the children referred to her. She knew of Jungle because Father Stephen had told her about her. He did this whenever a Nigerian and other Africans appeared on the street, plying their trade.

Nike's mobile phone rang and she picked it up. It was Sister Mary.

"I think you better come down to the Sanctuary," she said.

Nike grabbed her keys.

Thirty-seven

At first, Eyo spoke hesitantly, slowly and, at times, painfully. While she talked, she kept her face down, wrapping her hands tight around the mug of hot chocolate she was drinking. Sometimes, when she spoke, it was as if she was talking about somebody else. And indeed, she sometimes felt like she was talking about somebody else. It didn't seem possible that she, Eyo–an inhabitant of Ajegunle, the most notorious slum in Lagos, born to Olufunmi and Wale Adegbite–had really come to the UK to work and get an education. It seemed impossible that she instead found herself doing sex work, was now in a church refuge and was on the run from a man she'd tried to kill, a man she would certainly have gone back to this morning, if Sister Mary hadn't stopped her.

When she finished, there was silence all around the kitchen table. Eyo looked down, refusing to meet anybody's eyes.

Father Stephen gestured to Nike with his eyes. She followed him outside the kitchen. "What do you think?" he asked her.

"Well, I don't think we need to worry about Johnny any more. I've got an idea. You go and tell him that you've conducted dental tests on Eyo, which confirm that she's under sixteen. If he starts blowing off on the fact that she's an illegal, that she assaulted him with a bat and that he will press charges against her, explain to him that statutory rape is statutory rape, regardless of one's immigration status.

And if he has any ideas about reporting her illegal status to the Home Office, you tell him you have every intention of reporting him to Her Majesty's Revenue & Customs for living off immoral earnings and not declaring the income. How's that?"

"Sounds good. What about Eyo?"

Nike paused to think. "I'm not sure. We have to find out what she wants. Does she want to stay here in the UK or does she want to go back to Nigeria? If she goes back to Nigeria, would she still be accepted by her family? And what about the family she stayed with when she first came here? I would like to find out more about them. I have many questions, such as how come nobody noticed a ten-year-old girl living with them for almost two years? Like I said, there's a lot to do, but it all starts from one thing: What does Eyo want? Once we find out, then we can start figuring out what we're supposed to do."

They both nodded in agreement at each other and went back to the kitchen. Sister Mary looked up when they both came in.

"She wants to know what will happen if Johnny comes looking for her," she said.

Father Stephen sat down on the chair close to her. "Nothing will happen," he said firmly. "And I don't think that you'll need to worry about Johnny any more. He's history."

Eyo tried to smile with confidence. They didn't know Johnny.

Nike went back to her office and started making some calls. After two hours, she was forced to admit defeat. There were no available beds in safe houses, for Eyo. The government safe houses roster for trafficked women was oversubscribed, with a long waiting list. She tried calling every agency, organisation and charity she knew all over the country and the answer was the same: no beds. They couldn't put Eyo up in a residential hostel because she was deemed at risk, but Nike refused to give up. At four p.m., she left the office and went for a short walk around the block. When she got back to the office ten minutes later, she went through her messages and put her head in her hands. At seven p.m., after a few more hours of fruitless and frantic telephone calls, she packed up for the day and went back to the Sanctuary to deliver the bad news.

"She'll have to stay here then," Sister Mary said.

"What about Johnny?" Nike asked.

"I think he'll be in the hospital for another day or two. He's pretty much jacked up on painkillers, so we have another day of grace at the very least," Father Stephen replied.

"How is Eyo?"

"Fine," Sister Mary answered. "She hasn't said much since this afternoon. She sleeps for a while, has some food, then goes back to sleep again."

"At least she's eating," Nike said. "She is way too thin."

*   *   *

Eyo looked through the window and into the busy London streets. Somewhere out there was Johnny who was going to come for her.

She wanted him to. She missed him and she wanted him back. He was her only friend in the UK, the only person who'd ever really understood her. He did not judge her for who she was and what she did. People like Father Stephen and Sister

Mary didn't understand. How could they? She looked away from the window and found herself facing the picture of the Madonna and Child. It made her think of her mother and Sade. It also made her think of her father alone with Sade.

Watch over my sister, Eyo implored the Madonna silently. Above the picture was a Christ figure nailed to a cross. Eyo averted her eyes away from him and went back to the Madonna. She looked through the window again, wondering when Johnny would come for her. She fell back on the bed. She hoped that he would come soon.

Downstairs in the kitchen, Father Stephen and Sister Mary thought about the next course of action to take.

"Well, she's going to have to stay here then," Father Stephen said.

"I made a few calls and Chelsea Abbey is more than willing to take her in," Sister said.

"You knew Nike wouldn't find any available beds in the government safe houses, didn't you?"

"The Lord knows that we would rather have her somewhere we can keep an eye on her. Chelsea Abbey is His way of saying He agrees with us," Sister Mary said, a naughty smile on her face.

Chelsea Abbey was one of a handful of convents left in central London. He wasn't surprised when Sister Mary mentioned it. He agreed with her that he would rather Eyo went to the convent than to the safe houses. Nike calling and rallying round the safe houses to take in Eyo was just protocol. They had both known the outcome.

An hour later, Eyo was packed and ready to go. As she

bent down to enter the car, she looked around as if looking for somebody and asked, "What about Johnny?"

Sister Mary gave her a gentle push inside the car and followed her in before shutting the door firmly behind them. "You don't need him anymore, Eyo," she said gently.

They both waved goodbye to Father Stephen and the car drove away, at first slowly, before picking up speed. In the back seat, Eyo turned around. Her last image of Euston was of Father Stephen watching them as the car sped away. She turned around and watched the passing traffic on her left. Johnny was out there somewhere, probably looking for her. She knew enough now about Sister Mary and Father Stephen to know that behind their compassionate and gentle façade lay resolves of steel. If he came looking for her at the Sanctuary, they would never say anything.

Sister Mary looked ahead. "Not long to go now," she said.

A tear fell down Eyo's cheek. She didn't bother wiping it away.

The
Emancipated

Thirty-eight

The convent was situated right in the middle of central London, although you wouldn't know it as it was secluded. Eyo woke up each morning to the sound of the first prayer of the day: Reading and Morning Prayer. She would lie in bed and listen to the nuns pray.

At first, she didn't do much except eat and sleep. For the most part, she was left alone. The head of the convent was Mother Superior, a lady with discerning eyes and a habit of looking at people, as if she could see inside their souls.

Eyo avoided her for the first few days, preferring her own company, which wasn't hard to do in a convent. Then she got bored and listless. She found herself getting agitated and angry. She didn't understand why she was cooped up in the convent. She wanted to go out. She wanted to see Johnny. She wondered how he was doing and who was taking care of him. The thought of Daisy being at the studio flat filled her with rage. It was her flat, not Daisy's. Johnny had rented it for her, not for drug addict Daisy. She wore down the long convent corridors with her furious steps. She stayed in the cloistered gardens for hours at a time, doing nothing, or thinking. A week after she arrived at the convent, just when she thought she would go mad with boredom, pent-up anger, her own company and missing Johnny, she was summoned to Mother Superior's office.

Mother Superior gestured to her to sit down. She put her glasses on and looked at Eyo intently. "So, Eyo, have you decided what you want to do?"

"I want to get out," Eyo said. "I'm tired of being here."

Mother Superior leaned back in her chair and took her glasses off her face. She stood up and reached out her hand towards Eyo.

"Come," she gestured.

Eyo followed her. She led Eyo out of the office and into the garden. She located a bench and sat down, slightly out of breath. Eyo sat with her. In the wintry February air, there wasn't much in the garden by way of flowers. The air was still, with only the faint singing of the nuns to shatter the silence. Eyo realised that this was the only instance in all her time in the UK that she'd ever felt the silence.

At the Sanctuary, she could still hear the doorbell being rung and Sister Mary going up and down the corridor outside her room, making sure she was nearby in case Eyo needed anything. Here, there was nothing but silence. When she first arrived, it was soothing, but it was now chafing her. She wondered what she was doing here when all she wanted was to be with Johnny, sleeping with up to ten men a night, who paid Johnny her boyfriend, protector, lover and bodyguard for the privilege. She pushed the last traitorous thoughts away.

"You are not the first to come here, but I'm going to ask you what we always ask the girls who do come," Mother Superior said.

Eyo turned to her expectantly.

"What do you want to do?"

Home, Eyo thought. *I want to go home to Jungle City, to Mama, Lanre, Sade and Mama Fola.*

She told Mother Superior.

"That's all I need to know," Mother Superior replied. They continued sitting on the bench, wrapped up against the chilly weather.

Eyo thought of her father waiting for her in that dark room in Jungle City. She pushed all thoughts of him from her mind. Just as she tried to push away all thoughts of Johnny.

*   *   *

Nike waited in Mother Superior's office for Eyo. It didn't matter how many times she came to the convent, it never failed to surprise her how far removed it seemed from the madness of central London. The door opened and Eyo came in. She looked better already. She had filled out a little, even though her arms were still rather thin. Her face didn't seem so drawn and her cheeks had a bit of colour. The bruises she sustained from her clash with Johnny were also fading. As she entered the room, Eyo offered Nike a hesitant smile. Nike nodded approvingly. Sister Mary was right to bring her here.

Nike gestured to the sofa and they both sat down. "You okay?" she asked Eyo.

Eyo nodded. Nike became brisk. "I just wanted to update you on a few things that have happened since you came here. Johnny did come back to the Sanctuary, demanding to see you and threatening to report you to the police for assault, but Father Stephen took care of it. You will never see him again, which is not a bad thing, don't you agree?"

Eyo nodded. She wasn't sure. Johnny had been a part of her life for almost two years. She wasn't sure she could let go of him so easily. She didn't even know if she wanted to let go of him. but she would try. If she was going back to Nigeria, she knew she had to go without him. She wanted to ask Nike how he was doing but restrained herself. Not for the first time, she wished she had money or a mobile phone to call him. To find out how he was. To say sorry. To tell him that she missed him and was coming back. But she didn't have money or a mobile because Johnny took everything. *She was his*, he said. He didn't want her to call up other people or hide things from him. Eyo didn't think she could ask Mother Superior for money either. Somehow, she didn't think she would approve if she called Johnny.

Nike watched the array of emotions flit across Eyo's face. She continued speaking. "I explained to you why we brought you here. It's safe and Johnny would never find you, plus we thought you needed somewhere to think, away from all the noise and people that you knew, so that you could make a decision on your own about the next steps you want to take. Lovely, isn't it?" Nike swivelled her head around the room and carried on speaking without waiting for a response from Eyo.

"Mother Superior has told us that you want to go back to Nigeria. Based on that, this is what we're going to do. We are going to arrange for you to go back to Nigeria, but before we do that, there are certain things that need to be done. Quite a lot actually. We need to get you a passport. Your case has also been passed on to a few agencies, including the Home Office, Social Services and even the police. They want to find out more about the people you told us about: Sam and his family, Big Madame…" Nike held up her hand when Eyo started speaking.

"I promise you that you'll be safe. And even if you don't want to, they will still try to find those people because they've done some terrible things. Not only to you but to other people. If they're not stopped, they will keep on doing it."

"I don't want any trouble," Eyo said quietly. "I just want to go back to Nigeria."

"There won't be any trouble, I promise. You've already said that all you want is to go back to Nigeria. That makes things easier. Some people have been through far worse than you at the hands of people like Big Madame, and they cannot go back home. Still, they remain in legal limbo because of the immigra…"

Nike stopped herself just in time. This was not the time for a political speech. She peered at Eyo. She had a lost look on her face. Nike wondered what she was thinking.

Eyo was thinking of her mother. She wondered if she would recognise her. She also wondered if she even knew the way back to their face-me-I-face-you in Ajegunle. For all she knew, they might have moved or, most likely, been chucked out by the landlord for not paying rent. If that was the case, how would she find them in that sprawling city of Lagos?

"It's peaceful here, isn't it?" Nike said.

Eyo nodded. She heard the small bell summoning the nuns to prayer. She glanced at Nike as if asking for permission to go. Nike nodded and Eyo left the room.

Nike went back to her office, her mind a whirl of activity. Social Services had an interest in Eyo. Eyo didn't know where Sam's family lived because she had been locked up in the house for pretty much the two years she was there. But from the descriptions she gave, Nike was pretty certain it was Clapton, an area of east London she knew well. Eyo had mentioned a few landmarks which she intended to check out herself, even though it was out of her professional jurisdiction. She worked for Camden Council, which covered an area of north London, while Clapton fell under Hackney Council, a sprawling London borough that covered a swathe of east London.

Hackney Council were interested in Eyo because she was an underage child who had lived in their borough for almost two years without going to school and had suffered unimaginable cruelty, and they hadn't known about it. It did not make them look good. If news of it ever got out, they would take a battering from the media and public together. Remedial action was needed. And fast.

The Home Office was interested in Eyo because she was an underage child who was effectively trafficked into the UK right under their noses. This did not make them look good either. It would suggest that the training given to their immigration officers at the port of entry was inadequate. It had to be, if a ten-year-old girl was brought into the UK, using a false passport, and they hadn't spotted it.

All the child protection agencies—the good, the bad and the media-hungry—were interested in Eyo because hers was a good story. It had all the elements of a tragic drama that they could use to point out the deficiencies in the government's immigration and child protection policies.

In a nutshell, everybody wanted a piece of Eyo. Nike knew that it was only a matter of time before everything exploded and the media scrum began. Before it did, she, Father Stephen and Sister Mary had to come up with a plan to keep Eyo out of the media glare and protect her.

Nike wasn't sure that was possible.

*　　　*　　　*

In the chapel, Eyo sat down and allowed the haunting Gregorian chants to wash over her. It was very different from the church services that she attended with her family back in Jungle City. Back then, she had never really thought about God. Church was something they did on Sundays. It was what everybody in Lagos did on Sundays. People did religion without giving it a name.

Eyo lifted her head. Right above the altar was a cross with a Christ figure nailed on it. As was customary, she averted her eyes from it and turned to the picture of the Madonna and Child instead. In that picture were her mother and Sade.

The nun's prayers washed over her. Suddenly, she felt alone and lonely. She wanted Johnny more than ever. If she went back to Nigeria, she would never see him again.

> *Glory be to the Father*
> *And to the Son*
> *And to the Holy Spirit.*

So many men, so many faces. She didn't often think of all the men she'd had sex with. Johnny did. He had a game he called, *How many men has Eyo had sex with?* He would start in a quizmaster's voice, *Hundreds? Thousands? Tens of thousands?* And then he would finish by saying that he was the only one who cared for her. Sometimes, he would talk about Sam, Mr Lau and the other men at The House. He would say things that she had never told him about, but she knew he got from Big Madame. He would even make her recreate some of the things she did with Big Madame's clients, with him. A lone tear fell down her cheek. She leaned forward and rested her head on the pew in front of her.

As it was in the beginning
   Is now
      And ever shall be
World without end.

She brushed the tear away and lifted her head. The cross was still there and the Christ figure was still on it.

I didn't ask to be born, she thought. *I didn't ask for all those things to happen to me. Why did You allow it?*

The figure on the cross did not answer.

Eyo leaned back on the pew. So many men, so many faces, none of whom she wanted to remember. Especially in a chapel. She had done well, using the robot technique to blank out all the things of the last five or six years. She had often thought back to her journey to the UK. Uncle Femi teaching her to flush the loo, with pride in his voice.

You see: no more shalanga *for you. This is what you'll be using in London. Just like on television!*

He was so proud to teach her and tell her that stuff.

The first time she slept on a bed was when she went to Big Madame's and it was with a client. It wasn't until she appeared at the Sanctuary and Chelsea Abbey that she could say she had a bed to call her own. Sometimes, she wished she could go back to her life in Jungle City, sleeping on the floor.

A still silence had descended on the chapel. Eyo kept her head bowed. When she lifted it up again, she faced Jesus on the cross.

A man, just like the others who'd hurt her.

But not Father Stephen. He hadn't asked her for anything. Eyo remembered one night he came up to her, trying to speak to her. Instead of her customary icy reception, she resolved to get rid of him once and for all. She disrobed in front of him, right there on the street. Johnny had laughed. "That's my girl!" was what he had said.

Eyo didn't know what she expected, but Father Stephen hadn't said anything. He merely averted his eyes and walked over to the next girl on the patch.

"Come on, Father! I know this is what you want! You're a priest! You're all alike!" she called out after him, with Johnny's encouragement.

The next night, he came back. It was as if the events of the previous night hadn't happened. Eyo had thought about disrobing again but changed her mind. Somehow, she knew that she would get the same reaction from him as before. So she reverted back to what she usually did when he tried to talk to her: She ignored him. Still, he kept on trying to talk to her.

That was Father Stephen. Johnny had always said that he was the only person who cared for her. He didn't care about her past or what she did. He *understood* her, he said, and the life they lived. Father Stephen had understood her life but hadn't flinched away from her. He didn't join her in her filth but had stretched his arm to steady her. He was ready to haul her out, if she so desired. Johnny had wanted her to stay in the filth because it would have been more lucrative for him.

Johnny didn't love her. He had owned her and used her as he saw fit. And she had loved him—*still* loved him—for it.

Eyo looked up at the cross and at the Madonna and Child. The tears started falling harder. She let them come.

*   *   *

Father Stephen hung up his mobile with a distinct look of distaste on his face.

"Johnny?" Sister Mary asked.

Father Stephen nodded.

"He doesn't give up, does he?"

"He soon will," Father Stephen said with an emphatic move of his head.

"What about the other girls he has with him?"

"Let's take it each day at a time," Father Stephen responded. They smiled at each other with the easy familiarity of old friends.

Sister Mary was right to ask and Father Stephen shared her concern for Johnny's other women, but somehow–call it gut feeling–he thought the girls were safe. Johnny would probably run roughshod over them for a few days, taking out his frustration over Eyo on them, but that would be it. He wouldn't be so stupid as to kill them or anything. He had a very healthy sense of self-preservation, Johnny had.

"I saw Daisy last night. She came at me with one of her heels, when I was talking to one of the girls," Sister Mary said.

"We need to keep a closer eye on her. Her drug intake has spiralled up, since Eyo disappeared."

Sister Mary nodded in agreement. "The girls said that Johnny had moved on to another girl. Daisy is not taking it well. Dear Lord, what a waste." She sighed heavily.

A companionable silence followed.

"I didn't think she would come to us," Father Stephen said after a while. Sister Mary knew he was talking about Eyo.

"Remember how we would try to talk to her? Just talk, you understand? And she would ignore us, blank us out completely. It was like we weren't there. Remember?"

Sister Mary gave a short laugh. "Yes. I also remember when she completely disrobed in front of you, on the pavement. At eleven on a Friday night, knowing full well there were people hanging round the pavement."

Father Stephen blushed. "Two years. We spent two years trying to talk to somebody who wouldn't spit on us."

"That's the Lord's work for you. I sometimes wonder what difference we make. We don't give them condoms. We don't preach at them. We don't do anything except talk, buy them cough mixtures and give them soups and beverages to keep them warm. And, of course, we let them know that if ever they needed anything, anything at all, the Sanctuary was there for them. There were times it seemed pointless," Sister Mary said.

"I know. There have been some victories: Eyo, Jane…"

Father Stephen's voice trailed off. They were thinking of the others. The ones who didn't make it. The ones who overdosed and died in their own vomit. The ones they didn't reach. The ones they buried, without anybody coming to their funerals.

"He never said it would be easy," Father Stephen said.

"And yet we persist."

"Because we're stubborn fools."

"No, because He's called us to do it. And, of course, because we're fools."

Across the kitchen table, they smiled at each other again.

Thirty-nine

Eyo held her head low and buried herself deeper inside the car. *If she tried any harder to make herself invisible,* Nike thought, *she would end up on the car floor.* But she didn't voice any of her thoughts aloud, choosing instead to concentrate on the landmarks around them. She spotted what she had been looking for: a local college. Eyo had mentioned a school that was close to a roundabout. She had also alluded to a train station close to the school. She took another look in the rear-view mirror at Eyo and tried not to worry. The girl was not looking good at all. By now, she was crouching on the floor, at the back of the car, taking deep breaths. That was a sign they were getting closer to their destination.

Nike glanced in the mirror again. Eyo had raised her hand and was now pointing at a Nigerian restaurant on the opposite side of the road. She quickly put her hand down again.

"Now please, let's just go. She'll see me. Please, please, let's just go."

There was a hysterical edge to her voice.

"It's okay. You've done well today. We're now going back to the convent. Well done."

Nike turned into a side street, reversed and headed back to the convent to drop Eyo off. After that, she went to her office and turned on her computer. First, she went to the Companies House website. Companies House had records of all registered businesses in England. She typed in Lolly's Delight, the name of the restaurant Eyo had pointed at. It was, as Nike suspected, registered to a home address. She opened up another browser tab and typed in the address into a popular street map portal. She printed out the map to Lola's home address and reached for the telephone.

She dialled a number.

*   *   *

Eyo. Her name had hung over the house like a lingering odour in the three or four years since she had disappeared. Her parents had never really given her an answer as to why she disappeared, brushing off all questions with comments about how difficult Eyo was. In time, Tolu and her brother had stopped asking. Until Tolu ran into her on the bus.

It was Eyo. There was no doubt about it. The defiant flash in her eyes, the thin arms and clear eyes that could chill people with one glance. It was definitely her. When Tolu got home that day, she had been subdued, knowing instinctively that she couldn't tell her parents who she'd seen. Seeing Eyo had brought back memories: Eyo helping out in the restaurant. Eyo sleeping on the mat in the sitting room. The little children who were dropped off at the flat. Eyo's bruised arms and the welts on her back. Eyo on her back, in the middle of the sitting room floor, whimpering. *Her dad* on her, his naked buttocks moving in forceful rhythm.

Yes, there were many memories. None of them made Tolu feel especially comfortable. She had known then that her parents were wrong, that they hadn't treated Eyo well, but she'd chosen to ignore it all because, well, what could *she* do? She was only ten or eleven at that time. The only thing that brought a smile to Tolu's face whenever she thought of those times was the knowledge that she'd taught Eyo to read and write.

She had never stopped thinking about her. Tolu now wondered who the guy Eyo dragged off the bus with her was. Her boyfriend? It didn't seem right. She had also taken into account Eyo's clothes. The skintight jeans and jumper. They screamed, *Look at me! Touch me!* And there was the way the guy was touching her...

Tolu was pondering all this one evening, when the doorbell rang.

"I'll get it," she called out, racing to the front door. She opened it and found herself facing two policemen.

"We're looking for Mr and Mrs Balogun," one of them said.

Tolu's hand went to her throat.

"Tolu, who is at the door? Close it quickly. It's freezing!"

It was her mother, speaking as she came out of the master bedroom. She stopped when she saw the policemen at the front door.

"Yes?" Lola's voice was not welcoming.

"Are you Mrs Balogun?"

Joshua managed to prise himself away from the television. He came to stand by his mother at the open front door. Alerted by the tone in his wife's voice, Sam came out of the bedroom. He was getting ready to start his night shift at the cab company.

"Dad, police."

Joshua's voice was subdued. He held on to his mother's arm. Sam joined them. They formed a semicircle at the door: Sam, his wife and their two children.

"Can I help you?" Sam asked the policemen.

"Are you Mr Balogun?"

"Yes. How can I help you?"

"Mr Balogun, we are arresting you on suspicion of rape. You do not have to say anything, but it may harm your defence if you do not mention, when questioned, something which you later rely on in court. Anything you do say may be given in evidence."

The policeman slammed handcuffs on Sam who was still standing there, dazed. The other policeman turned to Lola.

"Mrs Balogun, I'm arresting you on suspicion of assault..."

Lola didn't hear the rest. Doors were opening in their tower block and people were coming out, looking at them. Shame filled her. Suddenly, she was filled with rage. How dare they do this in front of her children!

"I'm not going anywhere," Lola said. She drew Tolu and Joshua closer to her, as if to shield them from the malignant influence of the policemen.

The other policeman spoke. "I don't think you understand. You're under arrest. You either come with us voluntarily or we call in reinforcements. You choose."

"Eyo." The name escaped Tolu's mouth, before she realised what she had said.

The two policemen gave her searching looks. Mrs Richards, their next-door neighbour, opened her front door.

"How is Eyo?" she asked the policemen.

"Madam, if you will just step back in..." one of the policemen said.

"It's Eyo, isn't it? I knew it. I tried and tried, but nobody paid me any attention."

"Madam, if you could just step back into your flat, it would be much appreciated."

The policeman looked back at Sam. *It's your call,* his look said. Mrs Richards gave the policemen a final, knowing look before going back into her flat. A moment later, the kitchen windows opened out onto the balcony and she poked her head out of the windows.

"I'm not going to the police station," Sam said.

The two policemen stepped back and conferred for a few moments before coming back to stand in front of him. They both started talking into their walkie-talkies, evidently calling for reinforcements.

"Fine. I'll... We'll both come to the station," Sam said quickly. Lola followed his example.

"Look after your brother," she called out to Tolu, as they were led away.

As they went past the window of Mrs Richards, the elderly woman called out loud and clear, so everybody in the tower block could hear her. "I know it's about Eyo. If you need anything else, let me know. I'll be a witness!"

Tolu led her brother back inside the flat and shut the door. She didn't want to talk to anybody or face the nosy neighbours.

"The police... Have mum and dad been bad?"

"No, Joshua. They're helping the police with something," she replied.

Joshua gave a look that told Tolu she hadn't fooled him.

"Why don't you go in the bedroom and play your computer game? I'll make you a sandwich and bring it to you," she said.

Joshua nodded and quietly went inside their bedroom. Tolu made him a chicken sandwich and settled in the sitting room to think. A few hours later, she was awakened by the sound of a key turning in the front door. She jumped up and ran to the door. Her parents came in and gave her a wan smile.

"Mum, Dad, what happened?"

"They released us on bail," her dad said.

"Tolu, go to bed. Your father and I need to talk," Lola said.

Ordinarily, Tolu would've protested but not now. She headed to the bedroom, while her parents walked on legs of lead into the sitting room. She noticed her mother didn't look at her *dad.* When they entered the sitting room, they pushed the door to close it, but it didn't shut properly. Tolu tiptoed back and stood by the opening.

In the sitting room, Lola didn't say much at first. Then she erupted. She knew that, in all likelihood, Tolu would be listening, but she was past caring. She had decided that the ghost of Eyo would be buried once and for all.

"You said you would take care of it. Is this how you take care of things? So now, because you couldn't keep your hands off a young girl, the rest of this family has to suffer. I will not allow you to do this to me or my children, you hear? I won't!" she said shrilly. She collapsed on the sofa and started crying. A creak made her look up. It was Tolu, standing by the door.

"It's about Eyo, isn't it?" she said.

"Tolu, this isn't the time for your nonsense," Sam started.

"No, Dad," Tolu said firmly. "You always do this: brush me off when I want to say something."

She didn't move from the door. Tears started falling down her cheeks. "Dad, I saw you with her. Right on the floor."

Slowly, Lola raised her head. "Tolu, be careful what you're saying."

Tolu sniffed. "No, Mum. I know what I saw. The two of them: Dad on top of her, having sex with her. I saw it all." She started crying even harder.

Lola went to her daughter and shook her violently. "Stop it! Stop it!"

Tolu broke free. "I know what I'm talking about. I woke up one night to go to the loo, and I heard a noise from here. The door hadn't been shut properly. I came in quietly because I was scared and I saw the two of them: Eyo crying and Dad telling her to be quiet. I didn't know what to do, so I went back to the bedroom. I saw you, Dad. I did. Why do you think I've never brought a friend home, since Eyo disappeared?"

Lola gave Tolu a harsh slap. She turned to give her husband a pitying look and left them both in the room without saying a word. She met Joshua in the corridor, looking confused. She ignored him, went to the master bedroom and collapsed on the floor in a heap, sobbing loudly.

*   *   *

A pall descended on the Balogun house. Lola barricaded herself in the master bedroom. Joshua wandered around the flat, wondering why everybody was awake and nobody was talking to him. Sam sat still in the sitting room, refusing to meet Tolu's eyes, choosing instead to stare at the computer.

Tolu left her father in the room. She met Joshua sitting on the floor in the corridor.

"I'm hungry," he said.

"I'll make you another sandwich," Tolu said. It was two a.m. Joshua followed her into the kitchen. Tolu worked mechanically. Bread from bread bin, peanut butter and jam from fridge. She turned on the kettle.

"I'll also make you some hot chocolate," she called out to him. Joshua came to stand by her, watching everything she did.

"Don't worry, Joshua. Everything will be okay," his sister said, although she knew it wouldn't be.

She finished making the sandwich and hot chocolate. She put them both on a tray and gestured to Joshua to follow her to their bedroom. As he ate, licking the peanut butter off his fingers, Tolu thought long and hard about what she intended to do. She ran her fingers through Joshua's hair, earning herself a smile from him. He was such a sensitive child. The best. She wondered what would happen to him, to them both, when she came back from the little expedition she planned to take. She already knew enough about her mother to know that Lola would never forgive her. But then, she, Tolu, had never quite managed to forgive herself for not saying something, when she saw her father and Eyo that night.

As for her father, she didn't have much to say to him. Indeed, since that night she saw him with Eyo, she didn't think she'd had much to say to him at all. Sam had blamed it on her teenage hormones, not suspecting anything, even when she would shrink from hugging him or resisting all physical contact with him. He never suspected anything or the reason why. Or maybe he did and chose not to say anything.

Joshua took a sip of the hot chocolate. "Tolu, can I see Mum?"

"Not right now, Joshua. Maybe later. And don't go disturbing Dad either. He's got a lot on his mind," she cautioned him.

When he finished eating, she took the dirty dishes to the kitchen and washed them. She had an image of Eyo doing this same thing when she was with them. She would jump every time she heard Lola's voice.

"Joshua, I think you should get ready for bed," Tolu said when she went back to the room. She left him to get changed in private and knocked on the door after about five minutes.

"Joshua, you done?" she asked.

"Yes, Tolu," he said.

Tolu went in and took her pyjamas from under her pillow, then she went to the toilet to change. When she went back to the room, she slid under her duvet and sighed.

"It'll be all right, Joshua. I'll make sure we're okay," she said, not really expecting an answer. She knew he would be asleep. He was a fast sleeper, for which Tolu was particularly grateful.

In the morning, she dressed quickly. She then headed for the front door. She took her coat off the clothes rack and called out to anyone who cared to listen. "I'm just popping out to Toni's."

Her mother and father didn't respond. As she closed the front door behind her, Tolu buttoned up her coat, adjusted the hat covering her head and set out for the short walk to the police station. She wanted to give her witness statement to what she had seen her father doing to Eyo all those years ago. She knew that by the time she finished, she would be single-handedly responsible for destroying her family's life. Her life and her brother's would never be the same again. She told herself it didn't matter. That it was the right thing to do.

She kept walking.

Forty

Bola watched the unfolding scenes on the television screen in disbelief. Her friend, Stella, was being marched out of The House, surrounded by policemen, under the glare of television cameras and flashing lights.

"Mark," she squeaked. Mark lifted their one-year-old daughter onto his shoulder and gave her an affectionate pat on the back before joining Bola on the sofa. He turned ashen when he saw Stella. She was wearing large, dark designer sunglasses and expensively cut clothes. Even on television, she exuded class.

She didn't bother replying to the myriad of questions thrown at her by the jostling reporters, preferring instead to give a small smile. As she was herded into a waiting police car, the camera panned to the female reporter.

"Yes, that was Stella Isidomie being taken to the police station earlier today. There are unsubstantiated reports from the police and immigration authorities that Stella ran one of the biggest human trafficking and prostitution rings in the UK and, quite possibly, in Europe. We are also getting reports of a young illegal Nigerian girl who was virtually a child sex slave and prisoner in this house. We understand that the girl, whose name has been withheld to protect her identity, provided some vital information leading to the arrest of Stella who was dubbed *Big Madame*. Back to you, Gareth."

The camera panned back to the studio where the newscaster promised viewers updates on the story as they unfolded. Bola took her daughter from Mark and hugged her fiercely. Stella would never betray her, Bola knew that. She inhaled Sunshine's baby scent and felt tears prick her eyes. At least Eyo was safe. She had always wondered about her.

"What now?" she asked Mark, her face buried in Sunshine's neck.

"We're married now and we have a beautiful daughter with a great name. There is nothing to tie you to that house. Absolutely nothing," Mark said. He took Sunshine from her and changed the television channel.

Bola took the hint. As far as Mark was concerned, the case was closed.

If only, Bola thought. Her mobile phone vibrated a few times and then stopped.

"If that's your no-good brother asking you for money again, tell him enough is enough. Who knows? Maybe one day, he'll actually call you instead of letting the phone ring several times and dropping the call, so that you'll have to call him back. You're too good for him," Mark grumbled.

"Yes, Mark," Bola said, taking the phone into their bedroom.

It was Michael, her husband in Nigeria. The fictitious story she told Mark about Michael being her money-hungry brother in Nigeria made it easy for her to send money home to her children, under the guise that it was for Michael's wife and his children.

Bola dialled Michael's number.

"*Iyawo oyinbo.* White man's wife. How's the UK?" his leering voice came on the line.

"What is it?" Bola had long given up any pretence at niceties with him.

"That's no way to talk to your real husband now, is it?" he laughed at his own joke.

"Can I speak to the girls? Please let me speak to them." Bola hated it when she heard herself speak to him like that, begging and pleading.

"Steady on. They're fine. They keep asking when you'll come back to Nigeria. I dare not tell them that their mother has married a white man and forgotten her family back home."

"You know that's not true," Bola said quietly, her eyes on the closed bedroom door.

"Do I? Do they? Aren't you the one who decided to go to Europe to make money? Maybe I should tell them the kind of job their mother did in Europe. You'd like that, wouldn't you? *Ashewo.* Slut."

Bola let the abuse wash over her. She didn't bother defending herself. That would give him too much satisfaction. She tried to remember when his feelings for her turned into contempt and worked out that it was shortly after she married Mark. She hadn't told him that she had a baby either. Mark had called and told him from the hospital, without her knowledge. He hadn't understood why she had gotten so upset about it.

"He's your brother, Bola, and the only member of your family alive. It's right that he should know that he has a niece," he said.

Bola turned her attention back to the telephone. "Michael, let me speak to my children."

Michael called one of them, the youngest, to the telephone. Pain shot through Bola when she heard her daughter's voice. She would be thirteen now. No doubt she would have started her period already. Without her mother there beside her. Six years. She hadn't seen her two daughters for six years.

"Hello, Mummy." Her daughter's voice brought her back to the present. "We got the stuff you sent. Thank you." Her voice was stilted, like she was talking to a stranger, not her mother.

"And you? How are you?" Bola asked.

"Okay, I guess."

Bola could hear muttering in the background, then someone else came on the telephone. It was her oldest daughter. Bola braced herself for the now familiar emotional onslaught.

"No, Mum, we're not okay. We want you here. Thanks for the things you send, but we would much rather have you here with us." She handed the phone back to their father.

"You hear that, Bola? The children want you back. They don't understand why you would rather stay in the UK and send them money than come back to Nigeria, where we can all be a family again."

"You're the one who wouldn't let them come to the UK. I told you I would've given a plausible explanation to Mark to allow them come and live with me. Even if you don't want to send the two of them, give me one," Bola pleaded.

"You want me to send my daughters to a man I've never met? Don't be ridiculous."

"You're not fooling anyone, you know. The only reason you won't let me have the children with me here is because you know that once I have them, you won't get any more money from…"

"My dear," Michael cut in, "it really doesn't matter whether or not they're here or there. The fact that I know what you're doing and what you've done to stay in the lovely UK…"

"Why are you doing this?"

Michael lowered his voice. "Bola, all I have to do is call the British High Commission here and you're history. *Ashewo*, marrying a man for his passport. Perhaps I should tell the children about the kind of person their mother really is. Perhaps I should tell Mark that his wife and the mother of his brown child is not really his wife. That your marriage is founded on false grounds. That you're a bigamist. Perhaps I should install one of my girlfriends in this house to take care of your daughters, seeing you abandoned them. Perhaps…"

"Michael, you started this. You told me to do it. Why are you behaving like this?" she could feel her voice cracking and hated herself for it. She heard footsteps, then the bedroom door opened and Mark came in, carrying Sunshine.

Bola gathered herself. "Tell your wife I said hello. And my love to the kids." She quickly hung up. Mark joined her on the bed.

"I hate it when you talk to him. You always end up upset, and then I get upset," he said.

Bola took Sunshine from him. Sunshine gurgled and a huge blob of saliva escaped her mouth. Bola wiped her lips tenderly, swallowing the tears that threatened to overwhelm her earlier.

"I know. I'm sorry," she said.

"He's the one that should be sorry. I've said it a million times and I'll say it again: You're too good for him."

No, Mark, Bola thought. *You're too good for me.*

*　　*　　*

It was late at night and Bola couldn't sleep. Finally, she flung the covers off the bed and went into the kitchen to make herself a cup of tea. She took it to the sitting room and sat on the sofa, thinking. She wasn't duly worried about Stella. She knew her friend well enough to know she would come out of *this*, as she called it when Bola texted her, unscathed. As if on cue, her mobile phone rang. It was Stella.

"I'm out on bail. Expensive lawyers are worth it. Things are a bit hot at the moment, so you might not hear from me for a while," she said when Bola picked up.

She sounded the same. Unshakeable. Unflappable. In control. But then, when had Stella not been in control?

"What about the girls? How are they? What about Nkem?" Bola asked.

"The girls are fine. You need not worry about them. They'll say nothing. As for Nkem, they took her away. I don't know where."

She didn't sound too concerned about it either.

"They talked about Eyo on the news."

"They talked about me in the news as well," Stella said and hung up.

Bola sipped her tea, taking stock of her surroundings. She thought back to that night when she and Michael had talked far into the night about her journey to Europe. It seemed like a hundred years ago, not five and a half–six, if one rounded it up.

Mark did reasonably well for a plumber. He had his own business and it was thriving. He was kind and attentive to her, all the things her husband in Nigeria had never been. She didn't love him, but she had grown to tolerate him and appreciate his good nature. He worshipped the ground she walked on and his waking thoughts were for her and Sunshine. He also suffered from crippling shyness, which was the reason he started visiting The House to meet women. One of his friends had recommended it as a classy place.

He never met Eyo in all the time he came to The House. Stella was too careful for that. But he knew enough about her from what Bola told him. When she came back that day to tell him that Stella had taken Eyo down south to London—she couldn't bring herself to tell him that Stella had given her away, like a worthless object, to a pimp—Mark had offered to look for her.

"You don't even know what she looks like, so how will you find her in London?" Bola had asked him.

"I don't know, but if there's a will, there's a way," he had replied.

She knew where he got his kindness from: his parents. They were good, kind people. The kind of in-laws all women wished for. In all respects, she couldn't fault her current life. Sunshine filled the gaps that were missing. So, why did she feel this yawning hole deep inside her? Because try as she might, she couldn't shake off the feeling that the European dream she had established for herself was a poor substitute to the one in her fantasy. The one where she was surrounded by her two daughters at their graduation from a UK university. The one where Michael featured as a beaming father and husband, having battled through the red tape to become a card-carrying British passport holder finally.

The red passport. She still hadn't gotten it. In fact, she was stuck. It was only a matter of time before the Home Office cottoned on to the fact that the passport number she had declared for her marriage papers was a dud. Mark knew about the fake passport. He accepted her story that she had to get a fake one as an asylum seeker to enter the UK. Despite her pleas for him not to bother, he was vigorously pursuing her legal residency in the UK by using the most expensive immigration lawyers money could buy. What the lawyers would uncover about her, Bola shuddered to think. In hindsight, Bola could see that she hadn't thought about her wedding to Mark hard enough. She had been blinded by the possibility that she could get away with marrying him and becoming a legal resident. She had let her ambition and duty towards her family in Nigeria blind her.

She had been incredibly stupid.

Sometimes, she felt cheated. Other times, like tonight, she would lie in bed, unable to sleep, convinced it was only a matter of time, before Mark found out the real reason she married him. Each time she sent money to Michael only seemed to delay that moment that she knew would come. And it would be Michael, the Home Office or Mark's own immigration lawyers who would give the game away.

The day was coming. It was only a matter of time. She took another sip and waited.

Forty-one

Mother Superior hurried to meet her appointment with Father Stephen and Sister Mary. She met them in her office.

"So, here we are," Sister Mary said.

"Where is Eyo?" Father Stephen asked.

"In the chapel," the Mother Superior answered. "She's been spending a lot of time in there lately."

Father Stephen and Sister Mary looked at each other in delight.

"Not so fast," Mother Superior said with a wry smile. "From what I can observe, she seems to glare at the cross a lot and look at the Madonna with a kind of slavish devotion."

"Anyone see the news last night?" Father Stephen asked.

Sister Mary shuddered. "I don't like to think of what went on in that house."

"The phone's been going mad. All the press…" Mother Superior said.

"I wondered about that. Who told them Eyo was here?" Sister Mary asked.

"Who knows?" Mother Superior answered.

She rose to her feet and gestured for all of them to leave the office and head for the alcove, just off the corridor, a few feet away from the kitchen. It was a snug room, with a worn sofa, a few plump chairs and a spectacular view of the garden.

"Eyo likes coming in here," Mother Superior said. "She'll be in shortly after prayers. That's what she usually does."

"That Big Madame on television," Sister Mary said, "She's…"

"A heck of a classy lady," Father Stephen finished for her. "That cool, elegant poise."

Sister Mary pretended to glare at him. They heard the faint ring of the doorbell and feet walking towards the door. Not too long after, one of the nuns popped her head around the door.

"It's Nike," she said.

"Well, send her in here," Mother Superior said. "The more, the merrier."

Nike soon joined them. Pleasantries were exchanged and she got down to business. "I'm assuming you all caught the news of Big Madame?" she began.

Nods all around.

"Good. I wasn't too keen on having all the media there myself for the arrest, but I was told it was all about sending strong messages to traffickers, etc. You know the drift."

They all nodded again.

"Any news of the other young girl in that house? Does Eyo know about what happened?" Sister Mary asked.

"The girl is safe; don't worry. I haven't told Eyo anything about what happened because I'm not sure I should. Let's take it one step at a time," Nike answered.

They all nodded appreciatively. Eyo entered the room. She didn't seem surprised to see them. She went to sit on the sofa next to Father Stephen and Sister Mary.

"Hello," she said to no one in particular.

"Good to see you, Eyo. I'm glad you popped in because I was just going to ask them to get you," Nike said.

She filled Eyo in on the latest events: the police going to Sam, Mrs Richards speaking to the police, Tolu's statement against her father, testifying that she saw him with Eyo. Sam and Lola's arrests and Sam's statement, which gave details of where the police could find Big Madame, her subsequent arrest. Eyo listened to it all in silence. When Nike finished, she was silent, thinking hard.

"I saw her," she said.

"Saw who?" Nike asked.

"Tolu. That night. I thought I saw someone, something, but she… It was gone so quickly, and he kept telling me to be quiet; otherwise, he would hurt me some more."

Eyo also wanted to ask about Bola but didn't want to get her friend in trouble.

"Eyo, have you thought about lodging a formal charge against Sam, Lola and Big Madame?"

"No," Eyo's voice was emphatic.

"It sounds terrifying, but…"

"No," Eyo said again.

Father Stephen caught a hint of the old steely Eyo. He raised his hand to Nike to caution her to be quiet.

"Eyo?"

"Father Stephen, I just want to go home to Nigeria. I don't want any of this. I just want to go back. That's all. That's all I want. To see my mother and siblings," Eyo said.

They all looked at each other.

"And that is what will happen. We won't speak of this again," Father Stephen said.

Nike opened but closed her mouth again, when Sister Mary glared at her.

"Of course," she said.

Eyo looked round the room, at all of them. "Thank you," she said.

Nike stayed for another hour, engaging in idle chit-chat. As soon as was reasonable, she raced back to her office and made a few calls. When she finished, she called Father Stephen.

"I know, Nike. But it's what she wants," was the first thing he said when he came on the line.

"All that work. For what?"

"She wants to go back home and put all this behind her. In any case, the police have enough to prosecute Big Madame, Sam and even Johnny, whether or not Eyo decides to charge them herself. Johnny and Sam for statutory rape and all three of them for living off immoral earnings."

"Father, it's not that simple. I've just got off the phone from the Detective Constable. He doesn't think we have enough to go on to charge Big Madame. Not for trafficking because none of the girls that were taken from The House would testify that she brought them to the UK for sex work. They wouldn't even admit that they did sex work, calling themselves escort agents. Apparently, Revenue & Customs are powerless to do anything because she runs a complicated network of escort businesses and Lord knows what else. That would take years—hear that?—years to untangle. And her company accounts are so thorough and complex that it would take them, again, years to put together and work out what to charge her with. As for the other young girl they saw in The House and who is now in a safe house? Well, it's her word against Big Madame's," Nike said through gritted teeth.

"I figured something like that would happen," Father Stephen said.

"I asked–no, pushed–the detective if he thought Big Madame would be brought to court and he said it was highly unlikely. She had covered her tracks too well. And besides, he said she had extremely good friends in high places."

Father Stephen thought he heard her sniff.

"And Eyo refuses to charge Sam formally. Can you believe this? After all that hard work, everyone gets away. Evil wins," Nike sniffed. She knew she was being overemotional, but she didn't care.

"Evil hasn't won, Nike. Sam's family is broken. His own daughter is willing to testify against him…"

"What do we do now, Father?"

"We leave the matter in the hands of the Home Office, Social Services and the police, and we concentrate on taking Eyo home. That's what she wants. And that is exactly what we will do."

Home

Forty-two

Eyo held on tightly to Sister Mary's arm, as they sat in the airport café, watching the check-in queue with interest.

"Nobody has ever really explained to me why Nigerians carry so much stuff," Father Stephen said, his eyes also on the queue. A family of five was unpacking and repacking their heaving suitcases, in full view of everyone around. The check-in assistant waited, her face unreadable.

"We're a nation of traders," Nike answered him.

Eyo turned her attention away from the queue to the world outside, peering through the clear sliding doors. The sun seemed to put up a fight with the clouds in its bid to give Londoners a glimmer of shine. As she shivered in the cold, she wondered what she would do with her winter jacket, back in Nigeria. Papa would probably pawn it. She stared into her hot chocolate. She didn't want to think of him just now.

"You okay?" Sister Mary enquired, rubbing her shoulders protectively.

Eyo nodded and thought back five or so years ago. She saw herself walking into the Lagos airport with Uncle Femi, gripping his hands tightly in awe, temporarily blinded as it were, by the glare of lights in the departure lounge. Her uncle had told her that there were no power cuts in London, unlike in Lagos. Johnny once told her that Nigeria had the highest number of electrical generators in the world. She didn't know if it was true. It probably was. Johnny knew things.

She had promised herself that she wouldn't think about him. She turned her attention back to the table to find Father Stephen watching her. He probably knew she was thinking about Johnny. She gave him a weak smile and took a sip of her chocolate. Her suitcase was packed with enough chocolate sachets to sink the Titanic.

"You want to go outside for a breather? We've got another ten or so minutes before we hand you over to the airline," Father Stephen said.

"Yes," Eyo said. They both got up and left the table.

"He doesn't want her to go," Nike noted.

"He'll get over it," Sister Mary said. Her voice shook and her eyes glistened with tears.

"What if she's wrong? What if…"

"You don't learn, do you? She's made her choice. Leave her be."

"But…"

Sister Mary's voice was firm. "Nike, let it go."

*   *   *

Father Stephen had good intentions when he woke up that morning. He was going to take Eyo to the airport with Nike and Sister Mary, check her in, pray with her and hand her over to the airline staff. Having an emotional meltdown in front of a child—and Eyo was a child—he was meant to protect was not part of that plan. He commanded his emotions to be still and took hold of himself.

"How about we walk up and down the pavement and get in the way of all these people coming and going?" he asked Eyo, a mischievous grin on his face.

Eyo smiled back at him, her heart heavy. She wanted to commit every feature of his face to memory, ready to retrieve as and when needed in Nigeria. This man and his sidekick, Sister Mary, never once asked her for anything in return for their kindness to her. All they wanted to do was help her, and this sometimes filled her with a sense of unworthiness. She had tried to apologise to them once.

"But you didn't know any better then," Sister Mary had said.

"And you still don't now," Father Stephen had interrupted, laughing.

Eyo got it then. They were telling her that it was okay, that they understood. Most importantly, they wanted her to let it go.

By nightfall, she would be in Nigeria, the country of her birth, the land of her mother and siblings. She would leave Father Stephen, Sister Mary and Nike behind. Probably never to see them again. It was a rather scary thought.

And Johnny. She would never see him again either.

Against her will, he'd intruded on her thoughts again. He was like a spider, his web stretching across London, clawing her back to him. She had money now. She could call him after Nike, Father Stephen and Sister Mary left the airport. She would tell him to come and pick her up and she would wait for him right here on this pavement, outside Heathrow. She was sure he would come. She didn't think he would still be angry with her. He might beat her, though, to teach her a lesson.

Her mind went back to those three days in the flat, with the two men and the dog and Johnny filming it all. No, her mind said. No. I want Johnny. But I don't want that. That was what she was going back to in Nigeria, with Papa and the landlord's predatory eyes. No, her mind said. I'm stronger now. This time, I will not be silent. I will fight back. For Sade. For me. For Mama and for Lanre. For us all.

She clutched the rosary Sister Mary gave her and started reciting furiously. Noiselessly.

Father Stephen patted her head and they kept walking up and down the pavement, getting in the way of people entering and exiting the airport.

*   *   *

When they got back to the table, Sister Mary and Nike were waiting.

"Eyo, it's time to go," Nike said.

To her horror and shame, Eyo started crying. Sister Mary sat her down and murmured platitudes in her ear.

"You're going to see your family. Your mother and siblings. You know there's nothing for you here except two boring, middle-aged, celibate ministers. The highlight of our week is an evening of *Coronation Street*. Is that the life you want?"

"But I like *Coronation Street*," Eyo sobbed.

"I know you do. But we would rather you lived the life God gave you in the real world rather than live it through a soap opera. You have that opportunity now with people who love you. Isn't that what you want? What you've always wanted?" Sister Mary asked, looking into Eyo's eyes, tears falling freely down her own cheeks.

Eyo sniffed. She was being stupid. She ought to be strong. She gathered herself and looked at each one of them. Then she spoke. "I'm ready," she said.

Sister Mary reached out and hugged her. They all started walking towards the departure lounge. They made a strange picture: a teenager, a nun, a priest and a social worker. They joined the queue, ignoring the curious glances from other passengers. At the departure counter, Father Stephen spoke to the officer. The lady dialled a number and, a few moments later, a security guard appeared.

"Look: You even get your own security guard. Just like a celebrity," Father Stephen joked.

Eyo gave him a wan smile, while Sister Mary wished he would be quiet. Eyo took another look at them, recording their faces for posterity. They gathered round her in prayer, Father Stephen placing his hands on her shoulders.

"May the good Lord Himself guide you and keep you safe. Godspeed my child." He kissed her forehead.

They all embraced her.

Then Eyo turned to the security guard. He led her through the gate. She turned back for one final look. They were huddled together. Sister Mary blew her a kiss and Father Stephen made a sign of the cross. Nike's face was glum. Through fresh tears, Eyo flashed a smile and gave them a wave. Then she turned towards the departure lounge. To Sade, Mama and Lanre. To Nigeria.

*   *   *

As the plane began its descent to Murtala Muhammed International Airport in Lagos, Eyo straightened her clothes in a conscious move. It was strange, but she felt more aware of her modestly dressed body than she did while on the streets of King's Cross, London. She reclined on the seat and tried to still her erratic heartbeat. She then looked pensively through the window.

Night-time Lagos was alight with millions of twinkling lights. Even then, she could see huge swathes of darkness: the places afflicted by either power cuts or no electricity at all. Somewhere down there was her family. Eyo felt the urge to stop the plane's descent. She wasn't ready.

The air hostess assigned to her came over. "I'll escort you down to immigration and hand you over to Father Ignatius. When I do that, he will call Father Stephen and Sister Mary for you so that you can talk to them. Is that okay?" She smiled at Eyo.

Eyo smiled back in return and turned her attention to the scene below her. Tomorrow, she would see her mother and siblings. Tomorrow, she would see Papa. She would look into his eyes and find out if Sade got away. That was if she found them. She couldn't even remember where they lived. What if Father Ignatius never found her family?

Her mind was running away with her again. She took a deep breath, just like Sister Mary had told her to do whenever the darkness came. "And remember: You can do everything through Christ," she had added.

"Why do you always talk about Him?" Eyo pretended to grumble.

"Because without Christ, we can do nothing, you impossible child," Sister Mary had replied in mock frustration, as they both laughed.

It hurt Eyo to think of Sister Mary.

The plane bumped and landed. The passengers clapped. A few prayed aloud. Eyo ignored them as she had done throughout the flight. She waited until everyone had disembarked. She then made her way out, with the hostess beside her.

Father Ignatius was waiting for her right by the immigration desk. He was easy to spot, dressed as he was in full priestly regalia. The hostess waved at Father Ignatius, went straight to the front of the queue and handed Eyo's brand new passport to the immigration officer. The officer stamped her passport and handed it back to Eyo. Inwardly, Eyo wondered why. It was unlikely that she would ever use it again.

"Welcome back home, daughter," the officer said, waving her through.

Father Ignatius signalled that they should follow him down the stairs to where people were loitering around an unmoving baggage carousel.

"Father Ignatius, this is Eyo," the hostess said. She turned to Eyo. "Eyo, this is Father Ignatius."

Father Ignatius held up his hand and dialled a number on his mobile. "Hello? Stephen? She's here. Talk to her." He shoved the mobile in Eyo's hand. Eyo held the phone to her ear.

"Hello, Eyo?"

At the sound of Father Stephen's voice, Eyo's eyes welled up with tears.

"Eyo?"

"Father Stephen, I've just met Father Ignatius," Eyo mumbled.

"Good. Remember, Sister Mary and I are praying for you. Father Ignatius will help you find your parents' house. And if you need anything, anything at all, tell Father Ignatius. He's a good man. He knows everything about you, and, listen, he doesn't *care.*"

"Yes, Father Stephen." She handed the mobile back to Father Ignatius.

"Well," the air hostess beamed. "That's my job done."

Eyo had the sudden urge to smash her fist into the air hostess's smiling face. Instead, she pasted a smile on her face.

"Thank you," she said.

"Yes, thank you," Father Ignatius echoed. He turned to Eyo. "Now let's get you out of here. I'll be taking you to one of the mission shelters, where the Religious Sisters live. And tomorrow, we'll begin the search for your parents. We couldn't find the house from the description you gave us, but let's not get into that now. We'll get your suitcase, which–knowing Sister Mary–must be over-packed. She never learns. Ah! The carousel is moving. Come, let's go get your stuff."

They picked up her luggage, went past customs, through the arrivals hall and into the milling crowd outside. The balmy Lagos night hit Eyo hard. She'd forgotten what the climate was like. To think that only this morning, she shivered in the biting cold of London. She walked with Father Ignatius by her side, her eyes taking in the masses of people. Did they know who she was, what she'd done, where she'd been?

A man emerged from the crowd and headed in their direction.

"Here comes the driver. I'll hand him your luggage and let him wheel it to the car," Father Ignatius said.

"Be careful with her luggage," he called out to the driver. "I don't want any backchat from Sister Mary. Be careful!"

Despite herself, Eyo smiled. It felt good to be home.

*   *   *

The next morning, as the jeep shuddered and shook its way down Malu Road, Eyo felt a deep well of excitement within her. She thought she even recognised some buildings, although she wasn't too sure that this was the Jungle City she had left behind. Some of the houses they went past could easily sit in any one of the richer areas in Lagos. They were tastefully painted, with high-end cars parked on the driveways. Bored security guards sat on benches outside towering gates.

The Jungle City she remembered wasn't awash with mobile phones, four-wheel-drive vehicles and a diet of MTV culture manifested in young men's swagger, baggy trousers, and diamante studs. In return, girls did their best to copy singing divas, with skintight jeans, tops and lots of costume jewellery. Maybe Jungle City had always been like this, only she hadn't noticed because the margins of her existence had been dictated by her family and their harsh life.

The area boys were still there, she noticed. Their shifty eyes darted back and forth, looking for any opportunity to fleece innocent victims by any means necessary.

The heat was still unrelenting, beaming down its punishing rays on the Lagos population. Only this time, there seemed to be more humanity constrained into an even smaller space than she remembered. The roads were still marked with boulder-sized craters. Lorries, cars and motorcycles blared their horns intermittently. The air was thick with smoke from the wood-fired stoves of the roadside kiosks, exhaust fumes and burning, uncovered drains. Traders, hawkers, pedestrians and public transport touts screeched loudly to make their voices heard above the din. And it was hot.

From the cool confines of the air-conditioned jeep, Eyo could see the heavy perspiration on people's bodies. The sweat clung to their clothes in damp patches on their backs, armpits and necks. She vaguely remembered their one-room home, the damp humidity and the rancid smell of rotting garbage that permeated it. She shook herself. She wouldn't think about that just yet.

She turned her attention back to the children balancing trays of wares on their heads. It didn't seem possible that she had once done that. Could she walk around Jungle City carrying goods for sale on her head again? She hoped she wouldn't have to. In fact, she didn't think she would. A girl suddenly appeared in front of the jeep, without paying attention to where she was going. Or rather, she was too busy looking at the road she wanted to cross to pay much attention to the jeep coming up behind her. Eyo stopped and looked again.

No, it couldn't be! She tapped the driver urgently on the shoulder.

"Stop the car. Sade!" she called out loudly, scrambling out of the jeep, with Father Ignatius in pursuit. "Sade! It's me, Eyo! I'm back!"

Eyo reached to where the girl was and tried to embrace. At first, the girl shook her off, thinking her to be an opportunist. Cars sped past them, and traffic soon started building up behind the jeep. Cars tooted, but the horns went quiet because of the appearance of Father Ignatius in full priestly regalia. No one would dare be rude to a religious leader in Nigeria.

"Sade! It's me! Eyo, your sister!"

Recognition slowly dawned on Sade's face.

"Eyo!" She dropped her tray and screamed. Behind them, Father Ignatius and the driver waited patiently.

*　　　*　　　*

Olufunmi saw the crowd of people following a jeep emblazoned with a church logo and hissed. *Honestly, people didn't have better things to do*, she thought to herself. She went back into the face-me-I-face-you and came back out again when she heard people shouting her name. The jeep came nearer the bungalow and stopped right in front of her. She saw Sade sitting in the front seat with someone that looked like… Olufunmi's heart skipped. It was Eyo. She gave a shout and ran to the vehicle, tears streaming down her cheeks.

"Eyo!"

Eyo didn't need any reminders. She was out of the car in a flash, shouting, "Mama!"

They fell into each other's arms, laughing and crying.

"Somebody, go and get Lanre at the carpenter's! Tell him his sister is here. Eyo is back home!" Olufunmi shouted. "My daughter!" She embraced Eyo again protectively, as if afraid she would disappear or, worse still, that it would be just a dream. By now, a crowd of people had gathered around, watching them. Whispers of London and Olufunmi's daughter went through the crowd in waves.

Olufunmi became aware of the priest waiting by the jeep. She went to him, each hand holding onto Eyo and Sade. She knelt down in front of him, a traditional Yoruba way of greeting elders and saying 'thank you', when mere words wouldn't do the job. Father Ignatius laid his hands on her shoulder and helped her get up.

"Give your thanks to God. He brought your daughter back," he said.

Olufunmi wiped her tears. The crowd parted as a voice rang out. It belonged to a teenage boy who flung himself on Eyo.

"Eyo!" the boy said. It was Lanre. They both laughed as they embraced.

Olufunmi sniffed and turned around. When she saw the crowd, she bellowed, "*Oya*, right, the show is over. Go back to your homes. Are you deaf? I said everyone should scatter!"

"You are a true Lagos woman," Father Ignatius laughed.

"You don't know what they're like. They're thieves. Thank God, I locked our room door before stepping out. You give it five minutes and a tenant will come screaming that something of theirs has been stolen."

Olufunmi turned her attention to her children, with a wide grin. "God is good. He has redeemed what the Devil had stolen," she said.

Father Ignatius banged lightly on the jeep's bonnet. "Driver, start unloading and stop gawking!"

*   *   *

Father Ignatius left with a promise to come back the next day. As they walked inside the face-me-I-face-you, Eyo noted the dark corridor and the tenants loitering outside their rooms, watching her family as they made their way to their home, the second room on the right, when one came in from the street.

Once inside, Eyo instinctively turned to the right to switch the lights on.

Sade laughed. "Eyo, have you forgotten? We don't have electricity," she said.

Eyo smiled sheepishly.

"But one day, eh, Eyo?" Olufunmi said.

"Yes, Mama, one day," Eyo said.

Nothing had changed. They might have moved to another settlement in Ajegunle but, essentially, this face-me-I-face-you was just the same as their old one. The concrete walls were still unpainted. The wooden planks they laid on the solidified garbage foundation were still there, as was the thin mattress. Mama's pots and pans were still stacked neatly against the wall and, to Eyo's eyes, the ten-by-six-foot room seemed to be even more claustrophobic. It was ten a.m., but the room was dark, although it was broad daylight and blinding hot outside.

I can't live here, she thought. And killed the thought as soon as it came.

She propped her suitcase against the wall and Mama did the same with the other. The room shrank even further in size. Olunfunmi shut the door firmly behind her and turned the lock.

"Nosy thieves," she said.

Eyo smiled and dragged one suitcase towards her. She sat on the mattress and flung the suitcase open.

"See, Mama! Everything in here is for you, Lanre and Sade."

Sade screamed in delight and dived in. Her brother followed suit. He held a football strip against his chest in wonder.

"This is for me?" he asked.

"Of course," Eyo said. He put it on immediately.

"He will never take it off," Olufunmi remarked.

"I didn't think he would," Eyo replied wryly.

Sade held a pair of jeans and a pair of pink, flashing sports shoes. "Oh, Eyo," she said.

"Yes, Sade," Eyo answered. "Wait; there's more," she said. She dragged the other suitcase to the mattress and announced theatrically, "Chocolates from London!"

Sade and Lanre squealed in delight. Eyo turned to her mother and dug into her jeans. "Here's eighty pounds. It's all I have. The London church people gave it to me," she said. Olufunmi's eyes widened. "London money?" she asked.

"Yes."

She took the money from Eyo and smelled it. "It even smells like London," she said.

"Eyo, thank you so much for all this. I will never forget it," Sade said, her mouth full of chocolate.

"Me, too," Lanre said, shoving potato crisps in his mouth.

Olufunmi wrapped her arms around Eyo. "My daughter, you have done well," she said.

Eyo beamed happily. She did not stop to ask herself why she lied to her mother. She still had another twenty pounds sterling lodged deep inside her pocket.

*   *   *

At night, Eyo lay on the sleeping mat, with her sister, trying hard not to think of her unoccupied bed in Chelsea Abbey. The mat was uncomfortable. And the room stank of rotting, foul garbage. The smell went up her nostrils and into the back of her throat, where it lodged itself like a displaced missile.

She wiped her forehead. It was slick with sweat. The dank, humid air hummed with flies. She told herself that it didn't matter; she was home. That was all that mattered. And then she asked the question she'd meant to ask ever since she came. "Mama, where is Papa?"

"He is no longer with us," Mama's voice was flat. "That's why we moved. He and the landlord… I've sent word to Mama Fola. She'll be here first thing tomorrow morning to see you."

Beside her, on the mat, Sade tensed. Eyo turned over and tried to sleep. She also tried not to notice how hard the floor was and how much worse the stench of rotting garbage seemed than she remembered.

She didn't like the direction of her thoughts. She decided to ignore the greasy, unpainted walls and block out the noise from the street outside. She reminded herself that she'd spent ten years sleeping in a house with a doorway that opened out into the street, without worrying about security.

Eyo clenched her legs tightly together. She needed the lavatory but was loath to go to the outback. The thought of getting up, taking the candle, walking down the dark corridor and going to the *shalanga* filled her with dread. She had visions of herself stepping into human faeces in the pit latrine and somehow falling headlong into the pit.

Bile rose in her throat. She breathed slowly, inhaling the humid, swampy, garbage air.

She musn't think of her clean, crisp bed, flushing toilet and pristine bath at Chelsea Abbey in London. She musn't.

"It's not like London, is it?" Sade said softly.

"This is much better than London," Eyo said. She took her sister's hand in hers, lifted it and put it back down again.

"I would have stayed in London and played football," Lanre said.

Forty-three

"Where is she? Where is my daughter?"

The knocking on the door was belligerent. Eyo jumped off the mat—not that she'd slept much anyway—and ran to open the door. It was Mama Fola. They embraced.

"My child! Look at you! Londoner!" There was pride in Mama Fola's voice. And then she started crying.

"I never doubted that you would come back. Your mother did, but I didn't. As for that Femi, the less about him, the better," she sniffed.

Eyo saw a look pass between Mama Fola and her mother.

"Mama Fola, come inside and close the door. These neighbours…" Olufunmi said sharply.

"You can see that she hasn't changed, eh, Eyo?" Mama Fola said, as she came inside the room. She sat on the mattress next to Olufunmi.

Eyo sat on the mat with Sade. Right next to them, on his own mat, Lanre still slept, oblivious to the noise. *Some things don't change*, Eyo thought. Another look passed between Mama Fola and Olufunmi.

"So tell me, how was London?" Mama Fola asked.

Eyo stilled for a moment before replying. "It's very different."

"Of course it is! It's London!" Mama Fola said.

"I still think that I should've gone," Sade said.

"Well, you didn't, so shut up," her mother said.

Sade got off the mat. "I'm going to bathe," she said. She took a half-empty bucket of water nestling against the wall and headed for the door.

"Watch the water. Money doesn't grow on trees," Olufunmi said.

Sade ignored her.

"She's getting worse," Mama Fola said.

Olufunmi shrugged. Eyo went to get one of her suitcases and opened it. She took a nightdress and some underwear and held them towards Mama Fola.

"You mean you remembered your aunty?" she asked.

"Of course," Eyo answered. "And here. This is for Fola." She gave her a Sindy doll.

"You remembered your little sister? Oh, Eyo, this doll is beautiful! It must've cost you so much," Mama Fola said.

"Why don't you just take the girl's gifts and stop asking questions?" Olufunmi said.

"You see, Eyo, that she hasn't changed one little bit?" Mama Fola said.

Eyo smiled at the two of them, wondering how she had survived without their banter for the past five and a half years.

"And the church man is coming back here this morning?" Olufunmi asked Eyo.

"Which church man? When you sent word that Eyo had come back home, you didn't tell me she had become a church wife," Mama Fola said.

"Aunty, it's nothing like that. They just helped me. That's all," Eyo said.

"With what?" Mama Fola persisted.

Eyo chose her words carefully. "Mama Fola, I suffered a lot when I was there. It was the church people who helped me."

"And we won't ask you again," Olufunmi said quickly, watching her daughter's face.

Eyo felt her mother saw and perhaps understood more than she let on. She forced her voice to be light.

"What about Uncle Femi? I would like to see him," she said.

A look passed between Olufunmi and Mama Fola. Olufunmi spoke. "Your uncle is now a big man. We have nothing to do with him and he with us. We entrusted him with you and he abandoned us."

"Mama, it wasn't his fault," Eyo said quietly. "He didn't know…"

"Either way, we are finished with him and he with us. And you will not talk about him any longer in this house. You understand?"

Eyo acquiesced. "Yes, Mama."

Sade came back inside with the now empty bucket, wearing a towel, water dripping from her body. "I've finished," she announced.

Eyo looked at her and thought, *I was her age when they sent me to the UK. Barely a year after, I was servicing Sam and his clients. And before all that, Papa was servicing me.* She hoped Sade had gotten away. She wished she knew for sure but had no way of asking.

"Eyo?"

Eyo blinked. They were all looking at her in concern. She shook her thoughts away to focus on the present.

"I'm okay. Just thinking, that's all," she smiled reassuringly.

Mama didn't look convinced.

"Mama, I'm fine," she said again. This time, a bit more firmly. "Can I go outside? I think I need some air," she said.

"Of course. Be careful. There are many tricksters around, and now that everyone knows you're here from London…"

"I'll be careful, Mama. I'm just going to sit on the bench outside. That's all."

"Fine."

Eyo went out to the corridor. She nodded a general greeting to the women cooking in the corridor and went outside. She inhaled the air in sweet relief before sitting on the bench. Every face-me-I-face-you in Jungle City had one or more of these outside their bungalows. From what she could remember, some people even slept on them overnight, preferring to be bitten by flies outdoors rather than to endure the suffocating humidity and cramped living quarters inside.

It was barely seven a.m. and the sun was scorching already. An open drain separated their building from the dirt road. Already, traffic was building up. A few women were busy setting up their roadside stalls in readiness for the day's trading.

Eyo was careful not to catch anyone's eye, choosing instead to focus on the horizon. This time yesterday, she was getting into the car with Father Stephen and Sister Mary. They were arguing about who was going to drive because Sister

Mary thought Father Stephen had taken it upon himself to do the honours as usual. Just like a typical male. Eyo tried to remember how they'd settled the argument and then she did. Father Stephen would do the inward journey, while Sister Mary would do the outward one. *They would do well as a comedy duo on television,* she'd told them once.

By this time of the day, at the Abbey, she would be in the chapel for first prayers. Or in bed, with a duvet to snuggle under. If she was with Johnny, she would still be asleep. Not unless he woke her up with his lovemaking. Afterwards, he would make her scrambled eggs, which she would inevitably refuse to eat. A screaming argument would ensue. He would slap her round, make her eat and give her hot chocolate as a reward. And like a dog, she would accept it gratefully.

Eyo winced when those memories came back. She heard footsteps behind her and then a voice.

"Eyo." It was Sade. "Mama wants to talk to you," she said.

Eyo went back inside.

Mama motioned for her to sit on the mat. Lanre was still asleep. Eyo saw that he clutched the football strip in his hand even as he slept.

"Let him sleep some more. He's doing an apprenticeship with the local carpenter. Besides, I need to talk to you," Mama said.

Eyo sat on the mat and faced her. Behind her, Sade busied herself, carrying the stove out to the corridor and preparing their breakfast, which Eyo guessed was *ogi*.

"Mama Fola and I were wondering what you intend to do now," Olufunmi said.

Eyo looked down. "I'm not sure. I was going to wait until Father Ignatius came back today to talk to him. I thought maybe...school, a training programme...something."

"We just want to know, that's all," Olufunmi said. "How about you go bathe so that you're ready when he comes, eh?"

"Yes, Mama," Eyo said. Then she realised that she would have to go outside to the backyard, in full view of everyone.

"It's okay. I'll do it later. At night."

They all laughed.

"Didn't think you would! Next time wake up early!" Mama Fola said.

*   *   *

Lanre, Sade and Eyo were sitting on the bench outside when the church jeep pulled up. Father Ignatius alighted and Eyo went up to him. They hugged and she led him to the bench.

"Mama is inside," she said.

Sade and Lanre greeted him shyly, and they both went inside. A few moments later, Olufunmi came out. She greeted Father Ignatius.

"Are you sure you don't want to come inside?" she asked. "It's cooler there."

Father Ignatius shook his head. "I'm okay. Please do not trouble yourself," he said.

"How about a cold drink?"

Father Ignatius shook his head again. "I won't be long here. Please, I beg you, don't trouble yourself."

Olufunmi searched his face. When she became satisfied that he wasn't being rude, she left them both.

Father Ignatius turned his attention to Eyo as they both sat down.

"Now tell me. How are you?"

"Okay, I guess," Eyo answered. "It's like everything's the same and nothing has really changed. You know what I mean? And it's hot. Hot. Hot."

"Yes it is," Father Ignatius conceded.

Eyo looked down at her feet. She was wearing trainers. She should be wearing slippers. Something more attuned to the practical needs of the climate and Jungle City's environment.

"I don't know what to do, Father," she said quietly.

"That's why I'm here. I'd hoped to get you on one of our training programmes—sewing classes, hairdressing—but there are no openings just now. There are on average fifty people to a class, and we're bursting at the seams. Even the secondary school classes are filled to capacity. And the waiting list..." His voice trailed off. "We're taking in more and more girls from abroad, who've suffered just as you have." He sighed. "It's an evil thing. This trading in flesh. Truly evil."

Eyo stilled as she listened to him. He was saying, in his own way, that he couldn't help her. "How are Sister Mary and Father Stephen?" she asked.

"I spoke to them today. They both miss you and say they're praying for you."

Eyo gave a faint smile. "I knew they would say that."

She would call them later that day. They would know what to do. How to help her. She cursed herself for her short-sightedness in London. She should've asked them to buy a mobile phone for her. Now, she would have to find a means of calling and talking to them. Not that it would be difficult. She'd spotted several telephone calling centres on her way here, while in the jeep.

Father Ignatius got up and stretched.

"Eyo, all is not lost. I'm working on this. Trust me." He gave her an envelope.

Eyo took it and looked inside. There was money in Nigerian currency and a piece of paper inside. She took a few notes from the bundle and put it inside her jeans, despising herself for doing so but unable to stop herself.

"I'll give the rest to Mama," she said.

"I know," Father Ignatius said. "And remember what I said about trusting me. I'm working on it. Just give me time."

"Yes, Father."

They both walked to the jeep. Father Ignatius got in. "My regards to your mother," he yelled through the window and waved as he drove off.

Eyo waved back and walked back to the house, a sinking feeling in the pit of her stomach.

Forty-four

"Ice water!"

"Ice water!" Eyo echoed Sade. Sweat streamed down her face, rushed past her neck and disappeared down her damp T-shirt.

"Say it louder and walk faster," Sade said.

"I'm trying," Eyo responded, her voice short. The tray dripped melting ice on her head. She gritted her teeth as the exhaust fumes from the congested roads lodged in her throat.

"I know it's not London, but you have to try; otherwise, the ice will melt completely and we won't be able to sell it at all," Sade said.

Stop talking about London! Eyo wanted to yell.

"I'm sure you wished you'd stayed." There was more than a hint of envy in Sade's ten-year-old voice.

"Sade," Eyo struggled to control her temper, "London is not like you think."

"And this is better?" Sade said. "I would've stayed. Instead, you came back and you're now selling ice. Like a commoner. Like someone who's never left the country."

Eyo didn't respond. She wiped the sweat off her forehead and walked past Sade.

"Ice water! Don't let the sun take you! Ice water!" she called out.

"Ice water!" her sister echoed.

At six p.m., exhausted and faint with heat, she limped behind her younger sister as they headed home. The smell and humidity of their room hit her afresh. Her mother was fanning herself lethargically on the mattress. Lanre was nowhere to be found. Probably playing football in the surrounding streets.

Eyo propped her tray against the wall. Sade did the same, and they both flopped on the mat. There was a knock on the door. They all looked inquiringly at each other. Sade went to open it.

"Mama, it's Kunle's mum," she called out.

"Then let her in," Olufunmi said.

Sade let her in. The lady came inside the room, giving Eyo surreptitious looks.

"Mama Kunle, come sit," Olufunmi said, patting the mattress. "Sade, here's some money. Go and buy her a Coke from the shop opposite the street."

Sade took the money and left the room.

"And this is Eyo?" Mama Kunle asked.

"Yes, Ma," Eyo answered.

"She even talks like an *oyinbo*," Mama Kunle said to no one in particular. "And you've been out hawking ice?" she asked Eyo.

"Yes, Ma."

"But you've just come from London. You shouldn't be doing that. You should be working in a bank. Like a big shot. Like…"

"For someone who's never travelled out of Lagos, much less the country, you have a lot to say," Olufunmi said sharply. "In any case, she's only been back a month. What else do you expect her to do? Sit at home and do nothing?"

Mama Kunle was quiet momentarily. "I'm sorry. I didn't know it was such a sensitive issue. It's just that… Well, we just weren't expecting her to start hawking so quickly. We thought, coming from London and all, she would… Well, you know how it is," she completed.

"She's a young girl. What exactly were you all expecting?" Olufunmi's voice was shrill.

It was getting dark. Soon, it would be dark completely. Then she would light a candle, make her way down the corridor and bathe outside. With the other tenants. In full view of everyone and anyone who cared to watch. That's if her mother could spare the water. Eyo realised Mama Kunle was watching her.

"I'm just going to sit outside on the bench," she announced.

"Very good," her mother said.

Eyo left the room and passed by two neighbours. They whispered when she went past, but she ignored them. The air outside was cooler. Eyo sat on the bench. Opposite her, at the other end of the street, Sade was crossing the road with a bottle of Coke.

"I'll come back and join you when I drop this off," she said, on her way back inside the building.

Eyo nodded and waited. A few moments later, Sade came back out and sat next to her. A young woman about Eyo's age came off the street and headed inside the building. She stopped when she saw Sade and Eyo sitting outside.

"Sade, you still haven't introduced me to your London sister," she said, her eyes fixed on Eyo, as one would study an alien.

"I know," Sade said.

The lady waited expectantly for an introduction. "Sade,

aren't you going to introduce me to your sister?" she asked, when none was forthcoming. "Your manners are even worse than usual today," she added.

Sade pointedly looked out to the street. Eyo smiled inwardly to herself. Sade reminded her so much of herself at her age. Evidently, Mama had taught them both well.

"I'm sorry. It's been a long day. My sister is tired. I've seen you around the building. I'm Eyo," Eyo said.

The lady proceeded to sit on the bench with Eyo and Sade. The bench groaned in protest. Eyo shifted and made to get up, but the girl pinned her down with a hand on her thigh. She leaned towards Eyo and whispered, "I want to go to London, too."

"Then go," Eyo said.

"But, how can I get there? You've been there. Tell me how you did it. If I was you, I would never have come back."

"Ayo, I can hear your mother calling you from the backyard," Sade said.

Ayo glared at Sade and lowered her voice even more. "When are you going back? I'll come with you," she said to Eyo.

Eyo stood up. "I'm not going back," she said.

By now, it was dark and flies were beginning to circulate. A few buildings were starting to glow with candlelight. She became aware of more than a few passers-by looking at her and whispering. She heard 'London' mentioned a few times. It was draining. This constant feeling of being under a microscope.

"But what will you do here? You can't sell ice forever."

"Why don't you mind your own business?" Sade said tartly. "Come on Eyo," she took her sister's hand and they both went inside. In their room, Olufunmi and Mama Kunle were still talking, evidently reconciled. They stopped when Sade and Eyo came in. Sade lit a candle and placed it on the windowsill.

"That's better," she said.

"I think I'll have a shower," Eyo said.

"There's not enough water for you to have two showers a day," Olufunmi said.

Eyo didn't bother responding but went back outside, fuming. Ayo was still there, staring dreamily into the distance.

"If I went to London, I would never leave," she said when Eyo rejoined her on the bench.

"Ayo," Eyo said wearily. "It's not what you think. It's nothing like you all think it is."

"I don't care," Ayo responded. "I still want to go and I will do it. I know a guy. I'll do it," she whispered to herself. "I refuse to waste away in this dump."

"Eyo?"

They both turned around. It was Mama Kunle.

Ayo got up. "Welcome back to Jungle City, Eyo," she said before going inside.

Mama Kunle joined Eyo on the bench. She waited for a few moments before speaking.

"There's something I want to ask you," she said.

"You want to go to London," Eyo finished.

Mama Kunle didn't bother denying it. "Yes. Tell me, how did you do it?"

Eyo smiled sadly. "I'm sure Mama told you."

"But your Uncle Femi is now an extremely wealthy man. He is also unreachable and untouchable. That is why I'm asking you."

"I don't know anything. I'm afraid I can't help you."

"Can't or won't?"

Eyo felt a flash of anger. "I can't help you," she repeated.

"How about a little something so that I don't leave here empty-handed? I'm sure those *oyinbo* church people gave you plenty of money," Mama Kunle said.

"I said I can't help you."

Eyo left her there and went back inside the cage, for that was what their room was beginning to feel like to her.

"What's for dinner?" she asked, when she entered the room.

"*Ogi*," Olufunmi said. "That was all I could afford. The money you gave me has more or less run out completely. The landlord was at me for rent. I had to give him something to get him off me."

Eyo went to sit on the mattress. She didn't want *ogi*. She wanted a Big Mac with fries, preferably eaten in an air-conditioned McDonald's with big electric lights.

She took in a deep breath. "I'll call Father Stephen in London. I'll see what he can do. If he can send me money or put pressure on Father Ignatius for a place on the sewing course."

"See, Mama? I told you Eyo would figure something out," Sade said, a big smile on her face.

"Yes, don't worry. I will," Eyo said, thinking of the twenty pounds and the money Father Ignatius gave her, now tucked away in her suitcase.

Forty-five

About three months after she got back, she was sitting outside the face-me-I-face-you, thinking of Father Stephen and Sister Mary when a woman in tattered clothes approached the building. She had a girl of about five years old with a distended belly with her. The girl was naked, save for the underwear she wore. Eyo stood up warily, wondering if the woman was lost.

"Are you Eyo?" the woman asked.

"Yes," she replied.

The woman pushed the girl towards her. "Take her to London," she said.

There was raw desperation in the woman's eyes. Eyo backed off and ran down the street. She turned at a side street and cursed out loud when she saw that she had stepped into a bag of excrement. This would never happen in London! She took off the shoe, flung it across the street and wept angry tears. A young man who'd been watching approached her.

"You're Eyo, the one who went to London and came back. What's there for you in Nigeria? Why did you come back?" he asked.

Eyo fled back to the safety of her face-me-I-face-you. The heat was oppressive, the walls pressing in on her. Flies buzzed around her face. She thought about opening the door to let in some air but changed her mind. She would only get unwelcomed visitors and enquiries about going to London. *They were all so ignorant*, she thought savagely.

She hated this room and everything it stood for. The key turned in the lock and her Mama came in. She nodded at Eyo and started arranging her pots and pans by the wall.

"If you have something to say, say it," Eyo said crossly.

"I wished that I could just sit down and be waited on, while everybody else left the house at half past six in the morning to make money," her mother replied.

"I'm tired of hawking ice," Eyo answered. "I'm trying to find something else to do. Father Stephen…"

"Enough of your *oyinbo* helpers! Face it: They're useless!" Olufunmi snapped.

"Stop saying that! All the money I've given you these last few months, where do you think it's coming from? Do you think they're like a cash machine and all I have to do is go there, key in a code and boom, they'll give me money? They have other people to take care of you know!" Eyo snapped back.

"Who do you think you're giving lip to? Just because you've been to London doesn't mean that I still can't take a belt to your behind."

"Go ahead and I hope it makes you feel better!" Eyo yelled.

"The rent is due and all you can think of is yourself." Olufunmi mimicked Eyo's voice. "'I can't hawk in this heat. It's hot and I'm tired.' Well, you should've thought of that before you decided to come back and burden us with an extra mouth to feed," Olufunmi yelled back.

Eyo had had enough. "You don't know what happened to me while I was there. Just because I haven't said anything…"

"What happened to you is no more or no less than what other girls go through…" Olufunmi screamed at her, then stopped and collected herself.

Eyo turned to her, painful understanding dawning on her. "You knew what Papa was doing to me."

"I don't know what you're talking about," Olufunmi said, but her eyes didn't meet Eyo's.

"That's why you threw Papa out. He was doing it to Sade. Why didn't you say something, when you knew he was doing it to me? Why?"

Eyo willed her mother to look at her eyes, but Olufunmi refused. She started rearranging the pots again. Eyo waited for her to say something. but she didn't. Instead, Olufunmi went to the door. She spoke without turning around.

"Eyo, I've tried. Really, I have, but I just don't know what to do. We don't have any money. I've just about pawned anything of value that we have. You…should have endured London. Sade still has a chance to live the life she ought to live. But you… Whatever hope there was for you… There is a guy; he sends people to London. Think about it."

Olufunmi left the room. Eyo wept. When she finished, she wiped her eyes and went to the calling centre. She telephoned Father Stephen in London.

"Help me, Father. I don't know what to do. I've just had the most awful argument with Mama. I'm so confused. I think I want to go back to London. Please help me find a way. There is nothing for me here. I shouldn't have come back. I was wrong," she bawled.

"Eyo, it's not that easy. You're back in Nigeria now. Getting a visa might be a problem. I'll speak to Father Ignatius as soon as I get off this phone and see what he can do. Please stop crying. I promise you, I'll help y…"

"Father Stephen," she interrupted. "Father Ignatius can't help. He's tried, but he can't."

"Eyo, don't worry. Leave it to me."

Eyo hung up the phone as he spoke and made her way woodenly back to the face-me-I-face-you. By this time, dusk had turned into night-time. She walked through the heaving crowd, unaware of everything around her: the noise and swarm of people pressing against her, each person trying to eke out a living in the prison of Jungle City. And then she knew. She shouldn't have come back to Nigeria. Her sister resented her for going to London. Her mother resented having to feed her, and her teenage brother had better things to do than to hang around a London has-been.

When she got back inside their room, Sade was lying on the mat, fanning herself with a newspaper. Her mother sat on the mattress, staring into the space.

"Hello, Eyo," Sade said. "Mama's gone into herself again, and I don't know where Lanre is," she said.

Eyo joined Olufunmi on the bed. She wrapped her arms around her shoulders.

"Mama, I'm sorry. I shouldn't have said all those things. I'll try harder. I'll endure," she said.

Olufunmi turned to her, tears in her eyes. "You're right. I should've said something then. I didn't know what to do. My Papa did the same thing to me, and when Wale started with Sade, something snapped. I…" She couldn't continue.

Sade went to sit on the other side of the mattress. She stroked her mother's back. "I'm okay now, Mama. See: Eyo is here. She'll help us. She'll make everything okay. Stop crying," she spoke soothingly.

"Eyo, all those things I said about your church people, I didn't mean them. They're good people. I know they are." Olufunmi wiped her eyes with her *wrapa*.

"I know," Eyo said. "Now stop crying. I said I would sort something out and I will. See?" She brought out the twenty pounds from her pocket. "I told you the church people would help us. This should keep the landlord off our back and maybe even buy us food for a few days at least, eh?"

Sade beamed. "See, Mama. Didn't I say that Eyo would find a solution?"

Olufunmi smiled weakly. Eyo thought of the money she'd siphoned off from what Father Ignatius gave her months ago, when she first got back. If that disappeared as well, she didn't know what she would do. She would be trapped here, in this room, in Jungle City, with no means of escape, just like she had been in The House, with Sam and with Johnny. A bleakness descended upon her.

"Mama, don't worry. I told you that I would endure and I will. I'll start hawking ice again tomorrow," Eyo said dully.

*   *   *

Eyo left the mission centre with whatever hope she had before going in dashed. Father Ignatius was sorrowful. They still had no places for her on any of the courses and funding was extremely tight. Their donors were tightening their purse strings. He gave her some money, though. Eyo knew that it was only a matter of time before that too stopped completely.

On her way back to their face-me-I-face-you, an hour's walk in blazing heat, she passed by a shop that sold mirrors. At first, she didn't recognise the girl with the wan, listless face and skinny arms, wearing rubber slippers and faded traditional *wrapa* and a *buba* top, staring back at her in the mirror. When she looked further, she realised that she was looking at herself, only it wasn't her. It was someone else. The real Eyo died the day she left Nigeria for England. The person staring back at her in the mirror was something other people had created and she had absorbed because she didn't have a choice.

Eyo raised her head and it was as if she could see Ajegunle properly, for the first time since she came back. She could see the open drains and the plastic bags of faeces fluttering in them. She saw the unpaved roads with craters the size of continents. She could see the roadside stalls with candles flickering on the tables, and she knew that it had been a mistake to come back. She didn't belong here. She wasn't the same girl who had left almost six years ago. She had changed. She liked having electricity. She liked having a working toilet, with a handle for flushing, not a *shalanga* with flies hovering around it in the backyard.

She should have stayed in England. She should've endured, not just for her own sake, but also for the sake of her mother and siblings.

"You're the girl who just came back from England?"

Eyo looked up at the voice. It was the same man who had spoken to her a few weeks earlier, when she had stepped into a bag of human waste. She nodded.

The man gave her a cool, assessing look, as if he was weighing her up for sale. Eyo knew the look. Her father had it, when he told her he was sending her to the UK. Sam had it, when he used to assault her and bring men to the house to have sex with her. Big Madame, the clients that came to the house, Johnny and all the men that slowed down by that pavement in King's Cross where she stood, they all had it.

Her heart fluttered slightly in her chest. She put her hand on it, making sure one of her fingers rested lightly on her breast.

The man's eyes followed her finger and its resting place.

"Yes," she said more confidently, with the practised smile she once used on men in England. *Strange*, she thought, *how it came back so easily.*

The man nodded and stroked her face thoughtfully. He reached into his shirt pocket and gave her a card. Eyo took it from him and turned it over. She didn't want to tell him that she was a poor reader. It was one of the things she'd hoped to correct once she came back to Nigeria. It hadn't happened. Just like everything else.

"It's an address," the man said, as if reading her mind. He gave her verbal directions to the house. "Go there, when you're ready to go back to the UK," he said. Then he left her there.

When she got home, there was no food in the house. Sade was playing with her Sindy doll.

"It's all gone. There's no money. I did tell you, didn't I? Two weeks ago, you said you would endure, that you would find a way. Is this what you mean? We're going to be homeless, you hear? Homeless and faced with starvation. And you swan in asking for food!" Olufunmi shrieked.

Eyo thought of the money Father Ignatius had given her: what she'd just received and what she'd hidden in her pocket. She grabbed a shawl and wrapped it around her shoulders. "I'll be back soon," she said.

Her mother and sister didn't utter a word. They watched her silently. Sade's eyes bored into Eyo's back. Eyo reached into her jeans pocket and took out all the money she had. She gave it to Sade.

"See, Mama. I told you she would find the money," Sade said. Olufunmi didn't say anything. Instead, she stood still and kept watching Eyo, her face expressionless.

"I'll be back soon," Eyo repeated.

She stepped out of the face-me-I-face-you. She had tears in her eyes, but she refused to let them fall. She didn't look back as she made her way to the man's house, chanting softly to herself.

Glory be to the Father

And to the Son

And to the Holy Spirit.

When she got there, she stood across the road and watched as a steady procession of women went through the security gates and inside the house. At one point, she thought she spotted Ayo among them, but she wasn't sure. She could hear Father Stephen's voice as clearly as she could feel Sister Mary's arms around her.

"For there is nothing you can do that will separate you from the love of God in Christ Jesus."

Eyo started walking.

THE END

What you can do about child trafficking and sex slavery

Support www.stopthetraffik.org and Africans Unite Against Child Abuse (www.afruca.org).

About the Author

Abidemi Sanusi is a former human rights worker, now author. Born in Nigeria, she now lives in the UK. A keen photographer and foodie, she can also be found via her website (www.abidemi.co.uk).

You can also follow Abidemi Sanusi on social media:
Twitter: www.twitter.com/abidemiuk
Google+: www.google.com/+abidemicoukcompany
Facebook: www.facebook.com/abidemiauthor
Pinterest: pinterest.com/abidemi

Lightning Source UK Ltd.
Milton Keynes UK
UKHW010628300919
350713UK00001B/10/P